"*Mian Mian's realm is one of wretched love affairs, hard drugs, promiscuous sex, and suicide. Her work is revolutionary for the People's Republic, and her own tale is one of personal liberation, excess, and redemption.*"

— GARY JONES, *Sydney Morning Herald Magazine*

AN INTERNATIONAL LITERARY SENSATION — now available for the first time in English translation — Candy is a harrowing tale of risk and desire, the story of a young Chinese woman forging a life for herself in a world seemingly devoid of guidelines.

Hong, who narrates the novel, drops out of high school and runs away at age seventeen to the frontier city of Shenzen. She falls into a relationship with a young musician, and together they dive into a cruel netherworld of alcohol, drugs, and excess, a life that fails to satisfy Hong's craving for an authentic self, and for a love that will define her.

Mian Mian's fresh, strident, and brutally honest voice illuminates the anguish of an entire generation. This startling novel is a blast of sex, drugs, and rock 'n' roll that opens up to us a modern China we've never seen before.

CANDY

A NOVEL

MIAN MIAN

TRANSLATED BY ANDREA LINGENFELTER

LITTLE, BROWN AND COMPANY   NEW YORK BOSTON LONDON

Back Bay Books / Little, Brown and Company
Hachette Book Group USA
237 Park Avenue, New York, NY 10017
Visit our Web site at www.HachetteBookGroupUSA.com

First English-Language Edition
First published in a different version in April 2000
by Zhongguo Xiju Chubanshe under the title Tang.

Back Bay Books is a division of Hachette Book Group USA, Inc. The Back Bay Books name and logo are trademarks of Hachette Book Group USA, Inc.

The characters and events in this book are fictitious. Any similarity to real persons, living or dead, is coincidental and not intended by the author.

Library of Congress Cataloging-in-Publication Data

Mian, Mian.
   [Tang. English]
   Candy : a novel / Mian Mian.
     p. cm.
   ISBN 978-0-316-56356-7
   1. Mian, Mian — Translations into English. I. Title.
PL2949.5.A5 T3613 2003
895.1'352 — dc21   2002043645

10 9 8 7 6 5

RRD-C

Printed in the United States of America

FOR ALL OF THOSE FRIENDS WHO HAVE VANISHED WITHOUT A TRACE

TRANSLATOR'S NOTE

Most of the action in *Candy* is divided between the author's native Shanghai and the enterprising boomtown of Shenzhen, in Guangdong Province. While Mian Mian mentions Shanghai by name, she refers to Shenzhen only as "the South." Once little more than a farming and fishing village on the train line linking Hong Kong and Guangzhou, Shenzhen began its radical transformation in 1980, when Deng Xiaoping, then China's premier, proclaimed it a Special Economic Zone (SEZ). Created as a response to the economic stagnation of the Maoist era, the SEZs were integral to Deng's economic reforms. In contrast to the central planning and state-controlled enterprises that characterized the rest of China, the SEZs were set aside as free of state control. The relaxation of state control and the relative freedom soon created a frontier mentality, and many forms of vice and corruption came to flourish alongside more legitimate private enterprise. Prostitution, drugs, and organized crime, which had been suppressed to a remarkable degree in post-1949 China, thrived in laissez-faire Shenzhen. At the same time, the influx of investment from Hong Kong, Taiwan, and the West was accompanied by a flood of cultural influences.

The personal and economic freedom represented by Shenzhen was extremely attractive to many young people all over China, and Mian Mian's protagonist, Hong, is no exception. In the rest of China, job seekers waited to be assigned a job by the government, which had the right to send people anywhere in the country. Often, people ended up in jobs hundreds of miles away from their hometowns, but they had little choice in the matter. Qualifications counted for something, but a recent high school or college graduate's display of devotion to the Communist Party was often also a key factor in securing a desirable assignment. In running away to the SEZ to try to make their own way, Hong and others like her were dropping out of this overly constraining system.

What may be remarkable to readers familiar with the last half century of Chinese history is how small a role the Communist Party plays in the lives of the characters who people Mian Mian's book. The omission is telling. The world portrayed in *Candy* is just one more reflection of what Orville Schell, in his lively and insightful book *Mandate of Heaven*, refers to as China's "gray" culture, one devoid of the "redness" that characterized the Communist culture of the first four decades of the People's Republic. "Gray" culture is apolitical on the surface but fascinated with gangsters and other outlaws. Its cynicism, irony, and seeming disengagement from politics have a great deal to say about Chinese society today. Whether it amounts to a loss of hope for political change in China or a subtle but effective form of subversion remains to be seen.

A note on currency: The Chinese currency is called the *yuan*. (There are roughly 8.25 *yuan* to the U.S. dollar.) There are ten *mao* (or *jiao*) to each *yuan*, and ten *fen* to each *mao*.

A note on language: Mandarin is the official language of the People's Republic of China. It is used in broadcasting, schools, and other official settings. However, in private life many people are more comfortable using the native dialect of their home region, such as Shanghainese or Cantonese.

AUTHOR'S NOTE

I created my own sweetheart, watching him move closer and closer to me. His undying fragility is his undying sweetness and beauty. This book represents some of the tears I couldn't cry, some of the terror behind my smiling eyes. This book exists because one morning as the sun was coming up I told myself that I had to swallow up all of the fear and garbage around me, and once it was inside me I had to transform it all into candy. Because I know you will be able to love me for it.

CANDY

A

Why did my father always have to push me in front of the Mona
Lisa? And why did he always make me listen to classical music?
I suppose it was just my fate, for want of a better word. I was
twenty-seven years old before I finally got the courage to ask
my father these questions — up until then, I couldn't even bring
myself to utter the woman's name, I was so terrified of her.

My father answered that Chopin was good music. So when I
was bawling my head off, he would shut me in a room all by myself
and have me listen to Chopin. In those days none of our neighbors
had a record player or a television the way we did. What's more,
many of them were forced to subsist on the vegetable scraps they
scrounged at the market, since meat, cloth, oil, and other basics
were still being rationed. My father thought that as a member of

the only "intellectual," or educated, family in our entire apartment building, I should feel fortunate.

Father said that it had never occurred to him that I might be afraid of that print hanging on our wall. Why didn't I just look at the world map that was hanging right next to it? Or the map of China? Or my own drawings? Why did I have to look at that picture? At length he asked, Anyway, why were you so afraid of her?

Many other people have asked me this very question, and each time someone asks, I feel that much less terrified. Still, it's a question I can't answer. Just as I can't explain why, from the time I was a very small child and barely able to talk, my father would have chosen to deal with my crying the way he did.

I have never actually taken a good close look at that woman (I'm far too afraid of her to attempt that). Nonetheless, my most powerful childhood memories are of her portrait.

As I grew older, certain ideas became fixed in my mind. Her eyes were like a car crash at the moment of impact; her nose was an order issuing from the darkness, like a ramrod-straight ladder; the corners of her mouth were cataclysmic whirlpools. She seemed to have no bones except for her brow bones, and those bald brows were an ever-present mockery. Her clothing was like an umbrella so massive that it threatened to steal me away. And then there were her cheeks and fingers. There was no denying that they resembled more than anything the decaying pieces of a corpse.

She was a dangerous woman. And I was often in this dangerous presence. I had very few fears, but she terrified me. In middle school history class, I was once startled to look up and find myself face-to-face with a slide projection of this painting. My throat tightened, and I cried out in shock. My teacher reacted by concluding that I was a bad student and making me stand up as punishment. Then he took me to see the assistant principal, who gave me a stern lecture. At one point they went so far as to accuse me of reading "pornography," like the then-popular underground book *The Heart of a Young Girl.*

That was the beginning of my hatred for the man who had painted her. And I started to despise as well all those who called themselves "intellectuals." My hatred had a kind of purity about it — I would open my heart and feel a convulsive anger pulsing in my blood. I named this sensation "loathing."

My unalloyed fear of this painting stripped away any sense of closeness I might have felt toward my parents. And it convinced me, all too soon, that the world was unknowable and incomprehensible.

Later I found the strength to deal with my fear. I found it in the moon and in the moonlight. Sometimes it was in rays of light that resembled moonlight, and sometimes I saw it in eyes or lips that were like moonlight. At other times still it was in the moonlight of a man's back.

B

When it rains I often think of Lingzi. She once told me about a poem that went: "Rain falling in the spring, / Is heaven and earth making love." These lines were a puzzle to us, but Lingzi and I spent a lot of time trying to unravel various problems. We might be trying to figure out germs, or the fear of heights, or even a phrase like "Love is a fantasy you have while smoking your third ciga-rette." Lingzi was my high school desk mate, and she had a face like a white sheet of paper. Her pallor was an attitude, a sort of trance.

Those days are still fresh in my mind. I was a melancholy girl who loved to eat chocolate and did poorly in school. I collected candy wrappers, and I would use these, along with boxes that had once contained vials of medicine, to make sunglasses.

Soon after the beginning of our second year of high school, Lingzi's hair started to look uneven, with a short clump here, a longer hank there. There were often scratch marks on her face. Lingzi had always been extremely quiet, but now her serenity had become strange. She told me she was sure that one of the boys in our class was watching her. She said he gave her steamy looks —
steamy was the word she used, and I remember exactly how she said it. She was constantly being encircled by his gaze, she said. It made her think all kinds of unwholesome, selfish thoughts. She insisted that it was absolutely out of the question for her to let anything distract her from her studies. Lingzi believed that this boy was watching her because she was pretty. This filled her with feelings of shame. Since being pretty was the problem, she had decided to make herself ugly, convinced that this would set her back on the right path. She was sure that if she were ugly, then no one would look at her anymore; and if nobody was looking at her, then she could concentrate on her studies. Lingzi said she had to study hard, since, as all of us knew, the only guarantee of a bright future was to gain admission to a top university.

Throughout the term, Lingzi continued to alter her appearance in all kinds of bizarre ways. People quit speaking to her. In the end most of our classmates avoided her altogether.

As for me, I didn't think that Lingzi had been that pretty to begin with. I felt that I understood her — she was simply too high-strung. Our school was a "key school," and it was fairly common for a student at a school like ours to have a sudden nervous breakdown. Anyway, it wasn't clear to me how I could help Lingzi. She seemed so calm and imperturbable.

Then one day Lingzi didn't come to school. And from then on, her seat remained empty. The rumor was that she had violent tendencies. Her parents had had to tie her up with rope and take her to a mental hospital.

Everyone started saying that Lingzi had "gone crazy." I started eating chocolate with a vengeance, and that was the beginning of my bad habit of bingeing on chocolate whenever I'm anxious or upset. Even today, eleven years later, I haven't been able to break this habit, with the result that I have a very serious blood sugar problem.

I sneaked into the hospital to see her. One Saturday afternoon, wearing a red waterproof sweat suit, I slipped in through the chain-link fence of the mental hospital. In truth, I'm sure I could have used the main entrance. Although it was winter, I brought Lingzi her favorite Baby-Doll brand ice cream, along with some preserved olives and salty dried plums. I sat compulsively eating my chocolates while she ate her ice cream and sweet olives. All of the other patients on the ward were adults. I did most of the talking, and whenever I finished saying something, no matter what the subject was, Lingzi would laugh. Lingzi had a clear, musical laugh, just like bells ringing. But on this day her laughter simply struck me as weird.

What did Lingzi talk about? She kept repeating the same thing over and over: The drugs they give you in this hospital make you fat. Really, really fat.

Sometime later I heard that Lingzi had left the hospital. Her parents made a series of pleas to the school, asking the teachers to inform everyone that Lingzi was not being allowed any visitors.

One rainy afternoon, the news of Lingzi's death reached our school. People said that her parents had gone out one day, and a boy had taken advantage of their absence. He had brought Lingzi a bouquet of fresh flowers. This was 1986, and there were only two flower stands in all of Shanghai, both newly opened. That night, Lingzi slashed her wrists in the bathroom of her family's apartment. People said that she died standing.

This terrible event hastened my deterioration into a "problem child."

I quit trusting anything that anyone told me. Aside from the food that I put into my mouth, there was nothing I believed in. I had lost faith in everything. I was only sixteen, but my life was over. Fucking over.

Strange days overtook me, and I grew idle. I let myself go, feeling that I had more time on my hands than I knew what to do with. Indolence made my voice increasingly gravelly. I started to explore my body, either in front of the mirror or at my desk. I had no desire to understand it — I only wanted to experience it.

Facing the mirror and looking at myself, I saw my own desire in all its unfamiliarity. When I secretly pressed my sex up against the cold corner of my desk, I sometimes felt a pleasurable spasm. Just as it had been the first time, my early experiences of this "joy" were often beyond my control.

This was the beginning of my wasted youth. After that winter, Lingzi's lilting laughter would constantly trail behind me, pursuing me as I fled headlong into a boundless darkness.

C

There was only one teacher I liked at my school. She was very young, and tall and slender. She liked to wear dark glasses, and from day to day she always had the same quiet, unhappy air about her. She taught my class just once, and before starting the lesson, she read us a poem, "I Am a Willful Child," by the underground poet Gu Cheng. No teacher had ever done anything like this before. Those ten minutes were the only moment of transcendence of my entire high school career — the spirituality of the teacher's chaste gaze, us listening to the poem, the classroom in the sunlight. A perfect day, a beautiful dream. Over the years, memories of that day have often come back to me, and they have never lost the power to affect me deeply. It was as though I had never been truly moved by anything until that moment.

The term that Lingzi committed suicide I dropped out of school, the only student who had ever left voluntarily. I had set myself free. I was hoping to find some other way to get into university, since I still wanted to go to college someday. But you can't get into college without graduating from high school.

I came to a conclusion: there was too much bullshit in my life. I didn't want anyone to bullshit me anymore, and I wasn't going to bullshit anyone else again either.

After I left school, I was introduced to a black-market booking agent, and that was how I fell into my brief career as a small-time nightclub singer. I love to sing — it gives me a kind of release. I would stand onstage, dressed up in ridiculous 1980s Taiwan-style outfits, making a big show of acting heartbroken. In those days I drew my eyebrows thick and dark, and I liked the plaintive and torchy Taiwan pop singers Su Rui and Wa Wa.

There was a dancer in our band who was even younger than I was. He had a clear gaze and was rather excitable. The two of us were very close and used to hang out together smoking Phoenix cigarettes. He went by the nickname Bug, but he was actually quite large and didn't bear the slightest resemblance to a little bug. Bug was a *niezhai* — a "debt of evil" — the illegitimate child of parents who'd been sent down to the countryside during the Cultural Revolution, and he didn't have a real home of his own in Shanghai.

Once, we had to go to Xining to play a few gigs, and this put Bug in especially high spirits. He hopped down the street as if he were performing his own version of the dance aerobics we all used to watch on TV. Bug had grown up in Xining. He loved the dawn in the Northwest. Sunrise there was more luminous than anywhere else, he said.

On the train to Xining, Bug told me story after story about a friend of his in the Northwest. The friend was called Bailian, "white face," like the villains in Chinese operas.

Everything in northwestern China was gray, everything except the sky, which was the bluest blue. I met Bailian, who turned out to be not much older than we were. His face was indeed very pale, but I was surprised that someone who had a reputation for having been in so many fights should be so good-looking. He had very dark, vacant-looking eyes and close-cropped, slightly wavy hair. I noticed that he had unusually tiny feet. He invited Bug and me to go to a dance hall with him.

It was 1987, before there were any discos. There were just dance halls where people could go to waltz and fox-trot, people of all ages. Dance halls in the Northwest were disorderly places, and competition over dance partners often ended in brawls. This struck us Shanghainese as a real novelty.

That night Bailian had a girl with him. She had a classical kind of beauty and appeared to be even younger than I was. Right in front of us, Bailian turned to Bug and asked him to trade partners. I didn't like this. If he wanted to dance with me, he could damn well ask me directly. Northwesterners acted very differently from us Shanghainese, I noted. But Bug happily agreed to his request, and I decided that I should give Bug some "face" and not embarrass him.

The song Bailian and I danced to was "Auld Lang Syne," and everyone there was dancing very carefully and correctly, as if this were the door to a new life.

The day after our second gig, Bailian came over alone and asked me to go out dancing with him, just the two of us. I said, Why are you asking me to go dancing? And maybe my tone wasn't very nice, since I was in a bad mood that day because the band leaders did nothing but argue over how the money should be divided up.

Or maybe Bailian just misunderstood what I'd said. In any case, I could see that he was angry. He looked at me and said, Why can't I ask you to go dancing? And I said, I didn't say you couldn't ask; I just asked you why. He said, Are you coming or not? I said, Are you nuts? Where do you get off talking to me like that? He repeated, Are you coming or not?

The whole time, Bailian's tone remained flat and unemotional, and he didn't raise or lower his voice. No! I said.

When Bailian had come in, I was lying on the bed in my guest-house room, reading a book of poetry, *City People*. When I said, No!, I flung the book away.

The next thing I knew, I'd been cut by Bailian's knife. I didn't see where he'd taken it from, I didn't see the blade coming at me, and I didn't see his hand returning it to wherever he kept it. All I remember seeing was him standing in front of me holding the knife, ashen faced, looking as if he'd pulled a muscle. The really interesting thing was that he wasn't even looking at me. He was staring out the window.

When he cut me, I went cold all over, and through the pain I was struck for an instant by the sensation that my body was separating from itself, and my spirits soared. Wave after wave of numbness hit me, spreading across my back, my mind went blank, and uncontrollable tears poured from my eyes. I started shaking, and I felt the same way I did when I read certain poems, or sang certain songs, or heard particular stories; but it was even more intense and came on more quickly.

Bailian was asking me, Are you coming?

He still wasn't looking at me.

became once again the face I'd seen at the bar, a face that was nothing like the face he'd worn when he was fucking me.

I said, You're the first guy I've ever been with. You fucked me. I had my eyes open the entire time and I watched you rape me. You were in such a hurry you didn't even bother to take all your clothes off.

He said nothing. His long hair was lying across my body, and he didn't move. The male singer on the CD kept singing, and the sound of his voice was the caress my skin was still waiting for. The simple rhythms kept spinning forward, and the world became smooth and flat inside the music. I didn't understand a word he sang, but the keyboard was like a vampire, sucking away my feelings.

I have to go to the bathroom, I said. I'm a mess, thanks to you.

I sat on the toilet and looked at his bath towel, and I don't know how long I sat there, but I felt as though my sex had been seriously injured. The face I saw in the crooked mirror was an ugly face. Never in my life had I felt so disgusted with myself. And ever since, I have carried the shame of that moment in my body.

The music playing on the CD that day was the Doors, and the brutality of the music seemed somehow connected to the brutality of my crude "wedding night," which violated the sexual fantasy I had held on to for many years. I didn't dare look at this man's penis, but I liked his skin, and his lips were very soft, and his tongue could put me into a trance. I didn't understand the strange agitation in his face, and I couldn't find anything there to fulfill the needs of my imagination. The girl that he held in his arms was like a kitten that was too miserable to cry.

I was nineteen. He buried me in pain, covered me with an unfamiliar substance, rude but authentic. Clutching my breasts, he moved in and out, in and out of the hole in me, and I couldn't see his expression, and no one will remember the way I looked that night, the night I lost my virginity. The self that drained out of my body was a nullity. As I tried to soothe my dazed body, the hazy mirror reflected my empty features back to me. He was a stranger, we had met at a bar, and though the ocean waves in his eyes were familiar, I didn't know who he was.

2.

That bar was painfully tacky and blazing with yellow lights that shone brightly on every sleazy detail. Sitting at the bar, I was as blank and luminous as the full moon. It was the first time I'd ever sat at a bar, and I felt a little nervous. Every now and then I'd turn and glance this way or that, making it look as if I were waiting for someone. I didn't even know that I was in a bar. I had only just arrived in this small city in the South. It was 1989, and in Shanghai, where I'd come from, there still weren't any bars, just a handful of small, unofficial street-side cafés. Maybe those tiny restaurants had bars, but I'd never set foot inside one.

Outside, it was raining hard, but I don't remember what music was playing in the bar. And I don't remember when I first caught sight of him, a tall boy swaying back and forth and smiling at nothing in particular. He was wearing an oversize white T-shirt and printed corduroy pants. The pants were wide enough to be a skirt, but they really were pants. He was there in the bar, all alone, rocking from side to side, with a whiskey glass in his left hand and his right hand dancing in the air. I watched his legs as, step by step, he moved toward me. His light blue sneakers had very thin soles, and it looked as if he was tripping over his own feet. His hair was long and straight and glossy, the tips brushing his upper back, and his face was very pale. I couldn't make out his features, but I was certain that he was smiling, even if I couldn't tell whether or not he was looking at me too.

I ate my ice cream. Before long, I became aware that a man's hand holding a drink had appeared at my right side. It was a large hand with sturdy fingertips, and I knew at a glance that he chewed his nails. This was something we had in common.

A curtain of hair filled my field of vision, and I smelled the faint, delicate scent of his hair. I looked up.

And saw the face of an angel.

He smiled strangely, and the naked innocence in his eyes filled me with confusion. For the rest of the evening I wasn't able to look away from that face, the face he wore then. And maybe it's my belief in that face that has kept me alive until now, because I believe in that face. It's my destiny.

He started chattering on and on about different kinds of ice cream. He said he also liked chocolate, and that his mother had told him that ill-fated children liked to eat sweets. He had a foreboding that because he liked sweets, he was going to be fat at thirty and bald at forty.

He asked me what I was doing in this town, and I said, Isn't everyone here to make money? I didn't graduate from high school, so I couldn't find a job in Shanghai. What else was left except to come here? He said, But you're so young; aren't your parents worried about you? My dad's pretty unusual, I said. He treats me like an adult. He wants to change his life and make a pile of money himself, so he encouraged me when I said I wanted to go off and earn some money. He asked me, Do you like money? I said, One time my dad helped a relative from overseas change some money on the black market. He thought that he could make a little commission for himself that way, but instead somebody snatched the cash from him, and he tried to chase the person down, but he couldn't catch him, and he ended up with a sprained foot. My dad told me never ever to tell anyone about this, because he'd slipped out during working hours to change the money, and that wouldn't look good to people. It makes me sad, what happened to him. I don't know whether I really like money or not. My dad's an intellectual; he's weak. I'll have to start now if I'm going to make any kind of money.

I had the feeling that this guy, who called himself Saining, was kind of interested in me. His clothing made him stand out, and each of the colors in his rainbow-hued pants made me feel happy. From his rambling monologue I learned that he played guitar, that playing guitar was all he wanted to do, and that he was looking for one or maybe a whole bunch of bars with stages.

Awestruck, I asked, Where in China are there places like that?

He said he didn't know yet, but he was definitely going to find out.

These words emboldened me — to me a bar with a stage represented the road to freedom. I looked at him, adoring his black eyes, innocent, heartbreakingly innocent eyes, large and liquid. Hey, I said, you know what? I'm a singer, and I'm not bad!

And he answered, Do you want to come over to my place?

This was the first time a man had propositioned me, and heaven knows why I agreed on the spot. My expectations were vague and poetic, and dark undercurrents overtook my fantasy.

He said, I like girls from broken homes who are crazy about chocolate and who love the rain. I've been waiting for a girl like that for a long time.

I said, My God! A chocoholic who loves rainy days — that's me!

3.

He'd fucked me into a state of numbness. I was off to a bad start with men. But as I saw it, everything that happened was just one more event among many, even the pain that pierced through my very heart, and those burning wounds. None of it was so different from any of the other things that would inevitably happen.

I went back to Shanghai. I listened to Cui Jian every day and lived on a diet of chocolate and Baby-Doll ice cream. Each week I made the rounds of the student dormitories at every university in town, peddling cloth dolls made by old people in the neighborhood production teams. I didn't have any friends. The first supermarkets had opened up, and although I didn't have any money, I could ease my loneliness by wandering the aisles. It made my life a little more interesting.

*   *   *

After a month or so, I'd set aside enough money to go back south.

When I caught up with Saining again, he was asleep. He came to the door in gray hooded pajamas. His lips looked very dry, and I found his aloof expression very beautiful. I believed that I had a real connection with this kind of beauty, and so I thought he was beautiful.

I'm back, I said. I've been looking for you.

He made himself a cup of instant coffee. In those days hardly anyone drank coffee, and drinking coffee was very hip and poetic. He said, Don't take it personally, but I never talk much when I first get out of bed. I said, I'm not sure what kind of relationship we had, or maybe I just forgot, so I came over.

Without raising his head or looking at me, he said, You've cut your hair. Only a little bit, I said. Your hair used to be longer than mine, he said. Now our hair is about the same length. I said, I'm hungry; can I have something to eat? Sure, he said. I'll make you some fried rice, how about that? I make really good fried rice.

He fried up some rice for me, with lots of different things in it, even apples. He insisted on feeding it to me himself, and looking at his eyes so close up, his soft eyelashes moving up and down, all of a sudden I felt my body get moist, and I wanted to touch his eyes, but I didn't dare. He knew I was looking at him, but he didn't look at me. He was feeding me more and more slowly, and my breathing was becoming ragged, and he knelt in front of me, stroking my sex with his hand. His fingertips were cold. This was his hand, and I loved his hand, the feel of his hand.

When he put his mouth on me, I was startled. I cried out. I didn't know you could do this. He was in such a strange mood, and the sensations I felt were so vague that I thought this was the most exciting picture I had ever seen, and like nothing I'd seen before. Because of this tableau, this man would live forever. I listened to the wet sounds of fluids mingling, sounds that made me think this man loved me. I called these vague feelings "love."

I spent the long afternoon playing a role that I didn't really understand, but I loved the way he made love to me. This is love-making, I thought. From then on, we made love in this way any-time and anywhere we pleased, and I felt that my body liked only his hands, his mouth, and that they were full of feeling. I didn't want anything more.

Once he said, This ought to be the most pleasurable spot for you. It's called the "little cherry," but you're not responding.

I said, Maybe I wore it out by playing with it too much when I was young.

He ate me, never asking for anything else, saying that he didn't care, that my sex had a nice scent. This didn't make sense to me. How could he think that I smelled good? I asked him, What is my scent? He said, It smells like your body, the smell of a body that has lots of secrets. I said, What does my body smell like? He answered, No one can know what their own body smells like. But I know your scent, and you know mine. I like your scent.

Sometimes he played guitar or violin for me. I always tried hard to understand his music. He said, Your brain is filled with too much crap; you need to wash it out. Music doesn't need to be understood; music is the closest thing to your body.

I moved out of my father's friend's house and rented a run-down little apartment. My landlord was like all of the local men, always eyeing me rapaciously and leering at me maliciously. He came right out and asked me directly if I was a prostitute. He said that all girls who came there from the provinces were "chickens" — whores. I said that honestly, I wasn't one, and that besides, I was from Shanghai. He said, Shanghai girls are smart — they all find married men to keep them as mistresses. They're even worse than chickens.

This was the first time I had chosen what kind of place I would live in, and how I would dress and look, and I wrote a letter to my father telling him that I needed to stay in this town. He sent me some money and told me that he had left his work unit to go into business for himself as an engineer. He said that it was extremely hard to do business on one's own, but he'd worked hard all his life and he was still poor, so he decided it was high time he made money for himself, and at the end he said he hoped that I would be able to find myself in this town. I remember it very clearly; he used the popular expression "find yourself."

I bought a CD player and had Saining get me some Western rock and roll CDs when he went to visit Hong Kong. All I knew about then was Cui Jian, and I still thought that the Madonna CD my father had sent me was rock and roll.

Saining brought me some marijuana, and I felt as though I were experiencing a mysterious freedom. It was the symbol of another kind of life, and I loved lying in bed with Saining, smoking grass and listening to music. The music in his room had a purity, and the music and the grass together were like keys that opened up my soul. It was good for me. Little by little, the huge stones blocking my ears were moved away. My hands began circling in the air, and our fingers moved with the music as if we were making this music ourselves. It was such a rush!

I felt really lucky. I listened to rock and roll and smoked marijuana, all in the company of this temperamental, beautiful boy. Wasn't this what I'd always wanted?

I spent my days hanging out, listening to music, smoking grass, and snacking. There was nothing else I wanted to do. I was nearly out of money, and it occurred to me that I might have to think about finding some sort of job, but Saining seemed to have plenty of money. Whenever we were together, it was his money we spent, and although I felt a little embarrassed by this, these were still happy times for me. One day Saining said, Do you know why I like you so much? Why? I asked. Because, he said, you're as lazy as I am.

Once, when I came to Saining's door, I heard the sound of lovemaking coming from inside. I couldn't tell if the woman with him was crying out in pleasure or in pain, but Saining's voice sounded entirely different from the way it did when he was with me. I had an intense desire to see them right then, but I didn't know what to do, so I ran.

I ran blindly down the street, back to my place, and up the stairs. As soon as I stepped inside my apartment, I called him up. There was no answer. I kept calling, and finally Saining came to the phone. I heard everything, I said. I want to see you right now or I'm going to die. I'll be there in ten minutes.

I set off again at a run, sprinting as fast as I could all the way to Saining's place.

He didn't open the door all the way but instead took me down-stairs. We got into a taxi.

He still hadn't said a word, and the anger in his face frightened me. We rode to the place where his band practiced, at a peasant's house out in the country. Saining introduced me to his good friend Sanmao.

So you're the girl who wants to figure out the meaning of life, Sanmao said. Who told you that? I asked. Saining, he answered. So, I asked, does Saining have a lot of girlfriends? Sanmao said, Not all that many. I asked, Why is it that men always have several girlfriends at a time? Sanmao said, Because we get bored easily.

I turned to Saining and said, I want to be with you. He said, Aren't we together right now? I said, I want to know your secrets. I want your secrets to become my secrets too. I want to know everything there is to know about you, I want to see you mak-ing love with other women, I want to see all of the different ways you are, I want to become one of those women who know everything.

You're only nineteen years old, Saining said, but you want to become a woman of the world. It's going to take some time.

Saining, you're only two years older than I am. You need to give me a chance to catch up with you.

He looked at me, and I looked at him looking at me. I started to cry.

Can't you do anything but cry? he said.

I said, I want to make love like that, I want you to be completely yourself, and I want to be with you totally. I want us to be together, really together.

I wanted to do things with him, and I wanted to hear him make

those sounds; I wanted it so much I could hardly stand it. But I
didn't know where to start, so I sat down on the floor, and the more
I cried, the sadder I felt. Saining ignored me.

At dusk we went back to Saining's and listened to music
together. Saining translated the Doors' lyrics for me.

Girl, you gotta love your man.
Girl, you gotta love your man.
Take him by the hand
Make him understand
The world on you depends.
Our life will never end.
Girl, you gotta love your man

Riders on the storm.
Riders on the storm.
Into this house we're born
Into this world we're thrown.
Like a dog without a bone
An actor out on loan.
Riders on the storm.

It was so smooth and supple, Jim Morrison's voice, and his spirit
drew us in, his soul caressing me, merging with me, quickening
me, drawing me on.

That day we didn't make love. Saining just held me, and we
spun into each other's dreams with the music. When we awoke, we
felt wonderful.

*   *   *

He never really talked to me about love. He was exactly what I'd been waiting for all this time. I was naked before him, he exposed me, and I felt close to him, but he couldn't make me easygoing, couldn't calm me down.

I said, Saining, what's a climax?

You'll know when it happens, he said.

He just wanted something light and sexy, a little fling, I thought, and I was the least sexy woman around, but I couldn't help that, could I?

Saining and Sanmao started a band of their own. Rock concerts were still rare, and the band often played the warm-up for other singers. They were usually booed offstage, but they didn't let it bother them. Saining said that he never turned down a chance to perform. As long as he got to play, he was happy. I always tagged along with them, although I wasn't sure what their music was about. I was only aware of their deep sadness, and I was in love with that melancholy.

I talked to Saining on the phone every day. I wanted very badly to see him alone, and I tried everything I could think of to please him. But he seemed unmoved. He might decide to take my clothes off, having me feel the rhythm of the music with my body, and he taught me how to move with the music and give him pleasure with my mouth. The scent of his penis was a secret we shared. I had no choice: I had to learn, I had to think of a way to make him need me. I think that every girl is like this the first time she falls in love.

Once, he was playing guitar and singing for me, and I was dancing around on his bed, and as he looked at me he sang me this question: Tell me, what do you want for your birthday? I said, I want you to be my boyfriend; I want something called love. His face darkened and he said, Boyfriends are for little girls. What women have is something else.

I started crying. He softened and came over and rested his head on my shoulder. There are many kinds of love, he said. If you only want one kind, you'll always be disappointed.

I said, Saining, didn't you once tell me that a woman who had never made love was a green apple, one who had made love was a red apple, and one who had made love too much was a worm-eaten apple, but that the last kind touched you with a special kind of beauty, a broken beauty? Right now I think you're a bastard! I don't want to be one of your apples! If you don't love me, then I don't want to see you anymore. I mean it.

Saining thought about this for a while and then said, OK, fine! Get out of here! I don't want you falling in love with me, especially not so fast. Get lost! I don't think I love you.

And just like that, without ceremony, that mean son of a bitch kicked me out.

4.

I stayed in town. In time, I found a job singing at a nightclub. I took to wearing cheap, low-cut, supershiny micromini "cocktail dresses" and singing Cantonese love songs.

I started cooking for myself and keeping my apartment clean. Every day I concentrated hard on trying to communicate with Saining by telepathy, calling his name in my head, calling him back to me. I wanted him because he knew how to make me love him.

And on an otherwise unremarkable night, my eternally baffling Saining appeared at my door. He pulled me to him quickly, saying, Baby, you've gotten so thin.

That was all he had to say. I felt weak all over.

Hand in hand, we went down to the street together — hand in hand like a couple of melancholy friends.

There were a lot of newly minted millionaires in town, and plenty of other people who were doing whatever they could just to get by. It seemed that everyone had come to this strange city to make money. It was hot and muggy, and the streets were always full of distraught people. Prostitutes were everywhere. They always wore black.

We went into the bar where we'd first met. When I ordered myself a cola, Saining said, You've got to stop drinking cola all the time. Women should drink alcohol.

A breath of moonlight drifted over Saining's face, and at this moment he became so peaceful and calm that he even seemed vulnerable. He looked down at the glass in his hand, and he looked as if he were dreaming.

I missed you so much, he said. You have that power. I used to be so depressed, before I met you. I want to give myself a chance, a chance to see if I can make something beautiful.

I was speechless. I just sat there, not believing my ears. I had never heard him say anything like this before. I was hearing the words of my first love. I said, I don't really know who you are, but I love you anyway. That must be what love is.

We called Saining's band mates up on the phone and asked them to join us. Saining told everyone that he had never thought he was capable of love, that he used to have trouble trusting women, and that he had assumed love must be something that would have to wait until he was middle-aged.

For the first time, Saining talked about himself. He had been bullied terribly as a child. Both of his parents were what was then known as "artistic political criminals." They had met at a labor farm somewhere in the Northwest, where they had both been sent for "Reform through Labor." His mother was a passionate admirer of the Soviet poet Sergei Esenin, so she named him Saining, which was the Chinese equivalent of Sergei. He was born at the labor camp. When he was nine, his parents were rehabilitated. They divorced soon thereafter. Saining said, Chinese marriages can withstand hardship and disaster, but they can't survive the good times. Sometime later, his mother remarried and moved to Japan. When he was twelve, Saining immigrated to England with his father. When I met him, he had been back in China for only a year.

His father had stubbornly hoped that Saining would become a violin prodigy. His first violin had been made for him by his father, out of bamboo, and the violin tunes of his childhood had all been hummed to him by his father. Saining said, Maybe this is why I got into the bad habit of always running away from things.

His parents had had to wait a long time for their political rehabilitation, but it didn't take them long at all to get a divorce. My parents are both really good people, he said, but they're both crazy. Until I was nine, we all lived at the labor farm. The three of us had been buffeted around too much already, and when it was all over, we just couldn't live together anymore.

Birmingham is a terrible place, he went on, an especially ugly place, and its streets are always full of worried people. I don't feel any connection to the place at all, but I truly loved the English countryside. If you haven't been to England, you can't possibly understand their literature or their music. England is unique, and the English don't like anybody who isn't English. When I traded in my violin for a guitar, I thought that my life was finally going to get interesting. Music was not going to shut me out anymore. But my relationship with my father deteriorated; we were always arguing. Things got out of control.

We pushed together a bunch of small tables to make a big one and began loudly extolling one another's virtues. Sanmao had brought along a U2 CD and he put it on the bar's sound system. The food at the bar was terrible, the beer was warm, and the waitresses were frank to the point of rudeness. When Sanmao caught someone spying on my man from the door to the toilet, our "wedding banquet" disintegrated into a free-for-all. Two opposing gangs turned the bar upside down while the bar owner just looked on without trying to stop it. I saw one guy who was missing not just one but both of his shirtsleeves, and meanwhile Sanmao had got ahold of a shovel and was standing stock-still in the middle of the room, and somehow Saining ended up with a tiny hat on his head that made him look like a train engineer's son.

Finally somebody in the other group yelled out, Stop fighting! None of us are from around here. Let's not give the locals an excuse to laugh at us!

The brawl ended instantly.

Saining returned the hat to its rightful owner, everybody contributed some money to the bar, and in the end they were all shaking hands.

You could call this "happiness": knowing for certain that that dead-of-night bar, in the darkness before dawn, is now very distant. Still, it's something I look back on.

5.

We started kissing, and we kissed until it became a kind of agony.

I'd never drunk so much alcohol before, and my head ached hotly. I'd never looked at a man's naked body until now, and I felt I couldn't distinguish between his skin and mine, couldn't tell for sure where my skin ended and his began, and we were enveloped in the softness of our own silence, and my desire lay hidden inside his body.

He traced a moist fingertip over my lips, saying, These are yours. When you're happy, it turns me on.

When he kissed my sex with his lips, I cried out. I had found the sense of total safety I had always craved.

He was slowly changing into another person, a sleepwalker, his hands getting heavier and heavier, his penis growing larger and larger inside me, and he let out a moan, this pitiful man. I finally heard that sound.

I said, Do you have to do that?

I hurt all over, but his cries had an eerie sweetness that made me reel, and I couldn't tell whether I was moaning with joy or with pain, and this made me feel ashamed. His sweat dripped onto my face, my breasts. I felt like a pathetic little girl. I looked up at him, loving the feeling of his sweat rolling across my body.

Finally he moved me on top of him, tonguing my breasts and breathing hard and warm against me. Suddenly I saw that his eyes were wet. He said, Remember me, remember me like you remember yourself.

My body broke with joy. I thought that this was probably a climax. Catching the scent of the substance flowing from inside my body, I saw into my own future, saw that I would become a woman with many stories to tell. But every story would have its price.

6.

Lying in bed in 1992, I thought back on that night three years earlier, thought back on all of the passion and pain and hunger and terror connected with it. I was still confused. Three years had passed, and I was still asking myself, What is love, anyway? The only thing I knew was that it was impossible for me not to see this man. We needed each other. There were secrets that only we shared.

And what was a climax? Qi told me that she had passed out once when she was coming, and this left me feeling more confused than ever. I loved the turbulent mood Saining and I shared when he was screwing me — this moment was more real to me than anything. I loved it when Saining screwed me like a total stranger while his lips spoke the sweetest words — it was only when he was fucking me as if he didn't know me that he would say things that really touched me. That was his style.

I know, language hurt me. Language hurt me, and there was nothing I could do about it!

One night, Saining repeated something he'd said to me early in our relationship, Remember me, remember me like you remember yourself! I didn't know if he was saying this to me again on this particular night because he'd just had a really good orgasm, or because I'd found out that he was cheating on me again.

God only knows how many illicit sexual encounters took place on any given evening at the nightclub where I sang. A lot of girls came from the countryside or from other cities to make a living here. Qi was just one among many transient "cocktail hostesses." She wore a perpetually quizzical expression; her face even looked like a question mark. I found out that her name was Qi, that we were from the same city, that she'd gone to university, and that she had no father. On another occasion, we were having drinks together, and after talking about Freud's *Dora: An Analysis of a Case of Hysteria*, we became friends. But one day she called me up out of the blue and asked me to come over to her place. She said she wanted to break up with her boyfriend and that she needed to have an audience. It had been a long time since I'd seen Qi, and this was the first I'd heard about her having a boyfriend. I also hadn't known that she had a place of her own — she'd always moved around a lot.

It used to be that I didn't like having a fixed address of my own, she told me. But then I met him. He looked after me, and I could be myself with him. Even though he knows what I do for a living, he still loves me. We can't keep our hands off each other. We just want to make love all the time. He helped me learn to love myself.

Qi poured me some Chivas, and I looked at her slim legs. Pretty Shanghai girls all had these beautiful legs.

I realized that she didn't have any mixers, but she said she liked her drinks straight. Saining also took his drinks that way, but I didn't like Chivas, and I especially didn't like drinking it plain. It was too much like being an alcoholic.

Little Qi was playing it cool that day, but it was all an act, because not once did she mention her boyfriend's name.

There were times I had turned my apartment upside down trying to find some book or other to lend to Qi. I told Saining how sorry I felt for her. Saining had reacted coldly, saying, What gives you the right to feel sorry for people? You just can't resist the weak or the sick, but frankly, it's immoral. You're a phony, and you just use people to make yourself feel better. I said, What are you talking about? You've gotten so weird lately; you used to love meeting new people. All I know is that she needs help, and I feel as though I have to help her.

I looked around Qi's apartment. I liked the way she had decorated it — simple, cozy, sensitive. I was thinking that I'd been right about her, that she had a lot of depth.

We sipped our drinks and listened to a Hong Kong radio station, and when we were just starting to feel a little bit drunk, we heard the sound of a key turning in the lock.

And who should step inside but Saining?

I screamed.

Is this your idea of a joke, Qi? I asked.

Saining stood stupidly in front of us, his full mouth hanging open, but his eyes were unclouded. He didn't appear to be the least bit uneasy or embarrassed.

Saining, I said, we're going home, now!

Without uttering a word, Saining made to follow me out, but Qi's icy voice was right behind us: I love him more than you do!

I turned and hurled my glass. Go ahead, I said. Take him and love him all you want — he's yours!

What the hell are you doing? Saining asked. What the hell do you think you're doing?

I said, Nobody has the right to talk to me like that!

I looked at Saining. My father had told me that this man wouldn't love me for more than a year. The bark of the poplar tree has the most beautiful eyes a hundred miles around, the saying went. Looking at Saining's eyes, those eyes that still had the power to hold me, I wondered whom I could believe. I didn't want to go; I wanted to stay and see what would happen next.

Qi walked over to us.

Saining, she said, do you love me?

Qi's face was the classic "melon seed" oval, her eyes were clear and liquid, but she also looked damaged, and her clear skin appeared almost bloodless. A long, narrow, classical nose, full lips that bowed upward, discolored teeth, a flat chest, tiny nipples. She always wore stiff, Chinese-made bras, had spindly, malnourished legs, long, skinny toes like Shanghai scallions, a thin waist, a flat ass.

Her sexual technique was average, but she was good at suppressing orgasms because sex for her was a means to other ends. She was a typical Shanghainese slut — they're the world's best fakers, the world's best liars. A lot of these Shanghai sluts become professional prostitutes. They aren't as businesslike and efficient as girls from the Northeast or girls from Sichuan, who meet, conduct their transactions, and are on their way. They excel at deception. They aren't afraid to spend a lot of time and effort on the slow seduction, because what satisfies them is a successful lie. And they aren't like girls from other parts of the country who sell themselves to pay off their fathers' debts, or to buy land or a house. They aren't driven into prostitution by hardship, because their lives aren't all that hard to begin with. They go into the business to feed their egos. This is the typical Shanghai slut. These are women who never tell you what they're thinking. They're smart, but almost always too smart for their own good. Most of them had useless fathers and capable but unlucky mothers. Like their mothers, they're status conscious, in love with Western things, good-hearted but naturally selfish, suspicious of men but in love with the gratification that comes from stealing another woman's man. I believed that Qi had genuinely fallen for Saining, but she wasn't about to throw away her rich clients on account of him. That's what Shanghai sluts are like; they want to have it both ways. They're good at letting slip, bit by bit, the details of their sad stories, not knowing themselves what's true and what's a lie. In bed they're apt to blurt out, Do you love me? And they're good at faking orgasms and feigning madness. They always have trouble putting their heart into what they're doing, especially when they're making love.

But who they were going to be, what they were destined to become, was determined long before they were born, by the men who fucked their mothers and the men who fucked their mothers' mothers.

I could easily picture what Qi had done to get Saining into such a mixed-up state.

Now she was telling me, Don't try to influence him. There's only one thing I want from him right now. I just want to hear him tell the truth, just once.

This was the first time Qi had looked at me since Saining had walked through the door. In my mind, this tiny woman was pure evil, but she had a hypnotic power, which had Saining and me standing there as though we were in some kind of trance.

I knew you wouldn't be able to do it, she said to Saining. I don't ever want to see any of these clothes again. You're such a bore!

Qi started tearing off her clothes and flinging them at Saining, piece by piece. With purposeful movements, she stripped down right in front of us, and as I watched, her "frailty" took on an unexpected power, became an object of respect. I discovered that this little whore was actually very beautiful. Until now, I wouldn't have been able to define her beauty. It was a melancholy beauty and inseparable from her body.

I've seen through you! Qi took a stack of CDs out of the cabinet and hurled them at Saining.

He knelt down and began trying to gather up the disks. He had a nasty expression on his face, which made me sick at heart.

Do you understand? I don't feel anything for you at all! I want you out of my life! I don't want you ever to come near me again.

Saining had heard enough, and with his arms full of CDs, he opened the door and went out, with Qi wailing after him: You worthless shit! I was so wrong about you! I'm always wrong about people!

I said to Qi, I'll say! You were dead wrong about him. He was already in love with me. He couldn't fall in love with you too. He couldn't have done it, and you shouldn't have expected him to. He and I are really in love. We love each other very much.

I started to cry.

Qi also began crying. I'm so sorry, she said.

I said, You're sorry? After all I did for you, you went and seduced Saining behind my back, and now you say you're sorry?

Qi's voice went cold. She spoke deliberately, choosing each word carefully: There's just one thing that I think you should know. Saining came to me. He got into my bed, not the other way around.

All of a sudden, things looked very different to me. In a panic, I burst out of her apartment.

When I got to the ground floor of her building, I found Saining huddled there, and a conversation that Qi and I had once had came back to me in a rush. She'd told me how she'd made love with a friend's boyfriend, that he'd really screwed her brains out, and we'd talked about how maybe a big part of the excitement came from the secrecy, from cheating on someone. Now I realized that the man had probably been Saining, and I cursed him, before running outside.

I tore down the street recklessly, my emotions in constant turmoil, until I became too worked up to calm down. Rushing along on foot, I couldn't stop picturing the two of them in all sorts of erotic scenes, and I was getting more and more upset, and I kept shaking my head, until finally even I had to conclude that speculating about other people like this was pretty disgusting. When I thought of Saining buying clothes and CDs for another woman, I started to shake. And whenever I start to shake, it's a very bad sign.

I thought he was mine and I was his, and that there was no one else in our lives. I thought that was love.

Maybe the kind of love that I'd believed in was something you could never have in real life. I felt a sense of bitter disappointment.

Later, when I got home, Saining was sitting in my doorway.

The moment he entered me, I knew once again that I couldn't be without him, and that nothing else in the world made sense to me except this, and that nothing else mattered to me.

I began to cry, and I said, Don't leave me; you're all I have!

My body shuddered with his, and my eyelids fluttered. It had been a long time since we had made love — I'd thought he was putting all of his energy into his music. Saining could put me into a dreamlike state when we made love. He became another person when we made love, someone absent, and he went somewhere else, somewhere outside of life, to a place that only he knew. He never spoke to me about what would make me happy, and he certainly wasn't an expert lover. He just wanted what he wanted. But I felt driven to make him happy. I didn't know how else to make him need me. When he was sick, I loved his sickness like my own. I wanted to be controlled by him because I didn't know it could be otherwise, and there was something absolute and pure about our need to obey our emotions, and this gave me a certainty. I reveled in the shameful feelings our couplings gave me, as if this was what I was living for.

We were drinking, and it had been a long time since we'd drunk together. Between sips I said, Saining, we have problems. He said, You're right. We do have problems. I said, Like what? He said, I can't really explain it.

At first light I got up and started to gather my things. And then I realized that Saining was behind me, like a shadow, sitting on the floor at my back. In the early-morning light his skin looked even paler and his eyes even brighter than usual.

Do you really have to go?

Three years ago you slept with one of our neighbors, and you left me feeling like I had no place in the world to call my own, but I stayed with you anyway. I didn't even blame you — I just held on to you tighter. That was a mistake. I should have left you and waited for you to ask me to come back. I won't make the same mistake twice.

Saining picked up an ashtray and struck himself on the head with it. I saw blood.

Grow up! Even if you were dying right in front of me, I'd still leave. You make me feel unclean, as if I'd had sex with millions of people, and I can't stand that.

Saining lunged at me and pulled me to him. He leaned against the door and said, OK, how about you wait until my head stops bleeding? Then you can go.

You're even more careless with your life than I am. I can give you a few more minutes of my time, but you're not going to convince me to stay with you. You don't understand love; neither of us does. Why else do these things keep happening?

How can you say that?

Saining, you became a father at eighteen. You said the mother was a prostitute ten years older than you, you left the child with your father for a year, and then you gave him back because you did some investigating and found out you weren't the father after all. Now you're twenty-four, your mother is in Japan, your father is in England, and you're on your own in China. You're not family, and I can choose whether or not to be with you. Nobody is responsible for you but yourself. You have to learn to accept the consequences of what you do. My father taught me this.

7.

I moved in with Sanmao. This time I couldn't tell myself that Saining wasn't to blame.

I was like a bird perching on a rooftop; I was stuck. My self-confidence had reached a low point. Sanmao said that my problem was that in loving Saining I had forgotten myself, and that a person who doesn't love herself is unlovable in turn. He told me, Love is something that has to be learned.

I went out every day to buy liquor, but I always threw up before I'd drunk very much. Sanmao said I was a sad and stupid girl.

Saining came to see me every Sunday night. He always brought presents, and sometimes he brought me songs he'd written while thinking about me. Saining's response to the world around him was mystical and highly original, but he hadn't had a decent Chinese education. There was no schooling for him at the work farm, and after he'd gone to England he wasn't able to study Chinese, so the songs he wrote were full of wrong characters, and I was usually the only person who could decipher them and make any sense out of what he wrote. He worked hard to express his feelings in the songs he wrote about me, saying that he couldn't bear to be parted from me. Soon he was even calling me "a woman as sweet as milk," but then the next thing I knew he was also calling me "a cookie laced with poison."

I asked Saining, Do you love Qi? He said, Yes. I said, What do you love about her? He said, I love her vulnerability and her selfishness, her beauty and her sadness. I love her stubbornness, I love her body, I love the way she doesn't love people. I said, Saining, don't I have a good body? Don't I satisfy you? Saining said, Her body expresses so much disappointment. I'm addicted to that feeling of hopelessness. I said, Well, you always say exactly what you mean. So, do you feel the same kind of love for her and me? He said, I feel the same kind of love for everyone; I only have one kind of love. I said, I only have one kind of love too, but you're the only person I love. There's no one else; I love only you. But you, if you love me and everyone else the same way, then why do you feel like you have to be with me? He said, Because I need to have some connection with you in this life. And he started to cry.

He couldn't do anything without crying. When we made love, he performed badly, often quitting halfway through. He played with my breasts until they got sore, and I was afraid that the good times we'd had in the past would never come back. This thought made me shudder. I really didn't know what love was; I only knew that if he were to be cut out of my life, I wouldn't be able to go on.

I tracked Qi down. I told her I could never forgive her for the pain she'd caused me and said I hoped that she would disappear from our lives forever. I said, Saining loves you, but he'll never be able to leave me. Do you want to be in love with a man like that? Qi said, You and Saining, you're both pathetic little good-for-nothings, just sponging off of other people. You're useless; you don't even understand each other! You're a pair of idiots, and you bore me to death!

She left, and I never saw her again.

I chose a blustery and moonless night to slash my wrists. Sanmao was at work at the nightclub, and I knew what time Saining would be leaving the house where he tutored, knew that he would be coming to see me that night. So I went into the bathroom a little before I expected him to show up. And when the knife in my hand pressed against my vein and finally cut through, I felt as though this was real, and I shook and felt my body approaching a state of bliss, and I was crying. I turned on the faucet, letting the cold water course over my hot veins. I sat on the edge of the bathtub, feeling dizzy and repeating to myself over and over, If he really loves me, he'll sense that something is wrong; he won't be late if I'm not meant to die.

Suicide isn't something you perform for an audience. You weren't trying to kill yourself, and you weren't proving how much you love me. You just wanted to be one of those stupid, crazy little whores. You're such a bore.

These were the first words Saining said to me after I woke up.

We were both crying. Saining never cried in front of anyone but me, and I found his tears seductive.

While I was in the hospital, Saining never left my side. He got me moved to a private room, and we listened to music together, sharing the headset, one earpiece for each of us. With him beside me, I was able to sleep, even though it was very hard for us to be intimate there, even though I didn't think that it was over yet. Sometimes I would tell myself, You're only twenty-two years old; you should get a job. You shouldn't depend on a man like this. You need to find your own future; this life you're leading is keeping you from growing up.

But I couldn't help myself; I couldn't fight it.

The day I got out of the hospital, I invited all of the band members out to a restaurant that specialized in snake. In the middle of the meal, I said abruptly, Saining, I've made a decision. I want to split up with you. I want to go back to Shanghai.

No! he said.

I said, Fine, we don't have to break up. So, you and Sanmao are always talking about how men in the Northwest like to beat their wives, right? I want you to sit right there and let me slap you on the face.

I was pointing to the center of the room, which was also the most crowded part of the restaurant, as I spoke. I'd rehearsed these words earlier.

Saining looked down without responding.

Stop it, you two! Sanmao tried to intercede.

If he loves me, he'll do it. He asked for it.

With a whoosh, Saining stood up while everyone looked on. Moving a stool over to the middle of the room, he sat down facing me, and before anyone had a chance to react, I had already gone over and given him a loud slap on the face.

I started to cry, and all of the shame came pouring out of me.

Many people were getting to their feet, but Saining held me tight, saying, Don't worry about it. It's nothing, really, it's nothing. She's my girlfriend, and I'm sorry if we disturbed anyone. This is between her and me.

We came back to the table and just looked at each other for a long while, and I couldn't hear anything going on around us, because I just wanted to look at him, and to look at him looking at me.

Let's stretch our legs, I said.

In the restaurant toilet I grasped his penis in my hand, and I suddenly felt upset when I realized that I'd hardly ever taken the initiative with him. It was 1992, I was twenty-two years old, and I was so useless. This made me start crying all over again.

A full moon was rising in the sky outside the window. I had to lock him up tight. I had the tools. I got down on my knees and started to pray. The rays of moonlight there were so hazy that I thought I was losing my mind. His flesh was soft in my hand, and I had to love it. Loving it would make it beautiful. I wanted to hold him, to squeeze him hard until I crushed him. I sucked him, sucking out his wet soul until the end, until that gateway to his life had closed. He was my one and only. I had learned how to give head, how to beg, how to pray. He had become my prey; I wanted to turn him inside out. God, how I wanted to turn all my caresses into curses and caress him all over, with limitless tenderness, until he would whisper to me soft and clear, I love you!

I swallowed, and with his semen inside me, I found myself again.

I moved back in. Once more, he and I were rushing, hand in hand, toward an uncertain tomorrow.

8.

Saining and I fell into a daily routine that continued, unchanged, for several years. We slept during the day, rising at dusk to go out to eat. We spent our nights at home relaxing, amusing ourselves. Occasionally we might go perform, or we might go out of town on a short vacation. We always made love in the early hours around dawn. The mornings were cold, and I liked the special sense of our place in the world that I had during these times. When the light penetrated the hazy atmosphere, I could always see Saining's hair spread out like wings on the pillow. I loved his hair; his hair was like the threads of my thoughts. Almost every morning, while it was still very early, Saining would stand by the window and play his violin. His guitar playing was spectral, plaintive, and cutting. But his violin playing was so classically pure and refined that I felt a sense of despair whenever I listened to it.

I worked for only a short time. Saining hated my singing at the nightclub, and he was always taking the outfits I performed in and cutting them up into all sorts of strange shapes, always trying to stir up trouble, always picking fights. During my brief stint as a nightclub singer, Saining would go for days barely speaking to me at all, not even when we were making love.

Saining also worked for a bit, tutoring a "problem child," a little boy from Hong Kong named Toby. Toby had a school phobia. He had been sent to live in Mainland China with his nanny, and he spent his days at home. Saining taught him math, English, and violin and how to play soccer. Saining and Toby had met purely by chance, but they trusted each other, and I was glad that Saining was Toby's tutor. I never imagined that many of the times when I thought he was at Toby's, Saining was actually sneaking around with Qi.

After the business with Qi, Saining convinced Toby to go back to Hong Kong. He said he wasn't up to the task of shouldering Toby's problems, and besides, Toby belonged with his parents.

Saining was skipping a lot of band rehearsals, and Sanmao was furious. Sanmao saw music as a way to change his life, but Saining simply liked playing in a band for its own sake, and he didn't have any ambitions greater than that. Saining didn't have the same chip on his shoulder that Sanmao did; he wasn't as worried about the fate of the nation. I watched their friendship ebb and flow, now close, now distant, in an endless cycle. Being in a band was just like being in love. Every time you broke up or got back together again, the memory of it was carved indelibly into your mind.

Sanmao said the way we were living wasn't healthy, with Saining depending on his mother for money, and me depending on Saining for money. Sanmao said that bit by bit we were going to rot. Sanmao thought that we needed to seek out hardship, to pay some dues. But I felt that as long as I could spend my days with Saining, I would be perfectly content to rot away. Whenever Sanmao castigated us, we just giggled like a pair of fools. There was nothing he could do to us.

Saining's mother kept on sending him money. All those Japanese yen went a long way in China, and we lived easy lives. For my part, I kept on spending Saining's money. I didn't want to work, since I hadn't been to trade school and I didn't know what kind of job I could expect to find. Wages in this town were pitifully low unless you went into some sort of business, legal or illegal, or wanted to sing in a nightclub. Of course, there were plenty of law-abiding citizens working in offices, but I didn't know what sort of job I could look for.

Saining and I had a lot in common. For one thing, we each had our own worlds, our own mute worlds, and because of this, we respected each other's silences. We both had asthma, both of us used to be picked on, neither of us had any grand ideals. We weren't interested in other people's lives, we were sensitive and self-doubting, we didn't believe what we read in the newspaper, we were afraid of failure, and yet the thought of resisting some temptation made us anxious. We wanted to be onstage, to be artists. We kept on spending other people's money, dreading the day when all of this would change. We didn't want to become good little members of society, nor did we know how. Anyway, we would tell ourselves, we're still young.

We knew that there were lots of people just like us, but we still felt especially lucky to have found each other. The two of us shared joy and gloom, vulnerability, humor, and shame. Every day we watched each other fall asleep.

Sometimes I thought that the love that Saining and I had was a kind of poison, for as we lay together in the soft depths of the night, the quiet and tranquillity left us speechless, left us never wanting to awaken.

9.

The street outside our apartment windows was the most famous street in town. On either side it was packed with unbroken rows of shops and big all-night restaurants. Every evening, as night fell, the street filled with throngs of women. They came from every corner of China, some around my age, some much younger, some much older. Their eyes followed the slow-moving stream of vehicles that drove by, tracking each car, while the men in the cars stared back, because some of those cars might stop for these women. The make and model of a car (they were afraid of military or police cars), the way the driver spoke, these were the keys to whether they would stay or go. People around there called them "chickens" or "roving orioles." The streetwalkers were the cheapest and most miserable of the prostitutes, but they also had the most freedom. Most of them also used heroin. They didn't have to worry about losing their looks and being cast aside, since anyone could work this street, no matter how ugly she was. Of course, they had a higher chance of being hauled in by the police here, and a higher chance of running into hassles like customers who wouldn't pay. The town's highest concentration of beggars gathered around these women, as did a crowd of pimps, drug dealers, young flower-selling girls, and shish kebab vendors. For years the Public Security Bureau had been trying to control this avenue, and they'd even held rallies there where they'd meted out justice. Occasionally a police vehicle covered in wire mesh would drive by, and you could see little clumps of people scattering in every direction, accompanied by the sound of the girls' screeching. Diagonally across the street from our building was a big movie theater, a theater that doubled as a place of business for the sex trade, mostly blow jobs or what they called "airplane rides" — hand jobs. Each contingent of cops had its own jurisdiction, so whenever the police showed up on the street, everybody ran into the movie theater, and whenever police appeared at the doors of the theater, everybody ran out into the street. Sometimes it didn't take anything more than for a van carrying frozen pork to drive by, but if even one person appeared to break into a run, all the others would take to their heels.

Everyone on the street spent their hours scurrying back and forth. Every night things got lively. And when the darkness fell away and the sun came up and penetrated the shadowy recesses of the endlessly cruising cars, you could always see a few girls still standing around, junkies who hadn't done enough business. This was the street where Saining and I lived, in a big apartment building, and I often stood on the balcony watching it all, until, over the course of a few years, it became a nightly ritual.

10.

Rock groups started cropping up in Beijing, and from time to time some of the embassies hosted underground rock concerts.

Saining and his band went to Beijing. While he was away, I went back to Shanghai. From there I planned to travel up to Beijing so that Saining and I could celebrate my twenty-second birthday together.

On the phone, Saining told me that he was going to be out at the Great Wall doing performance art on the afternoon when I was to arrive. I said, I'm coming just to see you, but you couldn't care less. Since when are you so interested in performance art? And what is performance art, anyway? He said that he had to go, that he was already committed, but that looking at the times, he was absolutely certain he would be able to meet me at the airport. I said, At five or six in the evening the roads in Beijing are bound to be jammed. He said he could guarantee that he'd be there for me on time. Lastly, he said he missed me.

The next day I waited at the airport for four hours. By the time Saining showed up, I was a wreck.

When I saw who he was with, the situation quickly spun out of control. The guy he'd brought along was someone who had stolen money from Saining in the past. He went around telling people he was a Buddhist, and while he clearly knew a lot about Buddhist teachings, he still struck me as a very immoral person. On top of this, I thought he treated Saining badly. Saining appeared to be well aware of this person's faults, but he nonetheless treated him better than he treated me. I was certain that he was the one who had dragged Saining into the performance art piece. Beijing was full of slackers like him.

I wanted to go to the most expensive place in Beijing for dinner, and Saining took me to Wangfu, where I ordered the priciest champagne on the menu. I was drinking on an empty stomach, and the alcohol hit me fast. That person I despised just sat off to the side, eating and going on and on about his lack of interest in me. After I'd had a bit to drink, I started berating Saining. He argued back. A lot of people were looking at us, and a waiter came over to intervene. The waiter said, He didn't do it on purpose; he didn't mean to. Saining said, You see? Even he can tell I didn't do it on purpose. When I heard this, I picked up my bottle of birthday champagne and broke it over Saining's head. Shattered glass went flying, and champagne sprayed everywhere.

The police showed up, and Saining dragged me into the elevator, where I started hitting him. We got out of the elevator, and Saining carted me outside and pushed me into a car. The door closed behind me. I felt like killing him.

I have never genuinely wanted to kill someone. Except for that night.

I pictured him sitting beside me, pictured him breathing his last breath right before my eyes, and my entire being was focused on this fantasy. I wanted to kill him. I thought of all the times he'd hurt me, and I started shaking. I took a penknife out of my makeup bag, imagining that this small but very sharp knife could kill someone. Just then, that son of a bitch got into the car. If I was going to kill Saining, I had to do it now.

The car started moving. I didn't dare try to kill Saining. I realized that if I killed him, his goddamned friends would know it was me, and I wouldn't be able to get away.

I took the knife and started gouging holes in the car. Saining said, This isn't my car. He glanced at the driver and added, And it's not his car either! I made a cut in Saining's arm. It was then that I realized there was blood on his face, and in his hair. I was crying, and then I was screaming and shouting. Saining yelled, Stop the car! He jumped out, pulled out my luggage, and then dragged me out of the car. He got back into the car, and as he was shutting the door, I said, Please don't go! I'm still mad at you! But the car kept going.

I finally calmed down. I thought that if I waited there long enough, he would come back, but I hailed a cab. I told the driver to take me to the airport. When we got there, the airport was completely dark. I said, Take me to the airport hotel.

After checking into my hotel room, I drank every bottle of liquor in the minibar before going off to sleep in the bathroom.

The next day I called up Sanmao's girlfriend and asked her for Sanmao and Saining's address in Beijing. I said, I want to kill Saining. Sanmao's girlfriend asked me why I didn't just call them up and ask for their address myself. I said, Because Saining knows I want to kill him, so I can't let them know I'm coming. Sanmao's girlfriend said that she didn't know their address either, since she was just like me and never wrote letters but always phoned.

I called Saining's place. A stranger answered the phone. Nobody else was home. He said they'd all gone to do performance art. I asked, Where is it happening? He said, There's one somewhere in Zhongguancun, one near Jianguo Gate, one in the Old City, and another one out near the airport. I said, Isn't there another one at the Great Wall? That was yesterday, he said. Then he hung up.

I set out from the airport, frantically searching for the performance. The immensity of Beijing made me reel, and as a woman, I wasn't being treated with the respect I was used to.

At nine-thirty that night I flew back south. The moment the plane became airborne, I stopped hating Saining and I remembered all the good things he'd done for me. His attraction for me was too strong to resist; loving him was a compulsion. I was just a pathetic and insecure little girl. The color of the nearing skies always blurred the colors that were right in front of me. I had nothing, I didn't understand myself at all, and I was so pathetic. But how could I fight the desire I felt for this man? No matter how he treated me, I would stick by him; I would even die for him if it came to that.

But where did that deranged woman I was the night before come from? What had happened? I really didn't understand myself anymore.

The airplane rose into the sky, and the more I thought, the more I worried. I realized that I had been in danger, that I had just had a very dangerous birthday.

I went away for three weeks. While I was gone, a couple of girls from Nanjing named Cat and Kitten stayed at Saining's and my apartment. I had met Kitten first. She and Cat had been friends since childhood. They both worked at the nightclub where I used to sing. Kitten was stubborn and haughty, and she had a quick temper. But when the two of us talked together, she came across as very gentle and sincere, naive even. I liked her a lot.

Two days after I returned to the South, another friend of mine from Nanjing, Nanjing Noodles, came over to my place for dinner. She brought along her boyfriend, Luobu, who came from Chaozhou. Kitten and Cat were there too.

After dinner, as I was carrying a huge pile of dishes to the kitchen, a pair of men barged in. They asked, Is Ah Jin here?

Who's Ah Jin? I asked.

You know, Ah Jin. Ah Jin from Nanjing, they said.

Kitten was watching the news, Cat was doing I don't know what, and Nanjing Noodles and Luobu were in the bedroom listening to the radio.

Kitten! Come here! I said. They're looking for a guy from Nanjing named Ah Jin.

No problem! Kitten said. I'll take them to where he is.

There was nothing in Kitten's face to make me suspect that anything was wrong. I carried the dishes into the kitchen, but when I came back out I saw that there were now three strange men in my apartment, and they were all sitting on my sofa. Granted, none of them was older than twenty-one or twenty-two, they were all wearing clean T-shirts and black leather shoes that had been buffed and polished to a high shine, and each of them was carrying a black backpack, the kind that high school students use to carry their books.

Ah Jin lives here, they asserted. He's brought us over here before. We'll just wait here until he shows up.

Kitten and Cat were standing off to the side. Neither of them said anything.

The apartment had two bedrooms and a living room. One of the bedroom doors was wide open. There were a few things stacked inside: speakers, guitars, an effects box, a violin, and a mattress. I shared the other bedroom with Saining. The door was closed. The light was on, and the radio was turned up loud, tuned to Channel 2 out of Hong Kong. Since Nanjing Noodles was also from Nanjing, I thought that she might know who this Ah Jin was. I shouted her name several times. The bedroom door opened, and Nanjing Noodles and Luobu came out grinning.

Before I could even open my mouth, three foot-long butcher knives came whistling out of the three backpacks. Those three boys with their sharp knives ordered us all into the bedroom, where a song by the Hong Kong pop star Liu Dehua was blaring. With two of the knives trained on us four women and one man, the other knife boy began turning the bedroom upside down.

They were speaking among themselves in Hunanese, and I got the impression that they were having some kind of disagreement. But I couldn't figure out what had brought them here, what their purpose was — was it robbery, tracking down an enemy, rape, mutilation, kidnapping? Maybe it was all a mistake. As the knife tip danced in front of my face, every possible scenario flashed through my mind. The boy who was going through our stuff found the place where we kept our cash, and he found all of my jewelry, both real and fake, but none of this appeared to interest him or his cohorts in the least. He pulled out our identification papers and rifled through them. He even checked under the rug. I really couldn't tell what they were after. Let them do whatever they want, I thought, just don't let them cut our faces! I prayed to all of the gods and spirits, Please, please don't let them cut us!

One of these boys with knives came across a new package of stockings. He tore open the plastic bag and came up to me, a big smirk on his tough but babyish face. He said, These are yours, right, miss? But you haven't worn them yet, so they're clean.

With that he pulled a pair of hose out of the bag and stuffed them into my mouth. Gesturing at the photograph of Saining and me, he asked, So that's your longhaired boyfriend, huh? I thought,

Damn him! Damn Saining! This was his fault! He'd gotten into some kind of trouble, and now these guys were here to take their revenge!

They took those clean, unworn stockings, and one by one, they stuffed them into our mouths. Then, one at a time, they stripped us of our watches and jewelry. They were rough; they shoved us around. I started to whimper when they took off the necklace that my mother had given me and a ring and watch that Saining had given me.

They took out a roll of wide packing tape and taped our mouths shut. Then they bound our hands with it and put us together and wrapped us up in a big circle. They were hitting Luobu, demanding between blows, What are you looking at, huh? What are you looking at?

The five of us sat passively, staring blankly ahead. None of our eyes met.

Finally they stuck pillows in between us to separate our bodies and threw a quilt over our heads, the same quilt Saining and I slept under. They strutted off and didn't close the door.

Luobu was the first to work free of his bonds. He yanked off the quilt covering our heads and pulled the nylons from Kitten's mouth.

Don't worry about us right now! she yelled. Go after them! Catch them!

Luobu did not dare. Kitten scrambled out the second-story window.

Nanjing Noodles and I couldn't stop spitting. We couldn't see Kitten or the robbers. There was nothing but the usual noisy activity in the street below. The street I lived on was famous, and tonight it was filled with the usual assortment of prostitutes, pimps, beggars, little girls selling flowers, police, vendors, passersby, and drug dealers.

I spotted Dalong sitting on the ground in front of a small shop.

Dalong was younger than I. He was an orphan, and his friends had brought him down here from Shanghai to be a pimp, but he'd set up a stall and sold kebabs, grilled quail, and roasted corn. Every night, Dalong came out here along with the prostitutes, and they plied their respective trades until dawn. He became good friends with the girls who worked the street. There was some secret ingredient that Dalong put in his meat skewers that made them addictive. Once, he was caught in the supermarket shoplifting some condoms for one of the girls, but fortunately I happened to be walking by just then and I paid his fine. I helped him out because I felt that his shish kebabs had real soul and that anyone who could make such wonderful food had to be a good person.

Dalong! I shouted across the road. I've been robbed! Can you spot me twenty *yuan* right now? I need to go get a loan.

Despite what I'd just been through, I felt great. I borrowed some more money from Sanmao's girlfriend and went to the supermarket and bought a bunch of food. I didn't think I'd be able to sleep much that night. I got home and found, for the second time that evening, several strange men sitting in my apartment. None of the lights were on, and nobody greeted me. Cat, Kitten, Nanjing Noodles, and Luobu were all still there.

I heard someone say in Nanjing dialect, Shit, Nanjing people do the stupidest things! And then all of us lose face!

I started sifting through our things. One of Saining's acoustic guitars was gone. That guitar had been with Saining longer than any of his others, and I wasn't sure how he would react when he found out it was missing. I started to feel upset.

I made a call to Beijing. The phone rang and rang for a long time, but no one answered it. I hung up and called again. Still no one answered. I hung up again, then called right back. This time, after two rings, a woman with a lazy drawl picked up the line. Is Saining there? I asked. Who's Saining? she said. He's my boyfriend, I said. Who's your boyfriend? she said. Who are you? I said. You have a lot of nerve! Don't you have any manners? she countered. Listen, I said, just because I ask you who you are doesn't mean that I don't have any manners. She said, What's it to you who I am? I said, Nothing, I hope. Otherwise, we have a problem.

I hung up on her and sat on the bed sobbing and eating chocolate.

Someone knocked on my bedroom door, and in walked a refined-looking young man in a ridiculous suit and white shoes. His hair was slicked back, his skin very pale.

I'm Ah Jin, he said. Honestly, I didn't have anything to do with what happened here earlier. I'm just as confused as you are.

Get out, all of you! I said. This noise is killing me.

They all left, and I got to work cleaning the place up.

An hour or so later, Cat, Kitten, Nanjing Noodles, and Luobu came back. The moment she stepped inside, Kitten dropped down on her knees before me with a loud thud.

I'm so, so sorry, she said. When you were gone, I brought some people over here, and there was obviously some kind of trouble among them. But they clearly knew our habits, the way they came and robbed us at seven o'clock at night. It's all my fault.

Don't say that, I said soothingly. You were robbed too. I can't blame you. Just forget about it, OK? Now, stand up!

And the four of us women had a good cry together.

There was something naggingly weird about the whole incident. Who was this Ah Jin, anyway?

Ah Jin, it turned out, was a pimp, and the previous week at the New Capital Restaurant one of his girls had ripped off a client to the tune of more than 100,000 *yuan*.

No way! Some guy was walking around with 100,000 *yuan* in his pockets? Why didn't he drop it off at home first?

Really, it's the truth. The whole Nanjing crowd knows about it.

Kitten and Cat started arguing loudly. When they got into arguments, they usually switched to Nanjing dialect, which drove me crazy.

Forget it! I said. Let's just forget about this whole mess. I don't want to call the police, and neither of you has any proof, so what's the point in reporting it? The truth is, I'm the one who screwed up. I didn't realize what they were up to, and if I hadn't called Nanjing Noodles out of the bedroom, and if the door to the bedroom had stayed shut the whole time, things could have been very different. From the moment they walked in the door, all those guys really wanted was to see who was inside that room, to see if there wasn't some other thug in there.

Kitten said, Actually, the moment they said they were looking for Ah Jin, I panicked. I just wanted to get them out of here. If I could lure them away, I wouldn't have to be afraid of them anymore, because I knew there was a gang from Nanjing hanging out in the food stall downstairs.

Things are pretty mixed up between me and Saining right now, I said. The last thing I want is for him to come back and find everything in such a mess. You two are going to have to stay out of trouble from now on.

I've been wanting to go back to Nanjing for a long time, Cat said. But I was waiting until I'd made enough money.

I don't want to go home! put in Kitten. I just want to make lots of money!

Oh, so that's how you go about making money, is it? countered Cat. By stirring everything up. And to top it all off, you rip off your clients too.

He insulted me, Kitten protested.

The way we earn money is an insult to us all by itself, do you understand? Why can't you just accept that you're being paid to be humiliated?

Kitten said, Fuck you! That bastard couldn't pay me enough for that.

The phone rang, and when I picked it up, the person on the other end of the line asked if she had reached such and such a number. A familiar voice and a familiar question. If some woman was always calling my house and saying she had the wrong number, I'd have to suspect that it wasn't a wrong number at all, just the wrong person answering the phone: me. So this time I didn't want to let her go so easily. I waited a moment before speaking and then I asked,

So tell me, who are you? Maybe there was something menacing in my voice, because I sensed fear in the way she hurriedly hung up on me.

After I'd hung up, I turned to Kitten and Cat.

Would you two stop bickering! Tomorrow I'll take you to a place where you can get jobs as salesgirls. You'll be on commission. Try it out for a while. If they make you this bitchy, you should quit your hostess jobs. The worst mistake you can make is to think that you're not qualified for anything except being a bargirl.

The next day, I took Kitten and Cat to meet a man I knew, a man that I knew liked me. His name was Ji, and I figured that he could help me with this. We all had dinner together, and afterward I went home to get some sleep. Ji said he wanted to take the other girls to the seashore.

Later that night I saw Kitten return home alone. She said that Cat had gone over to a friend's house.

First thing the next morning I got a phone call: my friend Ji had been robbed by my friend Cat.

Cat had lured Ji into bed the same way she did her clients, and she had not only taken more than ten thousand *yuan* in cash, plus Ji's watch and gold jewelry, but worse yet, she had stolen his good-luck charm. Ji said that a man only takes off his amulet at one time — when he's having sex. Now he couldn't go home and face his old lady, and he was going to have to spend his nights in a hotel. This was the first time I'd heard anything about Ji's having a wife. But I felt responsible for getting him into this trouble. By and large, I only went to see Ji when I needed something from him, so I felt a little guilty toward him to begin with. Now I felt even more guilty. Finally, Ji tossed me two thousand Hong Kong dollars, saying, Fly up to Nanjing and see if you can find Cat and straighten things out!

Once more, Kitten was begging me to forgive her. This time you can grovel all you want, I told her, but it won't do you any good. There's nothing I hate more than being lied to.

I asked Kitten if she knew where Cat's house was in Nanjing, and Kitten said she did.

Then in that case she won't go home, I said. Does she have a boyfriend in Nanjing?

Yes, and she's crazy about him. She only came down here to make some money for him.

Does he ever go out? I asked.

Sure.

Does he have a favorite hangout?

Yes. And I know where it is.

Good. We're going to Nanjing!

I decided to go to Nanjing to find Cat, with Kitten guiding the way. After some thought, I concluded that it would be wise for us to bring a man along. Dalong said he'd go. We should settle this business, he said. We have to get Ji's charm back. Let's go tomorrow!

As soon as we reached Nanjing, Dalong went to buy a knife. He said that we couldn't be halfhearted about this; we had to show people we meant business, because if we didn't, people wouldn't take things seriously. Kitten said, You don't need to buy a knife.

She said there were plenty of knives at her place. But Dalong went for a walk and bought me a very nice charcoal-colored toy gun.

I said, The girl has to be punished for what she did, and we're going to do everything we can to get justice, but we can't kill anyone. That scares me.

It took us only a short time to find the restaurant, where an older guy in his thirties was having drinks. Kitten said that he was Cat's boyfriend. I walked over to him.

Where's your girlfriend? I asked.

The man didn't answer.

Dalong brought me a stool, and I sat down. I repeated my question, but the man still didn't respond.

Dalong was wearing some new clothes I'd just given him, but on Dalong even new clothes got filthy in no time. He had big eyes and thick eyebrows, but he was very skinny, emaciated even, and extremely soft-spoken. You could describe Dalong as sensitive and entirely lacking in self-confidence. From time to time, the man would cast a disdainful look in Dalong's direction. Dalong was stung. I was furious.

Fortunately the man was alone. Emboldened, I pulled the toy gun out of my handbag, which was hidden from view by the table. Look down, I said. Over here. Take a good look.

As I spoke I started to shake, because whenever I get nervous I get excited, and when I get excited I get the shakes, and when I get the shakes, things get dangerous.

The old guy turned his head and looked down. He said, How's your aim?

In a split second, I thrust the gun between his legs, into his balls.

I never miss, I said.

As I spoke, Kitten and Dalong whipped out their knives. My face went hot. The knives didn't seem to scare him — maybe he was carrying a blade of his own — but the gun pointing at his genitals scared the hell out of him. Of course, if the gun I was pointing at him were real, why would I need to have Kitten and Dalong waving a pair of knives around?

But this didn't occur to him. We'd caught the old fart off guard, and he was still reeling. I was feeling off balance myself, and hearing myself say I had great aim frightened the hell out of me too. My arms started to go limp, but the man didn't move a muscle, and it was a good thing he didn't budge, because if he had I don't know what I would have done.

He had the restaurant manager make a call for him. I held my gun between his legs for twenty whole minutes, struggling all the while to keep my thoughts from running away with me. The man, Dalong, and Kitten all wore intensely serious expressions, and I had a powerful urge to laugh, but I knew that if I even cracked a smile, Dalong would break into a grin, and we'd be finished. The man was a seasoned old criminal, and he would never let us get away.

Cat came in. She handed over Ji's wristwatch and charm. The chain that went with the charm was gone, and so was the money. I didn't dare look Cat in the eye. I felt acutely embarrassed, even though she was the one who should have felt ashamed, and it was getting more awkward by the second. I even found myself starting to empathize with her. Suddenly I felt bored with the whole thing. I wanted to drop it, to forget all about it.

To hell with it, Dalong said. Cat's a stupid cunt, but she's had a crappy life. Let's just forget this ever happened.

I had only just learned that Cat was a single mother, with a four-year-old son, and this man had always been there to help her.

Without speaking to Cat, Kitten turned to Dalong and me.

Cat always gets mixed up in the sleaziest schemes, she said.

We wanted to go over to Kitten's place, but she didn't want to take us there. She came from a broken home, and her older brother was in prison. The house is empty, she said.

Kitten started working at Ji's company, and she moved to a new apartment. I couldn't picture Kitten lasting long in an office job, but she actually went to work every day, nine to five. Kitten and Dalong became good friends, and the three of us often got together at my place. Dalong cooked for us, and we always talked until dawn, mostly swapping stories about things that had happened on our street.

This was when I learned that Dalong had never set foot in any kind of school. He was from the poorest section of Shanghai, and I was shocked to find out that there were still people there who didn't have enough money to send their children to school. He said that the reason he liked to hang around with me so much was that I seemed to be so cultured and well educated.

Dalong liked to read the newspaper, and he always showed up at my door carrying a rolled-up newspaper.

Kitten liked reading books about antiques. From the time she was a child, her older brother had taken her around with him to pick out antiques. He was in prison for dealing in antiquities. She said that her brother looked a lot like Leslie Cheung.

*   *   *

Ever since my return from Beijing, I'd been phoning Saining every day, but I had yet to speak with him. Once, I asked Sanmao, Tell me the truth, does Saining have a new girlfriend? Why doesn't he call me? He doesn't care about me anymore. Sanmao said, I don't know why he hasn't called. But lately everybody's been busy doing performance art. I said, Didn't you go to Beijing to play music? Sanmao said, There's no contradiction.

When I thought about Saining, I couldn't turn off the voice in my head that went on and on about how Saining's favorite guitar was gone, stolen by that bunch of bastards, and I was afraid he was going to be sad, but what could I do?

One morning, about two weeks after the robbery, I got a call from the local police station. The police said that one of the thieves had been caught.

It turned out that Kitten had hired a few guys from Xinjiang to look for Hunanese all over town and to personally inspect all of the usual Hunan gangster haunts. Before long, they had caught up with one of the gang in a third-rate nightclub. I heard that Kitten went to where they'd tied him up, and she hit him and kicked him, shouting at him all the while.

The precinct office was calling us down to give statements and identify the suspect.

I saw an overgrown boy in handcuffs and recognized him as the one who had slapped Luobu. He was a real mess. He was dull-eyed and dirty, and he stank. His fingernails were especially filthy. I stood outside the cell and identified him through the iron bars of the door, and then I picked out the others from a stack of photo IDs. I knew that two of them had already been arrested. The police scolded me and said that by not reporting the crime, I was condoning it. When I asked the cops how the thieves might be punished, they said that these boys had done all sorts of bad things and might face execution — a bullet to the head.

I felt sick at heart for the rest of the day. Nanjing Noodles and I were both terrified by the idea of "a bullet to the head." My watch and jewelry had all been recovered, and the guitar too. The rest was gone, but I caught a glimpse of those boys' black backpacks. The police said everything would be held as evidence.

Saining came back alone, and he seemed depressed. I asked him why he'd come back by himself and ahead of the others.

The artists in Beijing have such an inflated opinion of themselves, he complained. They're all drunk with their sense of mission, and they're always jumping onto bandwagons, looking for ways to make it big.

He couldn't get used to this collective way of life; it was too chaotic for him. And the bands there had taken what should have been heavy metal, pure and simple, and stuck in all kinds of fancy effects that threw the music off kilter. On top of that, there were too many people with big ideas and too many hardships for Saining's taste. He couldn't relate to any of it.

Saining came over and held me, and we made love feverishly. He had changed.

That night I put ten sleeping pills that I'd set aside earlier into his drink. He slept for two days. He awakened several times, and I kept watch over him, never leaving his side, helping him to the bathroom. Seeing him in such a daze, I felt a sense of peace that I had never experienced before.

When he had fully awakened, I told him what I had done. I said I'd done it because he'd been ignoring me for so long that I doubted he loved me anymore.

Well, this isn't the first time you've done something like this, he said. But ten sleeping pills is the most dangerous amount you could have given me. Any more than that and I would probably have thrown up and been fine. But you didn't give me enough to make me sick, and when it's not enough to make someone throw up, things can go very wrong. I could easily have never woken up.

Then he came over and held me, saying, I'm not in love with anyone else. You shouldn't punish me when you don't have any real grounds.

I wasn't trying to punish you. That wouldn't get me what I want. All I want is you, all of you, forever. I've never stopped wanting you, not even for an instant. I was hoping that I could move God.

II.

After his return from Beijing, Saining would disappear without saying where he'd gone, and he all but stopped making love to me. Finally he confessed to me that he'd been using heroin and had become addicted.

You, a junkie? I was incredulous. Really? No way! Do you have any right now? I want to try it.

Until now, I'd only tried grass and pills. That ten-year-old boy from Hong Kong had smuggled pills past customs when he'd come here, and he would sell them to other kids. I didn't even know what kind they were, but I didn't particularly enjoy the synthetic, chemical feeling they gave me. Sometimes, when he was in Hong Kong,

Saining took acid, but he'd never brought any back for me to try, and he told me more than once that grass was really the only thing he liked.

He put a bit of faintly yellowish powder on some tinfoil and showed me how to "chase the dragon." I inhaled and vomited and vomited some more as I kept inhaling. It made me feel very sick to my stomach.

That night I talked a lot.

You've been doing heroin — how come you're so talkative? You're giving me a headache with all your blabbing. You obviously didn't get enough. I better give you more and knock you out.

When I passed out, my body had already dissolved, and my nose was full of the odor of photographic developing chemicals. Heroin was icy cold, and I didn't think I liked it. It seemed as if there were cotton wadding packed all around my body, and I couldn't keep from falling into sleep, and then, bit by bit, the cotton fell away from me, until at last it was all gone, and my body and mind became supersensitive.

Saining said that heroin made him euphoric, letting him forget what the world was like, bringing him peace and serenity, giving him a world of his own. But, he said, I never thought I could become addicted so quickly. I'm not used to this feeling of being controlled.

Why did you wait until now to tell me? I asked. How can you get high all by yourself?

I'm not high, he countered. I'm very low. Ever since I got back from Beijing I've been in a daze, and it's something I need to deal with myself, on my own. It's not that I don't love you, you understand? When you're feeling numb, the best thing to do is to jump into a whirlpool. As for me, I've stumbled into the heroin whirlpool, that's all. Heroin is me, my way of coping; it's my world, and who I am doesn't matter anymore.

One day Saining said he wanted to kick his heroin habit. He said that heroin was too dangerous, and when he was using heroin he spent the whole day worrying about money or, when he did have money, worrying about scoring. It was never enough, and it was making him uneasy.

He took to spending long hours outside on the balcony, sitting motionless and looking out. This solitude of his was more than I could stand, and I joined him and we watched it all together, the chaotic street below. The sunlight in this city was always so full of poison. A drug that was a stranger to me had put up a wall between me and my closest friend. I couldn't read his expressions, and I had lost the power to attract him, but I didn't exactly feel hurt, just agitated.

I was determined to get my lover back.

Bit by bit, we were losing trust in each other. Actually there was no reason for Saining to lie to me, but heroin had turned him into a habitual liar. It was like a hobby for him; he just liked to say things that weren't true. The medicines that were supposed to help him quit heroin were useless, and I watched him suffer torment every day. I didn't realize that withdrawal made you feel like you were going to die, so I believed him when he said that it was killing him. I was genuinely afraid that withdrawal was going to be too much for him and that he could die at any moment. So I went back and forth between helping him quit and helping him use. We spent our days like a pair of criminals, going to whatever lengths we had to in order to get the drug. Sometimes I got completely fed up. This drug had reduced our lives to vulgar materialism. I watched our money carefully, and I always made sure there was a little packet of heroin in my pocket, just in case Saining started going into withdrawal.

When he was in the throes of withdrawal, Saining was oblivious to me. And when he was high he didn't notice me either. Heroin had made him so boring. I'd tried it a few times, and I didn't like it. I was a spoiled brat, and a spoiled child on drugs is no fun for anyone. Saining also found heroin boring, but he thought that was because he was a coward, because he was vacillating between using and quitting, and he said that there was nothing more boring than that.

Saining didn't use a needle, and he didn't snort it, he just "chased the dragon" across a piece of tinfoil. But people could tell at a glance that he was a junkie. He had a junkie's gauntness and pallor, and a junkie's jittery nerves.

Saining disappeared again. I went out looking for him, wanting to find him before the police did.

After I became aware that Saining was using heroin, I discovered that people all around me were using heroin. It wasn't just popular with prostitutes. Nightclub performers — singers, musicians, and dancers — were also using. Gangsters and small-time crooks used. Even taxi drivers used heroin. Suddenly I had the overwhelming impression that the entire world was floating on a sea of heroin.

I came home one day to find Saining sitting, dazed, in the middle of the floor and clutching his famous pillow. God only knew how much he loved that pillow of his — he'd even taken it with him to Beijing, saying that he couldn't sleep without it. There were several guitars laid out before him. Altogether he kept six guitars at our apartment, and they were all different: different ages, different colors, different uses. He said, Each guitar has its own music, its own sensibility. I love them all, but they don't have souls until I look at them. Sanmao hated it when Saining talked this way, and he would glare at Saining and say coldly, Right! That's easy for you to say — you have money!

Saining didn't look up, and I ignored him too. I straightened the room, took a bath, did the laundry. I ate the winter-melon-and-pork soup that Saining had made me. He always made the best soups. When I finished eating, I went and sat down in front of Saining. He was playing the same couple of melodies over and over.

Saining, I said, I'm tired of this. I called around today and got the number of the rehab clinic, and I went over and had a look. I've never sneaked around behind your back like this before. But the doctors there were really nice; they won't treat you like a criminal. They said the government supports people who decide that they want to quit, and they'll protect your privacy.

I'm not going to that hole.

But those drugs that are supposed to help you quit are bullshit! Now, if you don't really want to give up heroin . . .

Can you go with me?

He looked up at me, his eyes unsteady. He always spoke very slowly, and the look of complete vulnerability on his face left me with the feeling that both of us were idiots.

The clinic has a strict no-visitors policy, but my heart will be with you every minute, I promise. Please, I'm begging you, please go! This stupid drug is ruining our lives!

Finally Saining agreed to go to the clinic. Early one morning I packed his things. My baby, my tears, he waited out on the balcony with a blank expression. He was so frail and so beautiful, sitting there in the first light of morning with his ice-cold hands hanging limply beside him. One of his songs went, "I know the shape of happiness." Another song went, "Girl, I stole the purse with your soul." Looking at him now, I thought of those two songs, and I saw the deadly pale of this winter morning cutting at him cruelly, but I could only watch him from another place. There was no way I could take him away from that place where he was.

I couldn't stop crying that morning. I felt sick at heart, and I wasn't sure that Saining really wanted to kick his heroin habit. I felt that that goddamned heroin had stolen my Saining away from me. All the way to the clinic, Saining held on tight to my hand. Neither of us could speak. The clinic gave me back all of the food I'd packed for Saining, and the portable CD player, the CDs, the mirror, the razor. The doctors and nurses searched his body thoroughly, but he never took his eyes off me. When the time came for an attendant to escort me into the elevator, I heard Saining softly call my name, but by the time I turned my head, he had already been taken into a room with a big iron bolt on the door. There was no sign of him — only the last brief, intense look he had flashed me, now etched so painfully into my mind that I wanted to die.

*   *   *

I began drinking heavily. Sometimes I would loiter in the neighborhood where the clinic was. I'd never equated drinking with taking drugs. I saw my relationship with alcohol as sweet and easygoing. It seemed natural. Alcohol had many moods, many attitudes. And it was useful. It relaxed me, warmed me up. I started to drown my feelings in scotch. I was having trouble sleeping, and soon I was keeping a bottle of booze by my bed. I recognized that this was risky business. But with Saining gone, how could I go on living if I didn't drink?

The day he was released from the clinic, I got all dolled up, put on a pair of satin mules, and went to pick him up. We'd never been apart for this long, and when he gave me that first smile, I felt excited about life again.

He seemed to have put on weight, and he had this brainwashed look on his face, blank and stupid. We studiously avoided the subject of drugs. I was thinking that all of that was over and done with, and that things were only going to get better from now on.

Saining didn't make love to me. He was very quiet, and he always seemed tired, but none of this bothered me, because everything was going to be fine now. Besides, when he was asleep, I could drink.

12.

The real nightmare began a few months later, when Saining started using heroin again. He said he'd suffered so much in the rehab clinic that he felt mentally out of balance, so he needed to start using again.

Heroin was disastrous for our love.

I said, I think we should split up. If I can't make love with you, I'll find another man.

Saining ran into the bathroom and started throwing up.

You make me sick! he said.

What's your excuse? I countered. You're young, you have money, you have your music, but you seem to think that if you don't do drugs and fuck around a lot, you're not hip, right? That's what you think, isn't it? You're such a stupid asshole; you're just like all the others.

Sometimes you really scare me, he said. How can I make love to someone I'm afraid of? I share a bed with you, but sometimes I'll be watching your face while you sleep, and suddenly I'll get this feeling like I don't know you at all. Have you ever had that feeling? Maybe you don't really know yourself, either. We don't know shit. We're just a couple of morons.

What are you talking about? What do you mean, you don't know me?

You can look for another boyfriend, but you won't be able to leave me. You and I have to live together.

I realized that if I left him I wouldn't have anything. It had finally sunk in, and I recognized that for the past several years I had been living for one thing only — gaining possession of Saining.

I didn't know what to do. In all our time together, we'd never talked about control. Now drugs were controlling Saining. He had changed, grown moody, sometimes up and sometimes down. But the most confusing and hurtful thing of all was that he no longer needed to connect with me. He used heroin. I didn't. We weren't on the same wavelength anymore; we couldn't connect. He was gloomy, antisocial, always felt cold, didn't like the light. He was constipated, and he had no appetite for food or sex. I tried everything I could think of to attract his attention, but it only made him more irritable. He said that the truth of the matter was that he needed a life that was controlled by something, no matter how inexplicable. Anyway, his drug habit wasn't going to drive him to steal or borrow a gun. It was just that he couldn't live without this particular drug, at least not for now. He loved music, but love was love and nothing more. He wasn't like Sanmao, with all of his lofty goals. Saining didn't really have any goals; he'd never had any goal in life until heroin became his purpose, his opponent. He was pitting himself against heroin. He said it was a dangerous game, but it held his interest.

Pitting himself against heroin? That was the weirdest thing I'd ever heard.

Finally he said, You might as well give up. I'm not coming back.

I drank Black Label and soda every day, just like an old man, stupidly thinking that it made me look tough. We weren't making ends meet, and I went back to singing in nightclubs. I bought myself whiskey to prove that I loved myself. Alcohol kept me company; I needed it to keep away my loneliness, and it gave me a sense of security. I started drinking as soon as I got out of bed. I grew increasingly withdrawn and rarely spoke. Although I almost never drank so much that I lost consciousness, I still needed to drink a great deal of alcohol every day just to keep my composure.

Whenever I had too much, I would end up in the bathroom, leaning over the sink and retching, promising myself that I would never again drink that much. Once, when I'd mixed my drinks and drunk it all too fast, I vomited up a mouthful of blood. The blood I spat out was nearly black, and for the first time I found myself thinking that alcohol was evil. It had taken me a long time to come to this recognition.

Saining and I felt the pain of lovers adrift in the world. Together we moved through the shadowy landscape, each confirming the other's existence. We had once been passionate lovers. Now we just looked at each other without interest; any supposed feelings of love seemed gradually to fade into a vague and tearful sentimentality. Neither of us cooked anymore, not that we wanted to eat anything. We were living together like a pair of hostile neighbors, and our lives took on a sordid air. The slightest thing could provoke a loud and violent argument between us. We snickered at the idea of heroes.

Our lives were crazy, and the significance of pain was lost on us.

Sometimes we became suddenly tender, and I would urge him to quit heroin and he would urge me to stop drinking, and we always spoke these words with tears streaming down our faces.

Then one day, out of the blue, Saining told me he had a gig singing in one of the newly developing towns on the outskirts of the city. I said I thought that it was too far away for him to ride the bus back and forth every day, and I suggested that he rent a place there. I added, I'm giving you two months. If you haven't given up heroin by then, I'm going to start using it myself.

After he became a "celebrity," we treated each other with more civility. Instead of renting an apartment in that little town, he spent four hours commuting each day. If he was using heroin, it was barely discernible, and I wasn't drinking as much. Too often, though, we were in a state of lethargy, and for the first time I found myself thinking seriously about death. I hoped that I would die naturally, in my sleep. I felt that I'd been fortunate, I'd enjoyed my life, and I hadn't really suffered very much. But lately I'd started to worry about money, and my desire for Saining was met with rejection, and with my boyfriend acting this way, over time I too lost interest in sex. Sometimes even bathing seemed like too much of an effort. I might as well have been dead.

One day, on impulse, I headed out to that little town on my own. I saw big posters of Saining's face pasted up outside several restaurants. I had no idea when the pictures had been taken. He had transformed himself into a "rock star," which was a ridiculous idea, something that the Saining I used to know would never have gone along with.

I went and watched him perform, and it seemed to me that not only was he still on the same old disastrous course, but he had become a sensationalist. Everything he did was designed to attract attention, and maybe it was deliberate, or maybe he didn't care, and then again maybe he just had to go through those motions in order to make a living. I didn't know, nor did I know any of the songs he was singing. The act was totally idiotic.

I didn't know whether to laugh or cry, and the most laughably pathetic thing of all was his band. It was made up of a handful of local teenagers, no more than sixteen or seventeen years old, the sons of peasants who'd had a little land of their own and built houses during the reforms and gotten rich by becoming landlords.

I couldn't figure out how Saining had managed to set himself up as the leader of this bunch of country boys in such a short time. I understood the boys themselves even less, however. Even though their performances invariably seemed more like rehearsals than actual performances, I was charmed all the same. Where had they come from? How had they learned to play?

The band had lots of fans, young people of all descriptions. Most, like me, had ridden a long way on the bus to get there. The night was hot and humid, alcohol fumes filled the air, and Saining was leading the band, and the band was playing, and the crowd was crude and unruly, all free-floating aggression. But after the satisfaction and ennui of drunkenness had passed, everyone went away empty-handed. Because the new Saining had nothing to offer. The singing and playing were a pathetic spectacle.

I watched backstage as a few very young girls sought out Saining. They were all speaking Cantonese, these daughters of rich locals, and they brought Saining all kinds of strange and bizarre gifts. I noticed that the same handful of girls appeared whenever Saining played, and I overheard one of them saying how much she wished she could trade places with Saining's girlfriend. This left me feeling all churned up: Girlfriend! I thought. Did she have any idea what it was really like to be his girlfriend?

I joined Saining for a late-night snack in a restaurant, and we had a big fight right in front of the band. He told me that he liked playing this kind of music. I said, You realize that what you're doing is total bullshit, don't you? They've only just started to learn about rock and roll out here. CDs are hard to come by, they have to depend on you, and you're totally misleading them, these fans of yours, these kids. Do you realize what you're doing? How can you do this to them?

Saining said, I've never tried to pass it off as rock and roll; I'm just trying to earn a living! Can you tell me what rock and roll is? Young people in this country love to talk about rock and roll, but that's all they do, just talk, talk, talk. It's sick!

Aren't you one of them too? Anyway, I don't know what rock and roll is, either. So what! Who cares if it's rock and roll or not? What's important is that your music has no soul. You have to stop doing this; you'd be better off starving!

One day I found a poem in English written on the little blackboard in our apartment:

Please believe me,
The little stream told me,
It wanted to hold me, hold me so tenderly,
Floating free,
Falling free,
And the stream rushes on, never stopping.
Underwater, I'll breathe in that stream, until the end of my life.
Only the stream knows how it will happen.
Please believe me,
If you don't need me anymore,
I'll be gone soon,
I promise you, promise
I'll drown my body in wine.

*　　*　　*

Saining spent his days running from gig to gig without a thought in his head. He didn't have time to think about what he was doing. That little town was a lawless place, full of all sorts of criminals, con men, and grifters, and fugitives from the North and from Hong Kong. One night, at the end of a set, a couple of plainclothes policemen went backstage and questioned Saining in low voices about whether he was carrying a concealed weapon. The poor bastard thought that they were playing a joke on him, and he laughed, saying, Yeah, and I have a pair of grenades too!

They arrested him on the spot. Nobody knew which department the arresting officers had come from. I asked my boss at the nightclub for help, and we drove off to look for Saining. We searched everywhere until finally we found him at a small station house, in the Bureau of Special Cases.

On the way home, Saining bought an armload of booze. He drank and vomited all the way home, stinking to high heaven. We didn't say a word, either of us, and the moment he set foot in our apartment, he went to dig up his stash of heroin.

Before he could stop me, I'd snatched the little paper packet from him and thrown it out the window.

I shouldn't have bailed you out; I should have let you stay there and go cold turkey. They could have taken you to rehab and left you there for six months. I'm sick and tired of heroin. Look at you! Look at what you're doing to yourself! I can't stand looking at you; you're disgusting.

Is this why you left Sanmao? Just so you could do heroin? Nothing else seems to matter to you anymore. Are you actually happy?

Don't go back there. I don't want you to waste your time playing that crappy music anymore. Do it for me. I don't want to live this way. I used to be unhappy because I was worried about your being with other women, but now I worry about smack. I'm sick to death of this life we're living.

Saining didn't respond, and I started pounding, first on his violin and then on his guitar. Finally Saining took the strings that I'd ripped from his guitar and tied me up on the balcony while our dog howled.

Saining's pallid face had hardened into resolve — dark, silent, and complete resolve.

He left without a word.

The noisy, crowded street lay below me. The whole world had gone crazy, and there I was, a prisoner on my own balcony, with nowhere to pee.

Seven hours later, I was listening to Saining's incoherent apology.

Saining, I said, I've always thought that our being together was a good thing, something to be happy about. Even though we've had our problems, we've grown up together. But it's getting hard to take. Because of you I peed in my pants, I'm wet, and I stink. Our lives are a mess; we haven't made anything of ourselves. In the years we've been together, I've dedicated myself to making you want nothing but music and me. I've been such an idiot! Because our feelings for each other just can't compete with heroin. And what is heroin? I haven't a clue, and neither have you, but you pit yourself against it anyway, right? I've never stopped trying to make sense of things, but I just keep getting more and more mixed up. I've decided to move out. Even though I won't be living here, we can still be together. But living with you is too nerve-racking.

Once again, I moved out. And this time my mind was a blank.

13.

Sanmao came back, and I talked to him constantly about all of my current troubles. Sanmao said, Reality is a wall that lies between us and our recovery. We have to bore through that wall, but music can save us.

Sanmao's words were a perfect encapsulation of the spirit of the late-1980s underground rock scene in China. He always drew connections between music and salvation, music and destiny. This gave him a serious and responsible air.

But for Saining, music was simply a passion. It had nothing to do with salvation. Making music wasn't going to deliver him from anything, nor was it bringing him any kind of peace. Saining thought that the only thing that could save your soul was religion, but you had to have been chosen for it. It had to be your destiny. Music wasn't a religion. Music was a form of expression, an embodiment of the spirit, a way of life, and the most natural thing in the world.

Sanmao explained that there were many reasons that Saining had been so unhappy in Beijing. He always felt slighted, Sanmao said. But that's nothing unusual around there. Nobody in Beijing takes anybody else very seriously. The thing is, Saining is one of those people who come back from overseas with an especially clear sense of themselves. His natural tendency is to be a bit of a loner, and in Beijing he became downright antisocial. It was the first time he'd noticed how different he was — he wasn't Chinese, and he wasn't Western. No one else could relate to his anger. Not many people in Beijing can afford to buy instruments, much less know as much about them as Saining does. Most of those guys can't even

beautiful. They were what set him apart from all of the other Chinese rockers.

Saining did not have a very good feel for the Chinese language, but he insisted on writing his songs in Chinese anyway. We used to write songs together, usually starting with his strumming a little tune, and then he'd tell me what he wanted the words to express. Most of his lyrics touched on fragmentary stories. He would write them out in English, and my job was to come up with Chinese words that made sense. I always felt happy whenever I watched Saining singing these songs up onstage. I felt as though he had granted me a special privilege, the privilege of being bathed with him in the bright halo of his music. I was enthralled by the extended trance of this music, and it was only then, when Saining was onstage and I was in the audience, that I understood his secret. Only then did I achieve a genuine sense of well-being.

I hadn't been to a gathering like this in a long time. In the past I'd followed Saining around from one noisy concert to another. We'd been each other's biggest, most loyal fans, and he'd been my guitar player too. We used the most basic setups and equipment and played for all kinds of audiences. Saining liked to watch me onstage with my long hair and short skirts, and I liked to stare at my legs swaying back and forth to the music of my own thin voice as I sang, my hair whipping around to cover my breasts or hide my cheeks, something that I thought accentuated the three-dimensionality of my features. And I foolishly thought that this helped me create an aura of mystery. In those days, performing was mostly a pretext for me to have a good time, a pleasure that was enhanced by the fact that I had an audience. Saining had a habit of buying me little silk kerchiefs; I have a large head and I wasn't meant to wear a kerchief, but he kept on giving me kerchiefs all the same. Accessories are very important, he would tell me. Whenever I performed, I always picked out one of those little scarves and tied it around the microphone stand. I couldn't write songs, so I sang Doors songs that I'd translated, and they lit up my hazy prayers with a power that was at once comforting and inspiring. Saining was one of the few people who understood and encouraged my strange passion for the Doors.

There came a point in the performance when Saining suddenly grew calm. Sitting down on the stage, he picked up a maroon acoustic guitar, and this last song that he sang sent icy waves through my entire body, making me feel so cold I couldn't even weep. The chill crept into me, filling me with foreboding.

— I have the key — Get married Allen don't take drugs —

Saining's acoustic guitar had a clear and unadorned sound that hit you in the face like a whiff of heroin and turned the whole world cold. He had set the fragment of the poem I'd written on our blackboard to music and turned it into a song.

The key is in the sunlight at the window, I have the key, Get married Allen, don't take drugs. The key is in the window, in the sunlight at the window, Get married Allen, don't take drugs, I have the key, Get married, Allen, don't take drugs, don't take drugs, get married get married get married, don't take drugs, don't take drugs.

After that night, Saining and I spent a lot of time together. He'd quit singing for a living, and we often sat with Sanmao, talking through the night, and it was just like the early days when we'd first met. After what had seemed like an eternity, there we were again, sitting down together and talking about our problems, about drugs and music, about fear and free will. But we never arrived at any conclusions. We always seemed to abandon our discussions halfway because it was much more fun just listening to music. And together the three of us listened to every kind of music there was.

Saining's mother came back to China to visit us, and when she and Saining looked at each other, the expressions in their eyes made me extremely jealous. I sensed that Saining's mother didn't like me, but she gave me a ring and told me, Saining loves you very much; be good to each other.

I moved back in with him. We went to bed early that first night, and we did nothing but gaze at each other, slow tears rolling down my cheeks as he looked at me tenderly. Such beautiful eyes, such a beautiful mouth, such a beautiful dream. He fascinated me, he was so intriguing, and there was some deep truth hidden in his face. I trusted that face, believed in it simply because I believed in it.

We made the decision to free ourselves from drugs and alcohol. Saining said he was quitting heroin for me and his mother. I said I was going to stop drinking because it was expensive, and bad for my skin, and my skin and our lives were equally fucked up.

Sanmao brought Saining some methadone, which we knew was approved by international drug rehabilitation organizations as a good medicine.

I stopped drinking.

We were both in low spirits, sleeping, arguing, drinking water, and throwing up all day long.

14.

Saining quit his heroin habit without any apparent effort. However, he soon realized that he had become addicted to methadone. Our town, Shenzhen, was full of places to buy this drug, something that would hardly have been possible in Shanghai. Just about anywhere you went around here, there were all kinds of "cures" for sale, but these were usually drugs meant for mental patients, or for people with terminal bone cancer. Some were antidepressants, or maybe just very powerful sleeping pills. All of these "medicines" meant to wean people from their dependence on drugs were nothing more than drugs themselves. He took one drug to help him get off of another drug, and then a third drug to help him quit the second drug, and so on. His health began to decline seriously.

Sanmao blamed me for not keeping track of what Saining took and how much he took. I told Sanmao that I was overwhelmed, that the shops downstairs on the street sold anything and everything, and that I was powerless to stop Saining.

I tried to convince Saining to go back into rehab, but he said that the clinic had a rule: If you went in for a second time, they would lock you up for a very long time, and he didn't want to go back to that terrible place again.

Saining ended up going back to heroin. He said it kept him on an even keel, that heroin was his destiny. But heroin itself no longer existed as a separate entity; it had become one with his breathing. It had pushed him into adulthood.

You're too weak, I said.

Why should I be strong?

Are you afraid of being alone?

The only thing I'm afraid of is not having enough smack.

It was Christmas night 1993, and I hadn't seen Saining all day. I gathered up all of his things and threw them outside. When he came home, I spoke to him from behind the locked and bolted door: Go to Hell, I said. You're through. And those were the only words I spoke to him that night.

Saining spent the night sitting outside our door and singing, and his singing was half mumbled, but every verse had *Merry Christmas* in it. That night I quickly drank myself to sleep.

When I awoke the next day and opened the front door, Saining was gone, but all of his things were still there. By this time my drinking was out of control, and I stumbled around all day in a stupor, my temper flaring.

In love, it was language that had hurt me. With alcohol and drugs, it was money that had brought Saining and me to harm. If we hadn't been able to get our hands on all that money, would we have found other ways to grow up?

We hadn't made love in an entire year. Sometimes I would tentatively touch myself, but the sensation did nothing to arouse me. Occasionally we would kiss, but neither of us felt like making love. Neither of us knew what love was anymore. Our love was more like familial affection, something for our earthbound bodies to lean on, and when this realization hit me, I thought that I had finally grown up. But adulthood left me feeling enervated and wondering how our love could have slipped away. I couldn't understand what had happened.

Die in the prime of youth, and leave a beautiful corpse: what an intensely beautiful dream that was, but we couldn't manage to pull it off. We had neither energy nor passion nor love. We had nothing to burn except time.

One day you took a red cloth
Covered my eyes, blocked out the sky
And you asked me what I saw
And I said I saw happiness

It was a good feeling
It made me forget I had nowhere to go
You asked me where I'd want to go anyway
And I said I would follow you

I can't see you or the road
You grip my hands tight
You ask me what I'm thinking
And I say the decision is yours

I feel, though you aren't made of iron,
That you're just as strong and fierce
I feel the blood that's in your body
Because your hands are so warm

And it feels good
It makes me forget I have nowhere to go
You asked me where I would want to go anyway
And I said I would follow you

It doesn't feel like a wilderness
Though it's true I can't see the cracks in the parched earth
I feel it, and I need water, need to drink
But you cover my mouth with yours

I cannot walk, I cannot cry
Because my body has gone dry
I will follow you forever
Because I know your pain better than anyone

— CUI JIAN, "RED CLOTH"

Saining had been gone for a week, and I started to worry. San-mao and I looked for him everywhere. We even contacted his parents, both of whom were living abroad.

I eventually discovered that his passport was missing from his overcoat pocket, and I found a note he'd written sometime before in the red case of his Fender guitar: "My love, if you find this letter it means that I am gone, that I've left this town. It's September 1993, and right now you are sleeping in my arms, drunk again. I love you! No matter who you are or what you become. But what is love, anyway? There is something that terrifies me. Honestly. So I have to go away. I'm waiting for a good time to leave. We've been together too long. We're both a little mixed up, so I need to go. It will be hard for me to get used to being away, and I'll miss you, but I have to leave. Otherwise things will never get better."

I came across Saining's cash card and a slip of paper, and his password was written on the slip of paper, but he knew that I knew his password already. I discovered that the card still had a lot of cash on it. He was just as arrogant as his mother!

What was "We've been together too long" supposed to mean?

That was all we had. We didn't have anything else!

I started to shriek. And then, with terror, I realized that I was having an asthma attack.

I remembered all of the sweet times I'd had with Saining. It was all coming back, and I couldn't bear it.

There was nothing Sanmao could do, although he did convince me to go do a gig in another province. He wanted to see me become a professional singer. Drinking too much was making my asthma progressively worse. Performances became all but impossible. I wanted to sing, but I couldn't because of the wheezing. My final concert was a nightmare for me and the booking agency. Because of the terms of my contract, I ended up owing them money.

I'd been jeered at by a bunch of idiots, and I swore I'd never sing again. I discovered that the idea that you had to suffer in life was just a self-fulfilling prophecy that was out of step with the times.

I didn't want to inflict myself on the world any longer.

During the Spring Festival of 1994, I had a foreboding that my Saining was never going to come back. This hardened my resolve.

With scarcely any hesitation, I chose heroin, having been brought to that drug by Saining's long affair with it. I said to myself, You might as well be dead; you're finished anyway.

My asthma became increasingly serious, often landing me in the hospital emergency room. I could have an attack at any time, almost without warning, so I always had to have an oxygen bag on hand. Each day's first suck of heroin threw me into a fit of shaking that never lasted less than fifteen minutes, but I didn't dare lie down to sleep. Every day, as soon as I awoke, I went looking for my stash. Every day as I awoke I was transfixed by the sight of my own sweat dripping down on my quilt.

The world was vanishing right in front of me. All the better. The best thing about heroin was that it let me drift without end into a dizzying void. I was empty from the inside out. Time sped up, and life and death seemed to dangle high above my head, like two palaces, and there I was, trapped and vacillating in the space between.

Saining had often said he used heroin to help him find a "hallucinatory tranquillity." I didn't know what other amazing sensations he got from it, but there was nothing beautiful about my life with heroin. Heroin was a petty thief, stealing everything there was to steal until I found myself with an absolute lack, a lack I had never before experienced. This emptiness gave me a sense of balance. The only meaning in my life was that my life was meaningless. I had never been free before, because until now I hadn't genuinely understood myself, my life, my body, my loves. Heroin and its frigid world had become the only freedom I could have.

*   *   *

Sanmao couldn't help me, and in the end he called my parents, who sent me to a rehab clinic in Shanghai.

After being discharged from the clinic, I flew straight back to the South and right back to heroin. Heroin had become as natural to me as breathing. What else was there for me to do except use smack? My first glimpse of my parents had frightened me. They were too normal. I couldn't be around normal people. They would never be able to understand the emptiness of using heroin or the terror that comes from quitting it. The days without heroin were a blank expanse. If I didn't have heroin, it didn't seem as if I could go on living. Life had no content, but I didn't really want to kill myself either.

I was blind to the light, deaf to sound. I didn't want to speak to anyone; I was hypersensitive, indolent, messy, and disorganized. My periods stopped, and I lost my appetite. Every night I watched the old black-and-white Cantonese movies they ran at midnight on TV — just the picture, with the sound turned off.

One day I realized that I had lost my voice. I would never be able to sing again for pleasure, just because I felt like it, and once again I told myself, You're finished; you might as well be dead! And I never sang again, not even in the shower.

Ultimately, heroin brought me strength of a kind: it freed me from my need for music. When I saw that this had happened, I knew for certain that I was completely fucked up.

Blindness guides our blood, from the beginning to the end. Losing control is like a series of conflagrations. The only thing I understand is that I do not understand why our lives are destined to slip out of control.

My good friend Dalong fell in love with a prostitute, and she fell in love with him. The girl used heroin, and Dalong tried to help her quit, but eventually he started using heroin himself. Sometime after that, the girl's father accused Dalong of kidnapping a minor, and Dalong became a fugitive. He no longer came and set up his shish kebab stall, and he stopped dropping by my place to hang out. Later I heard that Dalong had turned up dead, from some illness, somewhere on the outskirts of town. But I never believed these stories, not even for a minute.

Kitten became a legend. Carrying her packet of white powder, she lured men in and then drugged them, stealing their money. She sought them out in order to destroy them. And after each encounter, she would go home and count the money, tear up their phone numbers, and get high on heroin. The last I heard, she had been locked up in the Women's Reeducation Center but had escaped. The center was on top of a mountain, and the authorities had closed the pass for three days while they searched for her. Discovered by a local, she'd attempted to bribe him with the five hundred Hong Kong dollars that she still had. He took the money, then took her home and raped her. He raped her all night long and then took her back to the Women's Reeducation Center, but she didn't tell the instructors there what had happened. After that, she jumped off a building and injured her back, and she was released for medical reasons. But she never came and looked me up, although I really hoped she would.

All news of Kitten had come to me through Dalong, and after

he disappeared, I didn't hear about her again. None of my old friends came by to see me. I kept thinking I would see them again, and I kept hoping because the street I lived on was still there. Who could have guessed that I would never see any of them again?

The most shocking thing was that Sanmao, who had never given up trying to get me off heroin, started using it himself. Sanmao's wife told me that he had actually started using after Saining had gone away. We love our men, she said. But our men don't love us, so they feel bored, and when you're bored, what else is there to do but take drugs?

Sanmao's wife asked me not to have anything to do with him for a while.

I often thought that if Saining, Sanmao, Dalong, Kitten, and I could all get together and do heroin once, all together, it would be wonderful, and it might make heroin a little more interesting, or meaningful. Or it might make it even more meaningless — who knows?

I didn't see any of my friends anymore. I didn't sing anymore. I was twenty-two years old and dead on the vine.

What else was there to do but take drugs? My life was skidding into darkness at high speed, and I couldn't stop it, no matter how hard I tried. You could buy needles at any of the little shops in the street below, at any time of day or night. Each and every one of us who lived on that street had been absolutely convinced that we could never become junkies. But we all succumbed in the end. We could never be sure if the heroin we were taking every day was really heroin or not. But our lives had been completely transformed, until we were living like vampires.

E

I.

Little Xi'an, that was his name. At twenty-one, he was working as a bouncer at a nightclub in the South and had blocked a knife meant for a patron. That cut had changed his life. He was transferred to an illegal gambling den, where he served as the watchman. Born into hardship, he could now wear the best blue jeans, visit prostitutes, and eat red apples every day. He could also send money back home. He considered himself lucky. His job was to monitor the doorbell. When the bell rang, he had to look through the peephole to see who was there, and if it was someone who belonged, he would let them in. But if it was an outsider, he had to question them at length while at the same time signaling the people inside. Each day, huge sums of money traded hands as people's faces told the ever-changing story of their wins and losses. He took home lots of tips, and sometimes a guest would toss him a whole stack of bills.

One day he was inspecting his knives. He kept them in drawers at the club, five knives in five different drawers. He'd never had to use them, but every day before the gambling den opened, he would check his knives. On this particular day, he opened one of the drawers and found that it was filled with money. The money had been wrapped in newspapers, and he knew that this was the cash they used to open up the gambling house. They'd always kept it in the safe; what was it doing here today? He made a rough count of the bundles and counted forty, give or take, and each bundle must have held ten thousand *yuan*.

All in all, from the moment he discovered the money, packed it into a duffel, stepped into the elevator, rode down, stepped outside, and got into a taxi, roughly fifteen minutes elapsed. As he later told Little Shanghai, he did all of this without a moment's thought, because people in the gambling den were fond of saying that money wasn't something you earned, it was something you got for yourself. All of the people with money that Little Xi'an knew said the same thing, so Little Xi'an believed it.

He took the cab all the way to Guangzhou, or maybe it was Zhuhai, and he checked into the best hotel in town. He thought he ought to shed his old identity completely; he thought he needed a companion, a woman. After some consideration, he made a phone call. He called at least four girls, but each one of them had some excuse or other and turned him down.

The last thing I heard was that he'd been caught by some thugs who'd been sent by the boss of the gambling den, and that he'd been shot and killed. But by the time they'd got to him, he was broke.

Not long after that, the gambling parlor was shut down, and everyone who'd worked there dropped out of sight. I never saw any of them again.

2.

Little Shanghai was her name. Like Dalong, she came from the poorest section of Shanghai and was nothing like Qi, who'd lived on Huaihai Road in the French Concession. Little Shanghai was simpleminded, had never been to school, liked men, liked to sing, and was a very dedicated and hardworking prostitute.

Her first boyfriend made her go through two abortions before he finally dropped her. She tried to commit suicide, and it was the kind of suicide where she really did want to die, but he still didn't want her. All she wanted was a man — a real boyfriend. Another man came into her life. He was older, and his face bore what looked like knife scars, and you could tell at a glance that he had a bad stomach. He had no eyelashes. He said he was in the woolen sweater business in the South; he said that he wanted her because she was only nineteen, because she was pretty.

She felt loved, and it made her lose her head. He bought her many nice things, although the truth was that there was nothing she lacked. Her parents had opened a small business, and she was the youngest child in the family, so she didn't need money. What she didn't have was love, and that was what she wanted.

One day he told her he wanted to take her to Guangzhou — just for fun, he said. He said that he was going to a trade show there. And so she went, after saying good-bye to her parents, went with him to a guesthouse in Guangzhou. The guesthouse was frequented by drug addicts, pimps (what the Shanghainese called "chicken heads"), counterfeit-watch makers, and drug dealers. All of the rooms seemed to be connected, and there were lots of people crowded together in these rooms, and many of the floors were covered with bedrolls. Little Shanghai's boyfriend said to her, I spent fifteen years in prison, so you'd better do as I say, and I'm telling you I want you to be a "chicken." I know everything there is to know about your family, and if you refuse me, I'll make your lives a living hell. I'll tell everyone you're a whore. But if you do as I say, I'll protect you. I'll find a good place for you to do business, and when you've earned enough, we can go back to Shanghai together. We can set up a business of our own and get married.

A lot of men from Shanghai brought their girlfriends here on exactly this pretext. These men all dressed alike, in double-breasted suits the same pale green as pickled vegetables, all with identical gold-colored buttons. Each of these men in suits had spent a decade in prison, and each one of them had a face that betrayed a bad stomach. Even though all of the girls were marketable, not every girl who'd been convinced to sell her body would succeed at it. You had to have a natural talent, a vocation for selling your body. Some girls were born with the ability to sell their bodies, and some were not. The Shanghai girls these men scouted out were hungry for prestige, highly marketable, and yearning for a man they could depend on. Little Shanghai was no exception, and she couldn't escape, and that was how she entered a life where day becomes night and night becomes day.

He brought her to a restaurant here in this city, where they watched the other men's women picking clients, making lots of money, and referring to their own pimps as their *laogong,* their "old man." This brought out her competitive nature. Three weeks later she had gone to work.

Every night we watched her riding the hotel elevator, up and down, up and down. There was an illegal gambling parlor in the hotel basement, and where there's gambling, there are prostitutes. It's a custom in Guangdong: when you're done gambling, win or lose, you call a prostitute. Otherwise it's bad luck. Little Shanghai in the elevator, a condom hidden in her underwear, kept a running tally in her head. Each john was equal to five hundred *yuan*. She had a good feel for numbers, but money left her cold, and after every trick she went back to the room she shared with her *laogong* and turned the money over to him. She never saved any money.

That elevator was her world, and I remember it as the window on her life. She always wore a red short-sleeved wool sweater; she called it her uniform. She would stand in the corner of the elevator, right by the buttons, as if she were the elevator girl. She had soulful black eyes and a man she called *laogong*, and she thought she loved him. She had given him her heart. All she had wanted was a man, and now all she wanted was him. She would do anything for him, and besides, now that she was a prostitute, nobody else would ever want her anyway. Her love was in her heart, not in her body. She had always been that way. The man who was with her right now was pathetic, and the one before him hadn't been much better, but it didn't matter.

Every kind of prostitute worked in this town. There were streetwalkers standing by the road; there were girls who only worked in hotel rooms, girls who plied their trade in nightclubs, and call girls who wouldn't go out unless they got a phone call. There were the girls who lived off of a few wealthy patrons (not that they considered themselves prostitutes), and there were others who slipped past immigration to Hong Kong and Macao and only worked there. Little Shanghai was one of the less expensive prostitutes, one of the ones who turned many tricks each night. She was only a little more pricey than the girls on the street.

Men of every description and a handful of women stepped in and out of the elevator. The majority of the men were johns. Most of the women were like Qi, hostesses who worked in the nightclub upstairs, and they looked down on Little Shanghai because they made most of their money in tips from the clients they joined for drinks. Actually sleeping with a client earned them more than a thousand *yuan*. They thought of themselves as hostesses, while Little Shanghai was just a chicken, a cheap whore. A number of the Shanghainese hostesses were convinced that Little Shanghai wasn't really Shanghainese — how else could they account for her poor taste in clothes? They took her for a country girl from somewhere near Shanghai, or possibly a native of some place like Suzhou or Hangzhou.

Someone was playing the piano in the hotel lobby; she didn't know what song it was, but listening to it relaxed her. Almost all of the restaurants had the same background music, Kenny G. Little Shanghai didn't like Kenny G, but from 8 P.M. to 10 P.M. each night there was always live piano music, and because of this, she especially liked coming here during those hours to look for clients. She spent a long time in the elevator, standing in the corner, stopping at every floor. When the doors opened, she would quietly ask the concierges who sat at each floor, Anybody here? and the concierges would give a discreet signal. Sometimes she would step off the elevator, and sometimes she wouldn't. It was obvious to the men riding the elevator that she was for sale.

Her eyes communicated an innocent desire. Fixing a man in the elevator with those black eyes, she might ask, Do you want to do business? Some of them wouldn't look at her, but some of them did, not that she cared much either way. Little Shanghai was used to it. Sometimes a man would come straight over to her and start feeling her up, squeezing her small, firm breasts, reaching inside her pants to see how wet she was, and bringing their fingers to their noses to catch her scent. Every man who touched Little Shanghai in the elevator was hurried and anxious, and every man who looked at her had a rapacious gleam in his eyes. Little Shanghai always smiled at this, figuring that the men liked the way she looked as she leaned against the wall of the elevator and smiled.

She never swore, but she didn't object if men talked dirty to her, or maybe she was just used to it. She was like a dumb little girl who didn't know how to do anything but make love. But she gave an impression of cleanliness, of being as pure as the driven snow, and this brought her lots of business. On occasion, she'd follow a hunch and go straight to a room with a client, quickly pulling off his pants and putting his penis in her mouth. She knew how to handle a penis. To her, a penis was just a penis, neither good nor bad. She might also take off her own clothing, exposing her hard little red nipples, or she might put a finger in the crease between her legs, but whatever else she was doing, she kept him in her mouth the whole time. Her movements were tender but efficient. She did everything she could to persuade a man to go with her. She knew she couldn't stay in a room for long. If she was there longer than ten minutes, she would have to give the floor concierge a tip, whether she'd done any business or not. They were her partners, sending business her way and acting as lookouts. If they thought she was cheating them, she wouldn't be able to work at this hotel anymore. So she had to make sure that a prospective customer would decide within ten minutes whether or not he was going to screw her.

Every man liked to do something different with her body. Sometimes she had to do a "sandwich," with two women and one man, or two men and one woman. She was an apt pupil and learned a lot from having sex with so many different men. Whenever a man praised her technique, she felt happy. She watched the ceiling pulsing above her, and Little Shanghai's cries always sounded so joyful, unlike those of some women, whose cries made it sound as if they were in agony. Little Shanghai's cries were exquisitely beautiful. Whether she was genuinely enjoying herself or felt numb inside, no one knew, and she never said, because no one ever asked her this question. She knew that men liked it when she cried out, and she wanted it to be over quickly so that she could go brush her teeth and take a bath. She had to bathe many times a day, two baths for each trick. After the bath she could get paid, and after getting her money she might drink a cola, or sometimes a Heineken, from the minibar in the john's hotel room. And then it was back to the elevator again.

Sometimes she had clients who were impotent. She always told them, There's nothing wrong with you; you're a good man, you're just not used to being with a hooker. You're nervous, but I like you; you're a good person. The only way to deal with an impotent client was nonstop oral sex. The truth was that Little Shanghai simply couldn't bear impotence. Nothing bothered her more. It made her sad; sometimes it even made her cry. She thought that it had to be very depressing for those men to have this problem, so she spared no effort trying to help her impotent customers. If they still couldn't get it up, she only charged them half, but most of them paid the full amount anyway. Sometimes she'd get a customer who had taken too many drugs or had too much to drink, and he would fuck her for a long time without coming, and if he couldn't come, she only got half of her fee or, worse, nothing at all. When she ran into situations like these, there was nothing Little Shanghai could do but try her best. They might fuck her until her feet were half frozen, but she still wouldn't get paid. For her, that was the worst possible case.

Riding the elevator till midnight, Little Shanghai might start making phone calls, or she might go knocking on the doors of hotel rooms. But this was very risky. If a prospective customer reported her, she could get into trouble. Even if her *laogong* had paid off everybody in and around the hotel, there were still a few people who didn't accept bribes, and she was aware of this. If she were reported, her *laogong* would not be happy with her. He might beat her, or he might not talk to her for days and would be even less likely to sleep with her. She had genuinely fallen in love with him after she'd come back home to him from her first night on the job, and he had held her close. That was the moment when she'd started loving him. She needed to feel someone comforting her. What motivated her every day was what she felt at that moment. It was what she yearned for.

But she still had to go knocking on doors, because the elevator was emptying out and the few potential johns she saw were bringing girls back to the hotel from somewhere outside, or else the johns were drunk, and doing business with drunks was too time-consuming, and time was money, especially at night. When she brought in lots of money, her *laogong* treated her well. He liked gambling, and there were many other Shanghainese chickens and chicken heads living in this hotel. While the whores went and earned wages, the chicken heads made wagers. Little Shanghai's *laogong* gambled away all of her money. Even when he won, he would go on to lose his winnings, and sometimes Little Shanghai had to do business wearing a tampon. But she thought that her *lao-gong* was going to marry her someday, or else why would she call him her "old man" while he called her his "lady"? She believed her *laogong* was good-hearted. Once, somebody had given him a girl, and he'd wanted to keep two women, but Little Shanghai had gone into the bathroom and tried to kill herself. It only took that one attempt. He didn't try anything like that again.

After a year of this life, Little Shanghai had serious cervical erosion. Whenever she tried to have sex, she bled, so she went to Liuhua Hospital. The doctor said that she needed electrotherapy. The doctor was an older man, and every day there was a long line of girls waiting to see him. He was a famous gynecologist, and he was soft-spoken and gentle with his patients. After each examination he washed his hands with a very old and very hard-looking little piece of soap. He had unusually small hands, without any flesh on them, and the skin covering them was dark brown and crisscrossed by pulsing blue veins. He said that Little Shanghai needed a long course of laser treatment.

Little Shanghai started going to the hospital every two days.

One day, Xiaohong, Sister Morphine, went with her. Sister Morphine said she'd lost interest in sex, so she waited outside. Little Shanghai didn't think she would ever be able to make sense of a girl like Sister Morphine. What did not being interested in sex have to do with going to the gynecologist? How could anyone so young not care about sex anymore? And what did it mean to lose interest in sex in the first place? And what was so great about using heroin? You might as well light a match to your money and watch it burn. But Xiaohong was the only girl she knew here who wasn't a prostitute. They'd met at the hotel swimming pool. Little

Shanghai had been with a client. It was very unusual in this city to run into a Shanghainese girl who wasn't a prostitute, so Little Shanghai liked Sister Morphine.

After the laser treatment, the two of them took a walk in the sunshine. They weren't used to the daylight. As Little Shanghai walked along she began to smile, and with Sister Morphine looking on, Little Shanghai pointed out men in the street, saying, Look, look over there. You see that one? I've done him, and I've done him too. Really. Honestly. I don't want to come out anymore, I just can't.

When she had her laser treatments, Little Shanghai didn't feel anything. It was very relaxing; the only thing was, it wasn't cheap. After a few treatments, Little Shanghai went back to work. After a few tricks she started bleeding again. Once, the bleeding didn't stop. She was taken to the hospital, and she stayed there for several days. But as soon as she was out, she was back at work, only it hurt her to have sex, and she couldn't show off her technique anymore. Her womb had been destroyed.

Little Shanghai was washed up, completely finished! Everyone said so. But Little Shanghai wasn't convinced. She used her mouth and stayed in business. She only used her mouth, but in no time she was in high demand, and she became the "Flute Queen" of the hotel. But her *laogong* was on a losing streak, and even though he was stealing money left and right, he kept sinking further into debt. He gave up his room and went to Guangzhou, saying that he was going to pull off a few burglaries there, and then he would come back. Her *laogong* gave her some money he'd borrowed for her, and he told her to look after her health.

Her *laogong* came back, only he came back with another woman. He'd decided to go to Macao because it was getting harder to do business here. A lot of people had come to town from the Northeast, and the Shanghainese were moving on to Macao. But her *laogong* couldn't take Little Shanghai with him, because she could only use her mouth, and the false papers you needed to get into Macao cost so much money that her *laogong* needed someone who could do anything you asked. Little Shanghai felt that her *laogong* didn't want her anymore because she was crippled, but this was something that couldn't be changed. Who had given her such an unlucky fate? Why did so many other girls get away without being damaged? There were so many girls, some of them tricked into the business, some told at the outset what was going on. None of them had any money either, since they gave it all to their men, but at least they still had a dream. They were waiting for their man to marry them, or to give them some share of the money so they could go back to Shanghai. But what about Little Shanghai? Altogether she had earned enough money to buy an entire factory, but all she had to show for it now was five hundred *yuan*. In all the time she'd been working, she had never bought herself any clothing, had never been out to eat. Instead she'd packed a daily meal of fried rice with salted fish and bits of chicken, or maybe some stewed eggplant. Her favorite food was nothing fancy either — just simple Shanghai-style poached eggs — but since she'd come south, she hadn't even eaten this once.

Little Shanghai left the hotel and became a hostess at another nightclub. Her stint working the hotel had taught her speed and endurance, and because she could sing and dance (she sang only songs by Teresa Teng and told everyone that she had once won a singing competition), she became very popular. Every day she took home big tips, and sometimes she would spend the night with a customer. The nightclub patrons were much more easygoing than the men she'd picked up at the hotel, and they paid more. Now that she didn't have a *laogong*, she only had to make money for herself and didn't have to work as hard. She could even take a week off from time to time, and she felt that, little by little, her life was getting better, and her health was improving too. She was starting to think that the time had come to go back home to Shanghai for a visit.

But then a new man came into her life. He was from the Northeast, a thief, and a pimp. He stole shoes for Little Shanghai, and she fell in love with him. She decided to go back to the hotel for a while and work the elevator again, because in one night you could service a lot of customers. At the nightclub you could only be with one client each night. Little Shanghai and her new man wanted to make a little money so that they could go back to the Northeast and get married.

Little Shanghai went back to the hotel elevator, and we went back to watching her. But now she always wore clothes that were in style, and she always had a smile on her face, and every day she went out to eat with her *laogong*.

Her new *laogong* was very masculine; he didn't talk much, but he was always screwing her. He was ready to strip off his pants anytime, anyplace, and he was a perfect fit for Little Shanghai. She said that he screwed in a very thorough way, that he could screw all day without coming. He had brought Little Shanghai boundless pleasure, and because of him she was constantly wet. Of all the men Little Shanghai had been with, he satisfied her the most, and Little Shanghai loved him for it. She felt that for the first time she was having a normal love relationship with a man. This time she was getting to experience the normal run of happiness, hurt, jealousy, secret fantasies, and sweet talk. She always felt like making love with him. She wanted it all day, every day, nonstop.

The hotel had connections with organized crime, and somehow the management must have offended someone important, because it ended up being closed down, and even the manager was hauled away. The day of the raid, the girls and maids scattered, but Little Shanghai happened to be in the elevator just then and wasn't able to get away.

She spent her days at the detention center hoping that her *laogong* would come to see her and bring her a clean change of clothes. Since her *laogong* had her passbook, and since she'd put away a lot of money, she was sure that he'd figure out how to pay someone off and get her out. All of the other women had visitors, and some of them had even been freed after the right people got paid; but no one came to see Little Shanghai. Every day Little Shanghai would tell people how much her *laogong* loved her, and how he was definitely trying to work something out for her, there on the outside.

In the end she was sentenced to one year of reform through labor at a women's camp. There at the Women's Reeducation Center, she continued to repeat the same story. Everybody got sick of hearing about it, and they all started making fun of her. Although everyone ridiculed her, they still helped her out by giving her clothing and cookies. Little Shanghai was pregnant, so she didn't have to do any work at the Reeducation Center. After only six months, she was released.

She went from place to place, asking people everywhere if they knew where her *laogong* was. With her protruding belly, she rode the train to Shenyang. Her man said to her, The money's gone. I spent it all. Now get the hell out of here. He also said, It never crossed your mind, did it, that I couldn't possibly be serious about a girl from Shanghai? Shanghai girls aren't good for anything but fucking. He kept repeating this, over and over. Little Shanghai came to town, alone. She wanted to go to the hospital and have her pregnancy, already in the eighth month, taken out. A man went to the hospital with her, a man who was in love with her. He wanted to marry her, but he didn't have any money either.

After the operation, Little Shanghai found that she had totally lost her figure. Her face and body sagged; her black eyes were no longer black. Only her eyelashes still had their upward sweep.

Little Shanghai went back to work at the nightclub, but this time she couldn't get herself back in demand. She didn't have the money to buy herself any nice clothes, and that man from the Northeast had gotten rid of her old clothes. Sometimes Little Shanghai would cheat on her new *laogong,* going out with other men and sleeping with them to make money, but she didn't feel good about it, because her *laogong* strongly forbade this, and the two of them often fought about it. But Little Shanghai was happy inside. She felt that this man's love for her was normal.

One day a letter came from the man's mother. She wrote that she'd heard her son had a fiancée and she was so happy that she'd borrowed two thousand *yuan* that she was going to give them as a wedding present. Little Shanghai cried and cried. Two thousand *yuan!* She used to be able to earn several times that in just one night! With this in mind, she decided that she would go home with this man and marry him.

3.

Ye Meili, "Beautiful Evening," that was her name. From the time she was a child, she had been bought and sold many times by people who trafficked in human beings. She was nineteen years old, maybe twenty — she never told the same story twice. She was illiterate, and she spoke a bizarre sort of Mandarin. Her peasant accent was as coarse as her looks. She said she was a Uighur from Xinjiang, but none of us knew where she really came from. Only she knew the truth, and she liked to tell tall tales — that was her stock in trade. She first appeared in our midst when Little Shanghai's *laogong* brought Ye Meili to town from Guangzhou. Her pale face was covered with freckles, and the high bridge of her nose was an add-on, her large double-folded eyelids were the product of surgery, and her big tits looked like silicone implants. She was intense and hot-tempered, and when she saw Little Shanghai's pathetic exit from the scene, she resolved that she was going to use that man. She was going to use him to get herself to Macao. That was where she wanted to go. There were casinos there, and she wanted to gamble.

But with her "ethnic" looks, she didn't look Chinese, and her man couldn't get her the false documents she needed to cross into Macao. So he got false papers for himself and went on alone, waiting for her to slip into the territory by boat. The first time she tried this, there was heavy fog, and the boatman accidentally piloted the boat to Hong Kong. They didn't realize where they were until they stepped ashore, and they decided to turn themselves in. The police sent them back, and they were released after paying small fines.

The second time she tried to sneak into Macao, their boat was pursued, and Ye Meili stood in the boat screaming and yelling at the top of her lungs, How come you're going so slow?! Faster! The boatman was afraid she was going to shout too loud and give them away, so he sped up. The bumping of the boat threw Ye Meili around until her ass was covered with bruises, but they made it to Macao. Except that her old man wasn't there to meet her. She waited and waited until she couldn't wait any longer. The boatman didn't get paid, so he raped Ye Meili, grabbing her big tits and coming just like that. But as he was pulling his pants on to leave, Ye Meili sat down on his face with her big ass, with her pubic hair overlapping the boatman's beard, and she squeezed her legs tight, and she stuck her two hands in the dirt, and her two huge tits started to shake violently, and Ye Meili cried out, faster and faster, and every recess of her entire body was shuddering with joy.

By the time the boatman left, he wasn't steady on his feet, and his face was dripping with the fluids that had flowed from Ye Meili's hole, including his own semen.

Ye Meili crawled forward, slithered through a barbed-wire fence, and finally reached the road. She knew that in Macao no one would ask you for identification if you were riding in a privately licensed car, so she got into a private car right away. But nobody wanted to do business with her, since she was covered with scratches from the barbed wire. So she went to a public phone, changed some money for Portuguese escudos, and, even though it was risky, called up her man, who was at the time gambling at Chinese dominoes.

*　*　*

Ye Meili put on some pretty clothes and went to work. She didn't want to go to nightclubs; the nightclubs here were too "regulated." You had to learn from your supervisor how to do "cloud nine with fire and ice," which was a blow job with ice. You had to wear an evening gown, blow-dry your hair, and paste on false eyelashes every day. In addition, you had to leave your breasts half-exposed and pushed up like a pair of balloons. The girls, all of them from provinces in the interior, sat around the club holding numbered cards. Anywhere you looked, all you could see was rows and rows of ballooning tits. Being picked out of this lineup was too humiliating for her.

She decided to find herself a spot to stand in. You couldn't loiter on a street corner in Macao, so she stood outside the main salon of one of the town's casinos, the Lisbon Hotel.

Just like Little Shanghai, she did business with gamblers. But unlike Little Shanghai, Ye Meili wasn't about to hand over all of her earnings to her man. She did understand his situation — he had spent more than ten years in prison, had no other way to make a living, and liked to gamble, and none of this was going to change. But she wasn't so stupid as to actually think of him as her man. Naturally she held back some money for herself.

The only thing was that she really loved to have a good time, and the moment her man wasn't looking, she went shopping. She loved everything she saw, until she brought it home, and then she didn't like it anymore. She drank, and she screwed around with other men, letting all kinds of counterfeiters and forgers screw her for free, or sometimes spending money so that she could sleep with some guy she liked. She also went gambling, but since none of the casinos would let her in, she could only play the slot machines. She always lost, and when she was tired of losing, she cursed out loud, and when she was tired of cursing, she went shopping.

Once, when she was on her way to a disco, she was stopped and asked for her papers. And because she didn't have any papers, she was sent back to the Chinese immigration authorities in Zhuhai. But the Chinese authorities wouldn't take her. They said she was Russian and sent her back to Macao, where she was held in detention. At this point, Ye Meili remembered a client she'd once had. This client had a large glass cabinet at home that was chock-full of cigarette lighters of every description, and she wondered why it was that other people had so many lighters and she didn't have even one. This made her cry.

Her man put up the money to get her out of jail, and to keep her out of any more trouble, he locked her up in a hotel room and had her service her customers there.

But in the end she stole her man's money and slipped back onto the mainland. She wanted to be free. And so she came back to stand on our street.

4.

Sister Morphine is my name. I used to have a lover in this town, I couldn't stand to be away from him, and nothing was right without him. I thought that's what love was. When he left me, I started using heroin. My craving for it was so intense, and my tolerance grew, and I liked to keep chasing the dragon until I was totally fucked up, until I felt as if I was more dead than alive. When I was alive I wanted to be dead, and when I was near death I wanted to live. I never had to think about anything else, and I felt free at last.

Sometimes, when I'd had a lot of heroin, I would think about men. I longed for a man's lips. None of the men here knew how to use their mouth on a woman. It wasn't something men around here did; either that, or maybe they just didn't like to use their mouth on women they didn't know. I don't know what it was. I started going out with different men. They all flattered me with the same tired phrases. They said nice things to me, but they all used the same old clichés. None of them ever said anything new. And no matter who they were, they were all like children when they came. I was always on the bottom, and they didn't usually need to have me take my clothes off, and I was so overcome with boredom that I could hardly move. I took a simple kind of pleasure from it, and it all passed without a word between us.

But I absolutely loved watching any kind of man taking off his clothes in front of me. It was a moment of lyricism, the only moment of lyricism, and it always happened in a flurry and was over in the blink of an eye.

One day, I was seized with a sense of doubt, a sense that I did not love Saining. Because I didn't know what love was anymore. Maybe I was just hooked on the frame of mind he put me in. This filled me with loathing. When I thought back and pictured Saining and me making love, I was so filled with disgust that I thought I would die. From then on, everything seemed tainted. I no longer had any interest in sex. I was twenty-three years old, and my body was dead.

Because of my severe asthma, I could tell from the tightness in my chest just how much a batch of heroin had been cut with, say, rat poison, or an insecticide like 66 Powder. Drug dealers were always being caught and imprisoned, or simply executed, with a bullet to the head, so I was constantly scrambling to find new dealers. But none of them could fool my bronchial tubes. Poor-quality heroin made me instantly sick.

There were a few dealers I'd run into on the street, but I met most of my dealers in dark little rooming houses. Usually run by people from Chaozhou, these squalid establishments fanned out around the edges of this spotlessly bright and shiny city. They were like the underground sewers of this little open city, this embodiment of economic "reform," and they were crawling with rats. I'd never seen such gigantic rats in Shanghai. The junkie prostitutes lived in these hotels, where many people were crowded into a room. I felt as if I didn't understand men at all. These girls were bags of bones, with ashen complexions, and their skin was covered with ulcerations and needle marks. But they could always find a man to do it with them, even the down-and-out and junkie whores with missing teeth.

Heroin made me hypersensitive, and I couldn't stand living in the same apartment I'd once shared with Saining, so I decided to move. But before I'd found a new place to live, I moved into one of these hotels. Sanmao arranged a free room for me. I didn't understand how Sanmao was able to get me a free room in a place like that. His wife told me that Sanmao used to be part of the "black society," engaged in organized crime, and had been a gang member at one point. As she explained it, it had originally been nothing but a bunch of kids who got together and stole bicycles. Over time they moved on to bigger things and became a real gang. But once, during a fight, somebody had fired a gun, and Sanmao had fainted in fear. When he woke up, he vowed to go straight, and he took up singing songs by the Taiwan pop star Qi Tai. From there he got into rock and roll.

The smell of air-conditioning, the smell of heroin, real and bogus, the smell of condoms, the smell of blow jobs, the smell of fast-food take-out containers, the smell of frozen fruit, the black-and-white Cantonese movies, the smell of table lamps, the smell of sweet rice porridge, the smell of paper money, the smell of the hotel manager, the smell of vomit.

One day, Little Shanghai was wandering around the hotel, randomly pounding on doors, and she finally pounded on mine. She was holding a shiny red apple in one hand, and I supposed that a customer had given it to her.

I'm sorry, she said. Wrong door again.

Come on in, I said. You can give me a hand.

There was a man passed out in my bathroom.

Little Shanghai said, Dead people are heavy. The two of us can't possibly lift him. I said, He's alive; he just passed out. Dead or unconscious, she said, he still weighs the same. I'll have my old man come over and help you. He'll be able to do it.

The man lying in my bathroom was Little Xi'an; he'd been pestering me every day, and now he'd fainted in my bathroom after shooting up. I never used a needle, since too many people died injecting themselves with bad heroin, and there was nothing I liked less than watching people shoot up in front of me.

I was badly shaken and a little incoherent. So Sanmao's wife came to the hotel and picked me up. She apologized for having put me in a hotel like this. Honestly, she said, I didn't realize what a scary place this was. She told me she was going to take Sanmao up to Guangzhou for rehab, and she asked me if I wanted to go with them.

After the day Little Shanghai's old man took Little Xi'an to the hospital, Little Shanghai and I became friends. Little Xi'an was a regular customer of Little Shanghai's, and the man who later married Little Shanghai was a friend of Little Xi'an's. Little Xi'an hated pimps more than anything, so he found Little Shanghai a good man, a good man who was as young and handsome as he was himself. After this man's mother gave Little Shanghai that two thousand *yuan*, Little Shanghai left town and got married. And she never came back.

Sometime after the wedding, Little Shanghai got a phone call: I have a couple hundred thousand on me. Do you want to go away with me? Little Shanghai said, I don't think so. My husband happens to be a friend of yours, in case you've forgotten. What were you thinking? I mean, why me? Little Xi'an said, I was just thinking about the old days when we used to hang out together. I think you're a good woman, and people say you used to be supersexy. When Little Shanghai heard the words "used to be," she cut Little Xi'an off short and hung up.

It was just a city street. But in the days that followed, I couldn't stop thinking about that street. And while those memories tormented me, that street was still where I had grown up.

In the old days, the street was populated with prostitutes, pimps, johns, drug dealers, young girls selling flowers, beggars, and shish kebab vendors. Later on, the police descended on the place, a lot of police, and you didn't see all those people anymore. My street was gone; those warm but terrifying sounds were gone. The stores also disappeared, and new high-rises went up on either side of the road. Their dark eye sockets came to occupy a place in my life, their lights going on, their lights going off. They were always there, in my gray times, in my brightest hours, and there was nothing that could separate me from this secret. Sometimes I suspected that this secret had robbed me of the strength to wait for the future.

I often went to the boulevard, seeking out another pair of eyes with my blue-flashing, poisoned eyes. I needed to find someone to sell me that drug; it was more important than anything else in the world. Heroin was the only thing in my life. My junkie life was simple, but at the same time it wasn't easy.

One day I went to see Ye Meili. She liked me because Saining had left me a pile of money, and also because I was "educated." Ye Meili said that she just liked to make friends with people like me.

Ye Meili and I found ourselves talking to Little Xi'an on the phone at the same time. We'd been in the middle of an argument. Ye Meili was angry at me for taking a particular man home with me. She said that she liked him herself, that she hadn't planned on "doing business" with him, that she'd just wanted to have him over to hang out and party. And she'd wanted him to meet her friend, me. She said, But you had to haul off and take what wasn't yours!

Ye Meili was shouting, And you call yourself my friend! Do you even know what a friend is?

Just then, Ye Meili's cell phone rang, and Little Xi'an tried his pitch out on her. Ye Meili said, I can't go with you. Don't bother me. But someone you know is over here right now. She likes money; why don't you ask her?

Little Xi'an told me what he'd told her. I said, If you have that much money, I'm sure you can find a girl who's a lot more fun than either of us. Why are you asking us? Little Xi'an said, I wanted to find a woman who knew me before I had money. Ye Meili is the kind of woman who might walk out on you at a moment's notice, but I'd be happy to be with her for as long as it lasted, and I wouldn't be sad if she left. You're the cultured type, plus you're the only girl I still haven't fucked, and now I've got all this cash, so what do you say you come with me? I can send you to the best rehab clinic.

My refusal was blunt. No way! I said. And then I hung up on him.

I asked Ye Meili, Why didn't you take him up on it? He's cute and he's rich. Ye Meili said, Because I need my freedom. That's why I'll never commit myself to another man as long as I live, whether I love him or not. I don't care who he is.

With that, she left and went back to stand on the street again. It had really made her mad when I stole her friend away, because she never spoke to me again.

A few months later, I got another call from Little Xi'an.

He said, I'm flat broke. Will you come with me now?

I laughed coldly and hung up.

5.

Little Dove, that was her name. Little Dove was a little beauty, short but voluptuous. She was the one who brought the news of Little Xi'an's death. A child of the oil fields, Little Dove had come to this city to escape a life of poverty. She became a prostitute, but she was constantly reminding herself that Marx had said that the primitive accumulation of capital was evil. With a head full of such potent ideas, she quickly gave up prostitution.

Little Xi'an had met her the same way he'd met Little Shanghai and Ye Meili — they'd met while "doing business."

Little Xi'an had approached her because she seemed like a bright girl to him, and what was more, she had the same humble origins he did. He told Little Dove, You can be my leader. We can struggle together against the power of the establishment.

But he was in a truly precarious situation, and Little Dove saw this more clearly than he did.

Little Dove was the one who had sold Little Xi'an the false papers he'd used when he fled to Macao. She had sold them for a high price.

Little Dove and I had also met on that street, when she was looking for customers who might want to buy false papers from her.

Little Dove asked me, What do you think Little Xi'an was thinking about at the moment he died? No one will ever know. His only mistake was that he forgot he was poor. He completely forgot. He didn't realize how easily 400,000 *yuan* could slip through his fingers and leave him with nothing.

F

In December of 1994 I found myself caught in the middle of a gang war. I'll never know for sure what started all that bloody fighting, and there's nothing I can say about it except that someone shaved off all of my hair before giving me a sharp kick in the face. Those are some pretty eyes you've got, little girl, he said.

It was a horrible night. My eyes had been injured, and when I went to pay the nurse, she told me that all of my money was counterfeit. When I finally made it to the operating table, the anesthetic had no effect on me because of my tolerance, and I had to suffer through the entire operation anyway. After leaving the operating room, I wasn't allowed to leave until someone came with real money. While I was sitting and waiting, a drug dealer from the Northeast called Blackie came limping in. He'd been stabbed, and I took him to the operating room. I'd been needing a fix for a while already, but Blackie had no heroin and no money, since he'd just been mugged. Blackie and I ended up sitting there together, waiting for someone to bring us some money, but the people who'd promised to bring the money took forever to show up. I was wheezing because I needed a fix, and I was fretting about not being able to leave the hospital until after daybreak. I was going to have to go outside with my messily shaved head. I was worrying about lots of other things too, and so I sat there, crossing and uncrossing my legs, not knowing what to do with myself.

That night, I had a sudden realization of this very simple truth: heroin was a drug that brought nothing but bad luck. It was true for anybody; all you had to do was cross paths with heroin, and sooner or later you would find yourself up to your neck in bad luck, with no way out. In this respect, heroin was no fun at all.

My father came to town. Once again he sent me to a rehab clinic in Shanghai. It seemed that this gang war had been a stroke of good luck after all, because otherwise I'm sure I would have died in the South. It must have been fate.

Before I went back to Shanghai, Sanmao and his old lady gave me a whole load of hats, hats of all shapes and sizes, and Sanmao told me that he was going to go back into rehab himself. He said, I have a feeling that you're going to get better, that we're both going to get better. Y'know, you look great in hats!

Completely bald, with a gauze patch over one eye, and lugging seven big suitcases, I arrived at the airport with my father. I had hidden some heroin in my underwear because I knew the craving could hit me at any time. This was something my father didn't understand at all.

As we went through airport security, I kept looking at my father anxiously and thinking, He's such a good person, and I'm so bad.

The moment the plane left the ground, I fucking burst into tears. I swore I would never come back to this town in the South ever again. This weird, plastic, bullshit Special Economic Zone, with all that pain and sadness, and the face of love, and the whole totally fucked-up world of heroin, and the late-1980s gold rush mentality, and all that pop music from Taiwan and Hong Kong. This place had all of the best and all of the worst. It had become my eternal nightmare.

G

My nurse's aide came in and asked me what I wanted to eat that night. She said, Here are some New Year's sesame-and-rice dumplings in syrup and some Master Kang's instant noodles. Then she said, Do you want to wash your face? Do you need me to get you some hot water? I opened my eyes wide and looked at this person at my bedside, a woman in her forties, with prominent cheekbones and a ruddy complexion. Dressed in a maroon cotton blouse and pants, she looked like a factory worker, and I said, Why are you my nurse? And how come everyone here except me is wearing the same clothes? She said, Because I'm a patient too. I said, You're in rehab too? Her lips slowly parted to form a grin, and she said, You don't know what kind of hospital this is? I said, What do you mean? This is a rehab clinic, isn't it? She started to rock from side to side, and then she leaned forward and said in a confidential tone, We're all mental patients who have done something wrong. I said, What? Mental patients? What did you do? She looked me in the eye and said, I killed my old man's father. I said, You killed someone? Why did you kill him? Because he was always yelling at me, she said, so I put insecticide in his soup.

My crime was that I was dependent on drugs, and I was my father's nightmare. First I'd spent all my energy trying to get love and alcohol, and then I'd laid my body down on the altar of heroin, and I had always known that this meant I was lonely and crazy. My father had brought me here only this afternoon, but my reactions were noticeably slow because I was already on medications, and I suspected that my mind was not very clear, but I was still capable of being frightened by what I saw. I thought that the Communist Party (and that included my father) was pretty intense, putting drug addicts who were trying to clean up in here along with homicidal maniacs so that we could all be cured together. Anyone who could overcome her habit in a situation like this wasn't likely to want to start using again. When I compared myself to the other patients, I felt ashamed of what I'd done, because I had already begun to feel a sense of shame. Heroin had made me stupid. When I'd checked in that afternoon, I had wondered why I was the only person in my tiny room and why there were so many people in the big room outside. I'd wondered why all the drug addicts in Shanghai were so old.

During the most unbearable seventy-two hours, the doctors didn't try to use shock treatment on me, because of my serious asthma. They put me on some kind of drip, which made me really high, and every now and then, when no one was looking, I managed to speed up the drip. Every day my nurse's aide helped me use the bathroom, wash my face, and brush my teeth. She also swept the floor of my room.

Once, when she was helping me to the bathroom, one of the other patients said to me, Look at yourself! Look at the mess you're in. When you get out of here, you're not going to start using drugs again, are you?

The room was huge, and it had another very large room within it, which was the dormitory where the psychiatric patients and forcibly committed drug addicts slept. There was a sea of beds, each one covered with a snowy white blanket. The rows of blankets looked like racks of magazines, and they reminded me of the plain white covers of the underground art magazines in Beijing. The sinks and toilets were in another room, where it was always dark except for a filament of moonlight. Even sunrays looked like moonlight there, and it was as cold as a refrigerator. I was in the smallest room, equipped with two sets of bunk beds. This was the room for drug addicts who had come voluntarily.

*　　*　　*

The pale winter light was sometimes shot with lemon yellow, and the patients played cards or sat in the sun and picked apart rags. They passed the time of day, occasionally chatting with the doctors, their voices like those of little birds. I watched them from my room, and it all looked so peaceful. After lunch they would sing songs together, in a chorus, since this was a required class. They sang old songs like "The Light of Beijing's Golden Mountains Shines Everywhere." They also sang popular songs from Hong Kong and Taiwan, like "Grace in Motion" and "Thank You for Your Love," which came in with the steady stream of new drug addicts entering the clinic. They wrote them down on the little blackboard so that the other patients could learn them. After singing practice, they lined up for their medications, and then they took their midday naps.

I sat like an idiot, pumped full of medications, and the patients were there playing cards in the sunlight, and the big doors were bolted shut. Losing control of your life was this simple, and here it was, laid out plain and clear, like winter in the city, icily harboring its murderous intentions. My mind was empty, and I don't think that it was just the drugs. After I'd given up my habit of using heroin many times every day, I honestly didn't know how I was going to fill up my life. After they took out my drip, I ventured into the main room and sat in the sun. Just then, another patient came up close beside me and bumped into me, saying, Give me a cookie, OK? Her gaze was focused on some other place, but from time to time her eyes darted back to me, looking for a sweet. A lot of patients watched as I handed her a cookie, but they quickly looked away. Suddenly I became aware that all of the patients shared a habit of rocking their bodies back and forth, rocking back and forth and constantly shifting their weight from one foot to the other.

I was given permission to call my father. I said, Daddy, I'm doing fine, but I want a mirror. They took my mirror away, and I want them to give it back.

My doctor called me into her office, and she said, We don't let you have mirrors, because we don't want you to hurt yourselves or make trouble for the other patients, but you can have yours back now.

That night a patient approached me in the bathroom and timidly asked, Can you lend us your mirror for a little while? Just for a moment, and we'll give it right back. I looked at her, and I said, You can have it for five minutes, OK? I took out my palm-size mirror, and everybody was taking turns looking at themselves, and that night I didn't feel lonely at all. The one who'd asked to borrow it spent the longest time looking at herself. Another patient told me that the woman who was looking at her reflection was a virgin, that she'd already been here fifteen years. You're a virgin? I asked her. No wonder you look so young. She said, I'm not so young anymore. I'm old, very old. And hearing her say "old, very old" made me start to cry, because when you're in withdrawal, you cry easily, sometimes for no reason at all. I felt a little embarrassed about my tears, but nobody paid any attention. Trying to cover my sense of discomfort, I rushed to ask, Why are you in here? She didn't respond, but another patient told me that this woman had done something evil: she had killed all of her older sister's children. My God! I exclaimed. But the woman appeared not to have heard us and went on as before, stroking her face in front of the mirror. Someone said, She thought that they were demons, so she killed them. But someone else said, She did it because her sister didn't treat her very well.

I took back my mirror. I spent the whole night thinking, wondering why some people went crazy, crazy enough to commit murder, and why they hadn't been taken to the hospital and treated before things got out of hand. Lying under the moonlight, I felt extremely lucky. I wasn't insane; I was just a gutless little mouse, or maybe, as my father had said, I was just a good girl who had lost her way.

I got the same food as everyone else, a bunch of stuff I couldn't even begin to choke down, but I was permitted to ask the doctors to help me out. They would pick up a few packaged foods in the little hospital shop for me. Every day, my nurse would boil up some things for me to eat, and I always tried to get her to have some too, but she never accepted except when the doctors said, Eat. She won't eat until you do. Someone else told me, She killed her father-in-law, so none of her family has ever come to see her, and they won't pay her hospital bills either. So aside from working as an aide, she also has to put on a pair of galoshes and work in the dining hall. It seemed to me that she enjoyed working. She looked happy as she went about her labors. Another patient snickered, Working is the only way she can get enough money to meet her expenses; she can't even afford soap or toilet paper. She always takes a square of paper to the toilet with her, but the second she squats down, she hides the paper in her pocket.

I saw a patient standing with her face to the wall, and I realized that it was the virgin patient. I went and stood beside her. She was looking at her feet, and she didn't turn to look at me. Someone said, She's being punished again because she's crazy and because she keeps saying the chief of staff is her husband.

One of the women was called into the office, and I heard the supervisor questioning her: You stole something from one of the rehab patients. What was it? After a while I heard her start to repeat, over and over, Pickles, apples, bananas, bananas, apples, pickles.

My release date finally arrived, and after I had thanked everyone, I had my father give the doctors a hundred *yuan*. I said, Use this money to buy my nurse's aide the things she needs, to thank her for helping me.

The second time my father brought me to the clinic, I was bald, one of my eyes was messed up, and I was so thin it was disgusting. I barely recognized myself. So who would have thought that when I approached the big locked door to the ward, one of the women would shout my name and cry out, She's back! She's back! And this time she's lost all of her hair.

And once again my father told the doctors, My daughter really is a good girl; it's just that she's too willful. But we're to blame for that, and we're willing to pay the price. The doctor told me, We were all moved by what your father said. I want you to ponder what he said. Later I was sent for HIV and syphilis testing. Then the doctors gave me some medicine, and this time they didn't use the same drugs they had the first time. They were going to try a different course of treatment. They said, This time we're going to have to let you suffer a little; otherwise you're not going to change.

Every day I took a bunch of little yellow, pink, or white pills. These drugs kept me from sleeping, and they made me feel hot all over, and I paced back and forth in my room, sometimes talking to myself nonstop, heavy-headed, dizzy, and staggering. One night, another patient slipped into my room. She said, If you want to get out sooner, don't take any more of those yellow pills. By the time I'd raised my head, she was gone, but she'd given me a scare. After a good cry, I decided to stop taking those yellow pills. I said to the doctor, I don't want to take the yellow ones.

After asthma, nightmares, and excreting every kind of fluid, I began gradually to improve once again. This time I went to work with the others, and one of the patients taught me how to play cards. I started to miss my mother. I missed her cooking, missed everything about her. Every day, I sang the songs on the black-board with all of the other patients. Except that I still couldn't stand the food. Oil-free and boiled to a pulp, it reminded me of the food I'd been given in that prison in the Northwest when I was younger.

Once a month we got to have cooked red meat, an event that was a high point for all of the patients. But I couldn't eat it. Someone asked me, How come you don't eat meat? How come? and my doctor overheard. My doctor was a Shanghainese woman, very beautiful, a fashionably dressed intellectual. She said, Why aren't you eating this meat? I said, I feel sick to my stomach, nauseous. Really. She said, Who do you think you are? Today I want you to eat it. I said, Honestly, I don't think I can force it down. She said, Do you want to get out early or not? I said, I do. Then eat it, she said. You're no different from any of the other patients here, and don't you forget it. I said, I'm not eating it. She said, Fine, I'll have your father come down. We'll see if you'll eat it then. She watched me eat a piece of meat and then looked on as I began to throw up, a bit at a time, vomiting and crying. She said, You're no different from anyone else, and don't let me catch you wasting food again. Remember the money you gave your nurse's aide the last time you were here? It was confiscated. You're no better than anyone else, and what you did actually hurt her because now she can't be a nurse's aide anymore. We can't be certain that she didn't do something for you that she shouldn't have. Be mindful of this.

One of the patients got a skin infection and couldn't work with us anymore. She sat alone on a stool, watching us work. When I walked by her, she asked me, Where did you work when you were outside? I said, What? What do you mean, where did I work? And I asked her, Where did you work? She answered, I worked at a disco, called JJ. Then she looked at me. I couldn't tell by looking that she was sick, but she had that habit of rocking back and forth and constantly shuffling her feet.

A contingent of drug addicts was brought to the clinic in a police van, and things got a bit livelier. They'd all been forcibly committed. One of them remarked to me once, You have such good veins. I bet you don't have any trouble at all. Just stick the needle in, and it's instant bliss. Two new girls moved into my room, Shanghai girls just back from Japan. They were always singing Japanese songs in my room. It was getting close to New Year's, and one day a tour bus came to pick us all up and take us to Pudong. After we got back, one of the others said to me, You know what? Life outside looks pretty good!

On Christmas we had a party, and someone ate some of my chocolate and started singing for everyone. She was the only patient who wore glasses. She was singing the kinds of Christmas carols that choirs sing. She had a beautiful soprano voice, and her real and falsetto voices blended naturally. When she was finished, I asked her, Where did you learn all these songs? She said, I'm a teacher. So how did you end up in here? I asked. I killed my husband, she said. I asked her why, and she answered, My old man was so tiny — just one squeeze and he was dead. After relating all of this to me, her expression remained perfectly calm.

I began hating myself. I swore I would never again ask another patient why she was in this clinic.

The song we sang in chorus that day was a little love song, and there were several dozen old women belting out,

Let me think of you, think of you, think of you,
Think of you one last time.
Tomorrow I'll be another man's bride.
I'm thinking of you deep inside.

They sang with great care and very little feeling, but it was genuinely moving. It had struck a nerve. I had not been touched like that in a long time, and I found my heart again.

Afterward I chanced to hear this popular song many times, and I found out that it was called "Words of the Heart." Every time I heard it, I would be overcome, and I would stop whatever I was doing and listen to the song until it was over. This song reminded me of where I'd been.

The morning after Christmas, I woke up early. My nurse's aide came into the room to take away my dishes, and she said to me, These dumplings are so good. Why don't you eat them? Every day she asked me the same kind of question, and every day I gave her the same answer: I'm not going to eat them, so why don't you? On this day she responded by picking up the dishes and carrying them out. Soon she returned with a mop and was about to start mopping when she abruptly leaned against the wall and blew a spit bubble. Afraid to call out, I kept one eye on her, and one eye on the space heater, worried that she might pick it up and hit me with it. Just then, one of the registered nurses passed by in the hall. I lowered my voice and said, Hey! What's wrong with her? The registered nurse came in, took the mop and placed it in the aide's hands, and had her grasp it tight. To me she said, She'll be fine in a moment. Don't worry. And a few minutes later, the aide straightened up and went back to mopping the floor, her face pale, her hair like wires. I wanted to get up and mop the floor myself, but I was afraid to move. After a little while, the registered nurse came in and said to me, She had that episode just now because she ate your dumplings. She eats your dumplings every day, but today a bunch of the other patients ganged up on her, so she got sick. In the future, if you're not going to eat your food, please make sure you give it to someone different each time.

It was almost New Year's, and everybody dressed up in clean clothes for visiting hours. One patient ate cake with her son. Another was talking with her husband. Another sat with her mother, who was probably in her eighties. Another patient was waiting around. All of the patients were shuffling back and forth. I sat by my bed, my hands jammed up my sleeves, my two feet rocking back and forth, left to right, right to left, and I looked at the chocolate my mother had brought for me. My mother had spent only ten minutes in my room. She said, The guard at the gate was very nasty to me. He said there was nothing anybody could do to help drug addicts like you. My mother said that now she felt like a criminal, and that she was going to have to leave soon. She didn't want to be subjected to another lecture.

My release date was getting closer, and I was moved to the large dormitory with all of the other patients. Every night, people talked in their sleep, and I couldn't sleep. I was always hungry, and I would get up at midnight and have some cookies while another patient watched me from under her blanket and laughed, saying, Why on earth did they move you into this room?

I went home. I said, I want to take a bath. There was nowhere to take a bath in there, and it's been way too long since I last had a bath. Then I said, The bathroom in our house is too cold. I don't like being cold, so I'd like to go to the public bathhouse. My mother gave me one *yuan*, which I told her was enough. I figured that she was afraid to give me more money than that, afraid that I would use it to buy drugs.

I was back in my old neighborhood, and now I was going back to the bathhouse where I'd often gone as a child. Wearing the wig my father had bought for me, I went into the baths. I was so weak, wheezing and gasping as I bathed, and my wig fell off. A middle-aged woman, stark naked herself, glanced first at the wig, and then at the fuzz on my scalp, before finally letting her gaze come to rest on my body.

After my bath, I left the bathhouse and spent two *mao* on a deep-fried Shanghai-style fritter, and the sugar-coated fritter stuck to my teeth, and I thought that it was incredibly good, and so cheap too. I was ecstatic at the thought that I wouldn't have to eat Master Kang's instant noodles or Danone Tuc crackers from the clinic store ever again. I didn't want to touch either of those things for the rest of my life. It seemed possible to me that I might be able to start my life over, beginning with this moment. I thought of my home, thought about how I wouldn't have to feel cold anymore, thought about the clinic I'd just left, and reflected that I was the only patient who had got out in time for New Year's this year. And then I told myself: Honestly, heroin is nothing but glorified shit.

H

I.

Roses have thorns, just like love. When the petals of a rose fall, they scatter one by one, like the tears of a young widow. This mournful rainy weather is sensitive, but there's something inauthentic about it too; I've always felt a particular connection with it. The sound of rain is heartless, it forms a barrier between me and this world, and the sound of my lover's singing drifts in the air. I can no longer kiss him, I can no longer plead with him, I can no longer thank him. I see my face buried under a big stone, and I want so badly to push that stone away.

The rain had stretched out my old leather shoes by a whole size, and my feet flopped around inside them. I kicked my CD player around with my ruined shoes. The man inside the player was too bourgeois. My CD player was skipping, and my shoes were wheezing in fits and starts.

Today, someone came from the South, someone who wanted me to pick out one of Saining's songs for inclusion on a CD. He said, We want to do a tribute to him, and we'd like it if you could do the vocals.

The word *tribute* made me want to laugh. I said, Saining was a broken poem. I didn't understand him. I can't possibly imitate the face he showed to the world, or pretend to bear the scars that filled his dreams.

I didn't tell him that I hadn't been able to sing for a long time. After I was released from rehab, I discovered Kurt Cobain. He was already gone, and I felt a sense of sadness and loss, but that didn't mean I understood him. Sanmao was drinking heavily, still making a living singing in nightclubs, singing pop songs from Hong Kong and Taiwan, giving his wife nothing but abuse. His wife was beautiful, and she worshiped him. She was as loyal and fragile as my little dog, Dangdang. More and more bands and stages were going over to punk, and there were more and more punk concerts all the time. The world was changing, and I felt as though I no longer had any heroes. I'd already had my Cui Jian. I was the girl who had run away while listening to the sound of Cui Jian's voice, and even today I still felt lucky in that. I'd long ago stopped wondering about the difference between blue skies and suffering.

The streets were filled with strange faces, all saying that the man I loved had disappeared. Fire and ash can never meet, just like yesterday and today.

It had been three years since Saining left me. He was the tears I couldn't cry, the words I couldn't speak; he was the terror I felt at the demon face in my mirror; he was the beauty of my death, the love I'd once had and would never have again.

His disappearance had distorted everything I was and knew, and sometimes I felt as if I'd been buried alive. But I recognized that this was how my life was. I didn't know how to talk about any kind of control (such as choosing suicide and actually going through with it), and I couldn't turn back my spreading misfortune. I certainly lacked determination. In this meaningless youth of mine, I was the victim and the assassin; I felt ashamed and unworthy, which was why I couldn't just end this weird trip I was on right then and there. In the end, maybe I forced myself to go on living, but it wasn't the fear of death that saved me; it was my own self-loathing.

It seems to me that love was invented by men. I used to think of myself as a woman who wouldn't have been ashamed to die for a man, and I saw it as a sign of my own courage and greatness. Inhabiting that man's world turned me into a weak woman for a long time. I was so weak, so desperate for love, and, deeply aware of my own pathos, I developed a knack for displaying my self-absorption and self-pity. That was my closed, intense inner world, and I thought that it was beautiful.

Now I had come to view myself as a completely unlovable girl; but I was also convinced that the weak woman I'd been had been destroyed.

Someone came from the South, and I have to admit that it felt like an intrusion, just like hearing all of the songs from the old days, songs that stirred up my feelings and reminded me that my love had gone far away. Even the stupidest songs could break my heart.

Saining and I were like a pair of curious cats, but curiosity can kill a cat. Sometimes, in his embrace, I would joke around and pretend to be the kind of girl who would marry him on the spot. Or I might pretend that I was the kind of girl who might run off with someone else at the drop of a hat. We liked words like *elope,* which to us suggested the road to freedom. But bombs fall on the most beautiful places, and happiness will steal away.

Losing control is like a series of conflagrations, and a huge blaze had taken away my love. He was gone, my love, carried away by a series of fires. Even before our five senses and our breasts had opened to the world, it was already too late for us.

A young woman's hands are stroking the guitar, but no matter how hard I strive for that impossible release, the scent between Saining's fingers will always be unmistakable, a darkness I will never be able to re-create. No matter how far away I travel, he will always call to me in my ashen hours, in my moments of flashing brilliance. Turn on the light, and he'll come to call, and he'll tell me my raison d'être. He dogs my heels, telling me over and over, You shouldn't be here. You belong with me because you have absolutely nothing else.

2.

It's time for me to disappear.

With these words I put my face in the shadows, although I knew that the expression on my face was not at all convincing.

Many years ago, I was a child like a blank sheet of paper, and I was exceedingly good at dispelling my anxieties by losing myself in reverie. My life had been changed by one terrible event, which had hastened my slide into the muck of being a "problem child." My sense of my own weakness and powerlessness was absolute. After I grew up, I became a singer, although fame and fortune eluded me. My voice, with its intimations of weariness, brought lonely people together amid all the confusion, like long-lost friends. And it made weak children who were having fits of temper go and comfort each other. The woman with the sandpaper voice, that's what my boyfriend called me. This bemused man, gentle as water, had once brought into my life the warmth I'd always yearned for, and he shrouded my sense of security in shadows. I was his smiling girl, his dazzling peach blossom.

The man I love has disappeared! I had never tired of crying out.

He was destructive and irresponsible; he'd hurt me, there was no question.

My face was ice. It was unreal and about to collapse. My prized miniskirts were threadbare, as worn out as my skin. I was a Playboy Bunny in a Santa Claus hat; I was a bucket the bloody color of raw meat. I was here, I was the shadow on the wall, and the shadow on the wall was mine. I couldn't erase my shadow. I'm a complicated girl, but my tears were simple and straightforward. My gaze is immaculate, but I've never experienced a sense of my own purity.

Loneliness, apathy, misery, helplessness, depression, and self-loathing — all together they combined to form my shame, my shame, my shame. I constantly felt ashamed.

In the winter of my twenty-fifth year, a naked purity I hadn't been looking for came to me in a flash. There was nothing for me to do anymore but leave a pretty corpse. My dead body, I despised the thought of my own dead body. I felt it was my responsibility to deal with my own corpse.

Monday morning, my bronchial tubes went into violent spasms.

The sun has risen,
Leaving the darkness behind.

The sun was so warm, and life was so beautiful; "My lover's scent is in the air."

One Monday morning, my elaborate plans for a "natural gas incident" were foiled by my father's unexpected return. He knocked down the door, and the next thing I saw was a pool of my father's blood.

Once again there was an ambulance in front of our building. A medic ordered my father to hold up the oxygen bag with one hand while helping to support the stretcher with the other. The sound of the medics' voices as they criticized my father for moving too slowly stabbed at my ears, and the sight of my father's old and haggard face sent me into unconsciousness.

|

I picked up the phone. It was Saining. Saining on the phone, saying, It's me, Saining.

Not long after that, I was in the coffee shop at the Capital Airport, looking at my famous Saining. He still looked the same, with the same long hair, fawn's eyes, and full lips. His hair was a mess, and although it was very cold outside, all he was wearing was a black sweater.

He had seen me first and called out to me. Then he'd walked over. I couldn't believe it was true. We stood there like a couple of oafs who didn't know what a hug was.

I thought it through, and I decided I should get in touch with you.

Why?

It was time, that's all.

But why did you leave in the first place?

I just wanted to go away, and I thought it would be good for you to do the same. That's how it seemed to me at the time, anyway.

Who are you living with now?

I have only one girlfriend. You.

Well, I slept with lots of other men. But that's all it was, just going through the motions. And I used heroin too — it was just something I did. But it made trouble for a lot of other people, and it didn't do that much for me, not really. I always thought there should be something special between me and heroin, but there was nothing, and I didn't have you either.

Maybe we were just meant to be a couple of good friends who got together to do drugs.

Is that what you think? You think everything would have been different that way? Have you ever wanted to do drugs with one of your relatives? Say, with your aunt? After you got off, you'd just sit around bullshitting together? Now, that would be scary!

It just doesn't interest me anymore. I'm sick and tired of heroin, sick and tired of that pointless crap.

I've been traveling around. I went to a few countries, did some odd jobs, and took all kinds of drugs. But I quit heroin. There are some drugs that can change your entire life, and there were times I didn't have any idea where my life was going. Those were the moments when I felt your presence. You came to me like an angel, and said to me, You fucked up. You have to stop doing heroin.

When you left me, Saining, you had the option of going just about anywhere in the world, but me, I couldn't go anywhere. There was nowhere I could go, nothing I could do. My voice was ruined. I'll never be able to sing again. Do you realize what that means? Who ever said we had to stay together? We split up. We split up, and my vocal cords are shot, and there's no fixing them.

There wasn't much to our conversation. Anyone looking at us would have thought that things were pretty good between us, as if we were completely removed from our shared history. The winter sunlight of Beijing, with its quality so unique to this place, poured over our bodies, and when I looked around this city, a city we'd once yearned for more than anything in the world, I saw that particular sunlight illuminating our personal disaster.

Who could ever have imagined that Saining would reappear like this, out of the blue? Once again, it was fate. My perverse destiny! I couldn't take my eyes off him, kept staring at his dewy eyelashes. Abruptly he lifted his head and looked at me, and his eyes had not changed at all except for the fresh dark circles beneath them. We drank the nearly undrinkable coffee and watched the crowds milling around us, and it seemed that all of these people led lives that were more substantial than ours.

Let's go home and talk some more, OK? Saining said.

Go home? The instant I discovered you were gone, it was like the sky came crashing down on my head. I don't know how you can ever right a wrong like that. Even yesterday, I was still in so much pain that I didn't want to go on living.

Saining, you can't know what true misery is until you've seen every tenderness turn to hatred.

Saining, I asked heaven and earth for an answer, hoping they would tell me what words I had to say to bring you back to me. And here you are at last. Now what?

I kept wanting to call you, and Sanmao too. But I just kept putting it off. I was afraid.

Am I that frightening, Saining? I thought that no couple was closer than we were.

Two hours later, I had Saining buy me a return ticket.

In the waiting area, Saining stood behind me, his arms around me.

I'm sorry, he said.

I felt his body, his breath, the warmth of his blood, but I didn't know if this was really my Saining or not.

I said, It would have been a lot better if you'd actually died, Saining. I'm missing those days when I stood at the window, crying over the news of your death.

*   *   *

After this, Saining called me every day, but our conversations were always rather awkward.

Once, I said, Don't call me anymore, but please let me know if you move. That way I can call you.

Sanmao and I spoke on the phone several times, and we both talked about how awful Saining was.

Once again I was convinced that, at least currently, I was a woman who had nothing to be happy for. I was looking forward to my thirtieth birthday because maybe after that some savor would return to my life.

I wrote a song about my trip to Beijing. I played the guitar Saining had left behind and sang into Saining's four-track tape recorder fourteen and a half times. It was a simple song, with a sweetly sentimental melody, but the lyrics were nothing but a bunch of profanity. I used the English that Saining had taught me, used the language of the bourgeoisie to curse the bourgeoisie, and while maybe there was one line that could have passed for cultured, the line that kept recurring went, "That's just the kind of bastard he is!"

I wrote down parts of Saining's and my story because I felt I had to. Writing had come into my life; it was the doctor's orders. And as I wrote, I kept hearing the words "That's just the kind of bastard he is, yeah, that's just the kind of bastard he is!" going through my head nonstop. I put together a bunch of literary techniques, like flashbacks, and I mixed them up with that song, and it all came out like something that might pass for pretty. My dad said, You must work hard. The effort will make you stronger. What I really wanted to get out of writing was to arrive at some deeper understanding of things; but the only thing I knew for sure was that writing had, at least for the time being, made me into a hard-working woman.

In the end, do we lose control in order to gain our freedom, or is freedom just one way of being out of control?

Marx really was a genius. He said that true freedom is grounded in the knowledge of the intrinsic nature of the world.

I knew that there was a state I would never be able to attain. What is Truth? Truth is like air; I sense its approach and its presence. I can smell its breath, but when I reach out, I can't catch hold of it. Over the years, I've been caught up in worldly things. How many times must I have brushed shoulders with Truth!

I'm sensitive by nature, but I have no wisdom. I'm naturally rebellious, but I can't stand firm. I think that's what my problem is. I watch myself with my body, I think with my skin, I believe in the absoluteness of physical sensations. I've asked myself, What is it to be high? I flew as high as I could fly, and then went higher still. But having tried it, I realized that none of it could liberate me.

And liberation and faith are alike in this respect — neither of these is a word you should use lightly.

Fate put a pen in my hand, and my dad said, If you want to write, you don't have to get a job.

The sky is all lit up, and that bright sky illuminates my devastation, illuminates my prayers, and I tell myself: You can be a naked writer.

J

I.

One night, Saining and I watched *Leaving Las Vegas,* and when it was over, we made love. He cried out as he entered my body. He said, You haven't slept with anyone in a long time! These words cut me. We became sadder and sadder as we made love, and each of us was wrapped up in our own thoughts.

That night I asked myself, Out of all the times I've made love in the past, which one was the best? It had been a few years earlier. I asked Saining when the best time had been for him, but he didn't answer.

Saining often came to Shanghai to see me, and we usually got together with Bug. He joined us as we sought out the new life of Shanghai, and all of this helped me feel a bit better. Lots of video rental stands had sprung up in Shanghai; they rented Hollywood movies and movies from Europe too. I saw some good movies and some terrible movies. I filled the evening hours of my drug-free life with movies from the West.

Bug took us to a little shop in Five Corners, out by the universities, to buy records, and we saw disks that had had notches cut into them with electric saws. Usually it was the last song that had been ruined, but the rest of the songs were still playable. There were other disks with a hole drilled in the middle, and those were completely playable, no problem. There were also tapes that had been cut, and all you had to do was buy them and take them home and stick them back together and they were fine. All of these Western recordings were incredibly inexpensive once they'd had holes punched in them. You could find any kind of good music you wanted, from the 1960s to the 1990s. Word was that these were surplus products sent by Western record companies as gifts to the children of our socialist country, but that customs had cut them, and then they'd been smuggled in. These notched and holey recordings were like a miracle, and nobody was really sure what the story behind them was. They were like a huge gift from heaven, and the whole thing was a deep mystery. At first we thought we were the only ones who knew about this wonderful stuff, but we soon learned that the same thing was going on in lots of other cities as well.

Sick and tired of waiting, we were finally entering a new world. We were hearing music that had never been available to us before.

Underground rock groups were proliferating in Shanghai, and some of the people that sold defaced disks got together and organized bands. Sometimes Bug and I would try to put together the money for a gig of our own. Over time, those of us who listened to hole-punched records came to be known as the Hole-Punch Generation.

Saining and I could still listen to music, watch movies, and smoke marijuana together. For some reason, the more I smoked, the more anxious I felt. Saining said that this was just a stage I needed to get through, and then everything would be OK again.

We did lots of things together, but we still didn't know how to become real lovers again. We just went through the motions. His hands were always cold, and his body had lost its heat, which made me ashamed, and my sense of shame seemed to spread to him. He'd changed; he'd become ashamed. When we made love, even the air was ashamed. And the moment his lips touched me, I felt a deep sadness, a bottomless sadness. We both felt depressed. It was a sickening cycle, of sadness giving way to boredom and circling back again, until in the end we were afraid even to try making love.

It was as though someone had filled our bodies with lead, as though we still felt and thought like addicts in withdrawal. But I assured myself that this was just part of the process.

One day, Kiwi turned up. He was an old classmate from middle school.

Bug tended bar at a club, and Kiwi had overheard him talking about me, so one night, Kiwi went to that club and waited for me.

There are some people whose feelings for each other are a mixture of yearning and fear. You can easily pick them out of a crowd. Kiwi and I were like this.

Kiwi had become an amazingly good sculptor when being a sculptor was still a brand-new profession in Shanghai.

I noticed that he had full lips, just like Saining, and I had a moment of clarity.

We came to his house, an old building on Maoming Road. In his bathroom I touched his lips and said, I've been longing for lips like these for a very long time.

I kissed him, caressed him. His skin glistened, and it was enough for me just to feel that smoothness. He took his time in peeling away my clothing, and my frail body gradually lost its strangeness.

His pale fingers, the waves in his eyes, his trembling lashes. His hair brushed my thighs, his lips calmed my body, and he brought me the warmth I had craved, lulled me as he moved in the space between my thighs. All of the good times I'd had many years before came back to me, and I said to myself, This is what I've been waiting for.

Slowly my skin grew translucent, my entire body became translucent, and I began masturbating at night even though it confused me and sometimes even left me feeling deeply depressed.

We always made love the same way. His used his mouth to give me pleasure, and I had to kneel beside him, my back to the mirror, thighs straight, twisting at the waist, with my arms hanging loosely at my sides. And he looked at the reflection of my back in the mirror and masturbated. I admired the way he masturbated; I thought that here was a man who really enjoyed playing with himself, and I watched him watching me in the mirror, with his left hand circling up, and his penis like the slash of the moon, because he needed to have me watching him in order for him to come. Watching him ejaculate sometimes made me tremble. But for the sake of his pleasure, I had to remain perfectly still until his cries of joy had completely subsided.

The sound of his voice when he came seemed to come not from his body but from the world of his dreams. The colors of the night made my breathing ragged, and we kissed, our bodies pressed close.

One night, after we'd made love, he blurted out, Did you know I was the boy who gave that girl those flowers?

He had his back to me, and I couldn't tell whether he wanted to talk about it some more or just wanted to say that much, but I was upset.

I said, Really?! Did it make any kind of impression on you?

He was silent.

Afterward each of us lit ourselves a cigarette. A while later, the telephone rang. As I looked out the window at Shanghai at night, I took in this news about Lingzi.

When Kiwi got off the phone, I said, Do you remember how I used to sit in the classroom, trying to figure out which boy had given Lingzi the flowers? I used to wonder, What is he thinking right now? I suspected each and every one of you boys in turn. And then I was struck by the sense that I could be sure of nothing in the world except for the food in my mouth. For a long time I wore that red waterproof sweat suit, with the two white stripes on the sleeves. It's still hanging in my bedroom closet. I love that outfit, no matter how silly it might seem. I love it because it's the symbol of my freedom, of my self-determination.

Kiwi said, I didn't think much about it at the time. Suddenly I'd learned that she was mentally ill. She was sick, but her illness had nothing to do with me.

Then he changed the subject. He seemed very cruel to me. All these years it had never occurred to me that it could be that way, and hearing him talk like this left me feeling unsettled.

2.

Kiwi and I often wandered around the city, sometimes stopping off at one of the restaurants that had been opened by Westerners.

Sometimes we stayed at home, drinking, listening to music, or watching TV. Sometimes we made love in front of the mirror, and it gave us a nice feeling. Actually, I thought up some other ways for us to make love, but Kiwi said he liked making love to me this way because I myself had said that I'd been missing lips like his for such a long time. He said that those words were what had attracted him to me.

Our attraction was mutual, and it was mysterious. I told myself that there were some things I didn't have to try to make sense of, especially because I was usually wrong. He and I couldn't even exchange ordinary pleasantries without feeling depressed, so we never talked about our pasts. He didn't know anything about my past, and he never asked.

One day I was feeling unsettled, and I shouted out right in the street, Love me! You'll never find another lover as good as me.

Alcohol was all around me, drugs were all around me, music was all around me, and men were everywhere. I was losing my bearings.

My mood was like my lover's hair. Love, for me, was partly a mood, just like that ultradopey bullshit music that I sometimes liked to listen to. That kind of music made me jumpy, but when I felt tense, I felt happy. When I felt tense, I also had to have chocolate. My youth wasn't over yet; fate wasn't going to abandon me. My youth and my nerves were as intimate as each other's shadows. And my lover's hair and I were also as intimate as each other's shadows. I was destined to eat chocolate forever, and every piece of chocolate I had ever eaten would live forever in hallowed memory!

Kiwi came up with a weird idea. He wanted to find a professional cameraman to videotape us making love. He said he wanted the video to be an investigation of the zeitgeist, presented in a form that would genuinely move people, a piece that incorporated faces and limbs. I thought his reasoning seemed a little dubious, and I figured he was looking for titillation, and you could film something private like this on your own. But Kiwi stubbornly insisted that he wanted a professional videographer. He said that he had been studying color and the subtle relationship between color and light. I thought he was too pretentious for words.

It seemed to me that he was trying to create something out of nothing, and that he was being a little selfish besides. But no matter how hard I tried to think of a way out, I couldn't find an excuse to refuse him. It occurred to me that maybe I'd been waiting to fall in love with him, and that this might have been the reason I was humoring him. These thoughts brought on an upwelling of the sweetest mood. My frail spirit shook, and my heart was no longer such a desolate place.

My one condition was that I would choose the cameraman. I looked up Apple.

Apple was an old classmate of ours. I told him that Kiwi had returned from abroad, and I told him what Kiwi had been up to lately and about Kiwi's and my relationship. I gave him lots of details, and Apple was intrigued. When I was seventeen I'd had a crush on Apple, and later on I'd found out he was gay. We'd always kept in touch, and he was the first person I'd looked up after coming out of rehab. He'd taken me to Huaihai Road, where we wandered through the new department stores, and he'd told me about all the latest trends. He might finger a piece of clothing and tell me something like, This is plastic. It's from England — plastic-coated fabrics are in right now. He took me to clubs, took me to the clubs with live bands. That little town in the South really didn't have much in the way of clubs with live music. Whenever there was something fun going on, Apple took me there. He gave me new clothes. And we spent a lot of time in his beautiful kitchen, investigating new recipes.

Shanghai had been completely transformed. It was no longer anything like the old Shanghai. It was becoming more beautiful and more hollow all the time. Fortunately I had Apple and Bug; otherwise I wouldn't have been able to form a relationship with this new city.

I started to like Shanghai, to like all those new names with foreign words mixed in. Some of the foreigners hosted lots of parties, but the air at those parties was both sweet and false, as if everyone had become white-collar workers overnight, and there were models, singers, and local artists, the genuine and the fake, and I didn't really know what I was doing there, in the midst of all of that. Everyone was speaking Mandarin or English; nobody spoke much Shanghainese.

So Saining was like a friend from another world entirely. I didn't want him spending a lot of time in Shanghai, nor did I try to conceal my relationship with Kiwi from him.

Saining said, I love you, and that's never going to change.

The problem is that I don't feel any desire for you anymore. Without desire, how can I feel sexy? Plus you've never once said I was pretty. You don't really feel any desire for me either.

Don't be silly. I still want to sing for you. How could I not desire you?

Heroin, stupid, shitty heroin. If you took all the heroin I'd sucked up and lined it all up, it would be as long as the Great Wall of China. Asthma attacks, hiding out in garbage heaps with rats scuttling about and waiting for drugs, getting mixed up with all kinds of people and all kinds of narcotics, having my hair shaved off, and once, while I was trying to get away from the police, I stuffed those drugs up my crack — I was so scared, so fucked up, I even stuck the little knife I used to cut up the powder into my crack as well. I'm saying all this just to scare you. I want you to be scared. What I mean is, the thing that you don't seem to understand at all is that stuff like this has completely wiped out any desire I ever felt for you, or what you represent. I need an entirely new life.

Apple agreed to videotape Kiwi and me. Apple had become a conceptual artist, one who made all kinds of video projects.

I felt that Apple was the best choice of a videographer. He was a professional, as Kiwi had wanted. Because he was gay, I wouldn't feel too inhibited in front of him; and because he and I went back more than a decade and truly cared about each other, I believed he would be discreet and keep our secret. He was also a little bit eccentric and a little bit crazy, and I was curious to see what kind of vision he would come up with.

We needed to schedule the taping soon, and Kiwi was constantly pressing me to commit to a date. It used to be that whenever we saw each other, we never had time to say everything we had to say to each other. Making love was only one part of our relationship. But now we spoke much less. And sometimes he had a look on his face that suggested he was losing control. Once, while he was watching me in the mirror, he started to cry, and on another occasion he buried his head in my chest and said, I love you; don't leave me. I became aware of a combined sense of happiness and unease that is difficult to describe, and I began to feel lost.

3.

We had our first meeting about the taping at Café Moti on Ruijin Road. Written by the door to the stairway were the words "If I'm not at home, I'm either at a café or on my way to a café."

The three of us never spoke Shanghainese when we got together, and when I was alone with Kiwi, or just with Apple, we didn't speak Shanghainese either. Right now, we three were sitting together and talking about our work.

I said, I want to find a way of writing that's as close to the body as possible.

But as soon as the words were out of my mouth, I was struck by the absurdity of what we were doing.

I suggested that we leave. We went out for Hunanese food, and we started telling racy jokes, and after we'd laughed long and hard, Apple told me, You'll be saved as soon as you start loving Truth more than you love men. These words instantly ruined my mood. I was getting fed up. I said, OK, that's enough for today. When do you want to get together again? But instead Apple suggested that we go to the Cotton Club, where Cocoa was singing 1930s jazz. Each of us ran into people we knew, and before long we'd all had too much to drink.

When it was time to say good night, we rode home in three separate taxis.

Later that night, Kiwi and Apple phoned me at the same time.

4.

I had stood numbly in the dim passageway at school countless times, a bottle of ink in my hand, and countless times I had imagined myself hurling that bottle at someone's head. With thoughts like these going through my head, I looked like a troublemaker. Once, as I was just about to throw the bottle at my beloved teacher, I wet my pants. In those days I often fantasized about being bullied or hurt, imagined that I was being abused by a merciless man, and this fantasy made me feel all warm inside, like some kind of chemical high. I believed that I needed to be protected, and in the haze there was a shadow — it was a man, and he had substance and specificity — and this shadow had come to protect me. I had been violated, and now I had been rescued. I felt wonderful. The death of that young girl set the tone for my entire life. Honestly, I've been terrified ever since; do you understand? The first time I made love, it was with a man. He broke open my body, and afterward I felt truly at peace. Love? I don't know what love is. I only know that I've always been myself; I've always lived for a flicker of recognition, a flash of understanding. Life is a series of beginnings, not a string of conclusions, and that's what makes life so beautiful. But I've never experienced a completely perfect day. Once, I saw that girl, in the space between waking and dreaming, and I felt faint, I couldn't breathe, and I drooled all over myself. There were many colors, many schemes, and I heard the voices of many ghosts, while my ass and my heart were at war with each other. I saw her, really, and she was so beautiful! Lithe and graceful, deathly sad, adrift, oblivious to what lay under the surface, completely unafraid, unblemished, she was the epitome of beauty. I had chewed my fingernails ragged. I didn't know if I was dreaming or if I was bewitched, but altogether I had gnawed away most of my fingernails. Maybe what I was feeling was terror, but I called it love. There was no difference between love and terror, no difference between blood and spit. Afterward I set out on my journey and began to study sculpture. I can capture a woman at the peak of her beauty; I turn women's faces into paintings, and I can control their beauty. I came back to China because I'm sentimental. And how do I feel about you? You're a beautiful woman, here with me, doing beautiful things. You have a stunning power, the power to bring comfort. I think I can say that. That is how I feel about you: this is the destiny you're always talking about.

5.

Today I realized that you're crazy. You want women and men. Do blood and spit mixed together make love? You're crazy, but I love you. Let's make love, for our tenderness and pity. Love is simply the looks, the gestures, the scent that I can't stop myself from sending your way to make you remember me always. But it's a comfort to me as well, something you've given me, and I'm touched by both of you. I believe in my body. More than anything else, I believe in my body, and my body conceals limitless truths. I need to live in my emotions. A pair of eyes is watching some fool or other, and these eyes don't need to be understood at all. What these eyes like best is to run our lives at several speeds. We're the same. And these nightmares, trampled underfoot, have touched off the madness of hallucinations. Our goodness is a goodness of the body, and our speed is the speed of the body. This is destiny.

6.

I will never forget him, not as long as I live. The older students were bullying me, forcing me to give them blow jobs. They used to stand in a line, and it all left a taste in my mouth that will never completely go away. My tears dripped into the toilet, black flowers blossomed, my every breath was filled with terror. The stars made their slow revolutions, and night descended like a sickness. My problems always surfaced at night. You were a day student, so you couldn't have known what went on among the boarders. If I didn't do as I was told, a line of tacks would appear around my bed as I slept, or I would awaken at midnight to find a cigarette burning between my toes. They always cornered me in the bathroom. Maybe that was where I first became excited by men's penises. But that doesn't mean I liked what they did to me. It's important that you understand this. I'd never imagined that life could be so terrifying, one dick after another — it seemed endless. I decided to quit school, and my parents rushed up from the countryside. They had no idea what was going on with me. Why did I want to give up my studies? Such a good school! I couldn't tell them anything; I didn't think it was something you could talk about. That was when I began to see that everyone has secrets. I can tell you these things now because I'm proud of who I am today. These memories can't hurt me anymore. I survived; I had the will and didn't let myself be broken. Eventually my father found me a place to live near the school, but even though I didn't live in the dormitory anymore, they still came over and bothered me. And this is where he finally comes into the story. I didn't hear what he said to them, but I saw the steely look on his face, and they went away. After they'd gone, he said that if they didn't do as he said, he would kill them all, one by one. He said he'd come up with a plan. He'd make all the boys in our class get into fights with him, which would settle this business of mine once and for all, while at the same time putting them in their place. There were always one or two boys in each class whom the others could turn to. He wasn't one of these class leaders; he was just fearless. I took his coming to help me as a sign that God had taken pity on me. Really, for all these years I've never stopped believing that he was a gift from God, a sign of God's love. Later on, his mother would curse me, and curse him for being with me and neglecting his studies. Afterward, that evening, as dusk was falling, I stood in his doorway for more than an hour because it was the first time I'd ever felt that I was important in any way. I could bring down someone's grades, and I was moved to tears.

7.

Everything is crazy today, and for some unknown reason, everyone is talking about the past. Talking about the past turns everyone into a poet. I could never have imagined this, not even in my dreams, and I'm grateful to you for not telling me about it back then. I couldn't have taken it; I can't even take it now. I wonder why. I used to show up at that run-down house of yours every day because I'd dropped out and didn't want to study anymore. I often came over at night, wearing that waterproof red sweat suit of mine, bringing you a few treats that I'd stolen from home, all packed up in little plastic containers. I liked you. You were pretty, and I've always liked pretty boys, ever since I was a child. You had large hands, and the saddest eyes, and your lips were full and still very red, and your little ass was like an apple. I don't remember what it was that we talked about. I felt incredibly excited every day, and my heart would always pound. My mother thought I had a boyfriend. One day you kissed me, and I went home and told my mother. I said, Mama, I'm not too young. We're just very close, really, and we want to be friends. Mama, is that love? My mother made me go into the bathroom, and she gave me a quick rundown of all kinds of birth control, and later I learned that everything she had told me was the opposite of the truth. My mother and I are equally mixed up. But there was nothing she could do with me then, and she tried her hardest to get me to take what I was doing seriously. Later, you got into college, and I went to see you off in pink plastic sandals, and when the train pulled away, I didn't think that you would ever come back. I sent you lots of telegrams. I liked the speed and simplicity, the plainness, of telegrams. Those were my first writings. The people at the post office all came to know me, and a hundred or more characters cost me something more than a *yuan*. Then you came back, and when you told me that you were definitely gay, I slapped you, and this was when my bad habit of slapping men whenever I have problems with them started. It's a sickness, a wrong I usually commit in a room that is closed up, carpeted, and air-conditioned, and where there's no music. When a man won't get together with me, I do lash out, and even though I've only done it a few times, I've always regretted it, always felt like a failure.

8.

I got mixed up in his problems entirely by chance. The smell of the toilets was a warm, dark smell, a terrifying smell. I was also afraid, since there were potential threats all around us. It was a time for questioning, and we often asked ourselves, Why are things this way? It didn't seem as if anyone was bullying him — at least that's how it looked. It was a mystery to me. When he showered he used the cloth head of a mop to seal the door because he was afraid of being watched, and I couldn't stand it. I felt I had to help him. My soul had already taken flight because of that girl. Aside from me and her, you're the only person who knows what happened, and it's a secret I'll take with me when I die. I forced myself to muster up a sharp and steely spirit; it was an opportunity for me. Yes, he was extremely grateful to me, and he developed courage, consciously holding his head up when he walked down the street, and eventually nobody dared bully him. But the threat never went away completely; it was there when he turned out the lights, that scent was our shared history, and it became our shared secret. This is very painful, but also very compelling. He liked to be with me. He and I often walked together in the winter streets. He said that walking gave him a sense of excitement. I remember that on one of the corners of the street we used to walk down, there was a flower shop, and around dusk they always turned on a little lamp. There was something unearthly about the lamplight, and it flickered with a mysterious warmth. The first year I was in America, I sometimes spent entire days longing for that little street.

9.

We forget most of what's happened to us. So how do you explain tonight? Even the moon is waxing nostalgic. And all the world is a poet. Tomorrow night there's going to be a moon-cake party. It's in an old 1930s house. I really should be at home tonight so that I can try out a few outfits and decide what to wear to this "party." Everyone uses the English word these days. Moon-cake *party*, five-chrysanthemum *party*, golden stem and jade leaf *party*. Shanghai is the mother of all "parties." So many foreign companies have cropped up, it seems as though everyone is living better. I don't know what kind of fun an out-of-work person like me is going to have, though. When I go to parties on the weekend, I often run into the same bunch of people, even though the locations are always different. I always put a lot of care and effort into picking out whatever clothing, jewelry, and makeup colors I am going to wear, and I need to walk around in a cloud of perfume and to have many secrets. I don't know why this is all so necessary for me; I just can't help myself. My old boyfriend never got used to this aspect of my personality. He was always saying, What are you in such a panic about? Stop worrying about other people's being hipper than you. Is being cool really that important? I said, I'm just trying to blend in. I need to. It's my way of falling in love with this city, because the truth of the matter is, I never stop thinking about leaving. I've always felt it wasn't right for me, but where else can I go? So now I'm just asking you, please, try to understand me. I want to go to bed now so I won't have black circles under my eyes when I show up at the party tomorrow night. I need to go get some rest. This doesn't mean that I don't like listening to you talk. You can come by tomorrow and put on my makeup for me and pick out my clothes, because I'm too mixed up today to pick anything out. You guys have got me all worked up.

10.

Every day I think of you, and every day I wonder. Old habits die hard, and so my sweetheart has lost her heart. Why do you hesitate, all alone? I don't suppose you're afraid that the sea will rise up in big, stormy waves. If only flowing water could look back. Please take me away with you. If flowing water could be changed into me, then tears would fall. If I were clear flowing water, I would never look back. Time never stops flowing. It passes by, never to return, and the flowers on the trees burst into bloom, the blossoms so beautiful. Flowers fade and bloom again, but who can understand? I'm a star; you, a cloud. Was our love too shallow, or was it fate that kept us apart? Today you must accept all that lies before you. You love me; I love you. Don't ask where love comes from, where the wind comes from. Love is like a song or a painted scroll. I hope you won't forget me. The wind came to ask me what loneliness is, but I'm too young. What do I know of loneliness? Another cloud drifted over and asked me, Is love a kind of happiness? But until I understand romance, how can I know if it's a kind of joy?

Kiwi had a long-standing habit of writing down a bunch of words before he went to sleep, and it was more or less the same stuff every time, the same snatches of songs by Teresa Teng and others.

Later he would take diet pills, and after swallowing them down, he'd turn out the lights.

The sky broke with a crack, and the shattered pieces of the moon crashed down against the window. Kiwi's eyelashes fluttered. There are some problems that the moonlight won't let you forget. The things he always thought about after the lights went out and he closed his eyes and waited for sleep — those were the things that Kiwi had never in his life been able to unravel. No matter which of them he thought about, he always came to the same conclusion: that they were among life's big, unanswerable questions.

The early-morning sunlight was very sweet, like vanilla ice cream lightly spread across the sky, a gentle light that didn't stab at the eyes, but Apple couldn't see it, because at that moment he was still asleep. He never got out of bed until the afternoon, and then he would imagine the look of the morning's sunlight, which gave him that just-awakened feeling. That began his days.

He always felt at loose ends upon first waking up. He might decide to brush his teeth, or he might decide to smoke a cigarette or listen to some music. He always listened to the same music when he woke up: violin, Paganini. Or he might fiddle with his body for a bit and then call some friend or other so he could hear that person asking him how he was doing.

When this day began, he couldn't see a thing that was in front of him; he needed his contact lenses. He thought that his eyes looked better with gray contact lenses. But he always stood in front of the bathroom mirror without his glasses, often wondering whether the man that other people saw when they looked at him was the same person he saw when he looked at himself. After all, other people's eyes weren't his eyes, and without the aid of a mirror or contacts, he couldn't have seen himself with his own eyes.

He could spend a long, long time in the bathtub. Every day it was the same.

Water was his most trusted mirror, and gazing at the hot water that quietly enrobed him like an invisible sugar coating, he would lie back, counting his toes, often counting eleven or twelve toes floating level with the surface of the bathwater.

That day he counted and counted until he cried. The only place he ever cried was in his own bathtub; it had been this way for many years. The tears he cried in the bath weren't in his tear ducts but in his skin, in every pore of his fingertips, knees, and heels, and between his legs. When he was in the bath, all of his pores opened up, and his tears seeped out. At first he cried out of narcissism or because he felt moved by himself, but later on he might cry for no reason. Sometimes, merely getting into the bathtub would make him start to cry. Occasionally he would turn on the tap, letting the showerhead cry along with him. He wondered, If the shower had eyes, would it be sad? And there were other times when he felt like a tisane of *pangdahai*, slowly swelling in the tub like steeping leaves, and he would stand up, the droplets of water rolling down his skin and dripping into the bath one by one. This made him feel like a towel that was being wrung out.

He felt clean.

Then he might trim his nails, eyebrows, pubic hair, and the hair around his anus.

Finally he put on his contact lenses. He liked the self he saw in the mirror — virtuous, free, clever, sensual, and young.

I used to be a lot of trouble, a serious "problem child." I had problems because I was both ignorant and passionate. I was on fire and I let it show, and during the periods of my worst excesses, I used to say to myself, Take it all the way, take it too far. If you push yourself over the edge, things will turn out right.

I might be doing something like brushing my teeth and suddenly feel as though I just wanted to die right then, and then, as if my life depended on it, I would try to get in touch with all of the friends from my past. I often focused a lot of my energy on planning my death, but I always concluded that the desire to die was just an urge like any other. Like a common cold, it would come and go.

Because what would happen to my parents if I died? Whenever I thought about this, I abandoned my plans. In the past I'd never so much as considered other people's feelings. Love is something that has to be learned.

I am someone who sees herself as a problem. For me, writing is a method of transforming corruption and decay into something wonderful and miraculous. I used to be the sort of person who was always on the lookout for excitement and novelty, but now I've somehow come to sense that if any marvels are going to appear in my life, they will undoubtedly spring from the act of writing. Actually, the prospect of marvels doesn't really excite me anymore. I feel that writing is the only thing that has meaning for me (lately I've been playing that depressing game of "What is the meaning of my life?" yet again).

I'm still spending my parents' money, and I don't know when I'll get a job, but I do know that I am in the midst of a process of getting better and better, and I am gradually recovering my will to live.

II.

This weekend, Kiwi and I went to a moon-cake party, where most of the guests were gay men. It wasn't the Mid-Autumn Festival, but somehow our host had happened on a large supply of moon cakes. Apple didn't want to go; he said that they were certain to show some movie about Old Shanghai, since nowadays everyone wanted to bask in the reflected glory of Old Shanghai, for reasons unfathomable to me.

There were parties every day, but an evening spent in an old house with gardens, where people in black velvet evening gowns danced the tango — that was something different. The living room was filled with every oil painting that our host had ever painted of the lakes and rivers of the lower Yangtze, and they seemed to cover every square inch of wall space like slate-colored bricks. Kiwi and I danced and our feet flew by the slaty walls, and the scratchy and soft language of Old Shanghai was playing on an old vinyl LP, hinting that Old Shanghai, modern and disappointed, was irretrievably lost to the past. With a dignified and graceful bearing, Kiwi held my waist and whirled me around the dance floor, I saw my neck, arched to the limit like a swan's, and when I rolled my eyes, I had the illusion that I looked like a swan spreading her wings and taking flight from the marshes.

We didn't know the first thing about how to dance this dance; we were faking it. I imagined that Kiwi's shoulders and skull were the lights leading me through the darkness, the three lights of Buddhism, and I felt happy. He was always like a breath of fresh air, and that night he kept on telling me how beautiful I was. He said, You can't understand beauty until you've really loved.

We went from the party to DD's. They hadn't been in business for long, and they'd taken their name from a dance hall in Old Shanghai. DD's was on Happiness Road, and it was the first club that played vinyl records and put Shanghai in sync with the international scene and got everybody dancing.

DD's was the sort of place where Western guys could pick up Shanghai girls. These Shanghai girls came to hang out, and they spoke English, most of them with heavy American accents, though some had Italian accents or Australian accents, and a few of them spoke with the accent of Chinese college students. But none of them spoke with an English accent. Of the foreign men in Shanghai who could speak Chinese, most of them talked like Shanghainese girls speaking Mandarin, in a kind of flirtatious baby talk, which sounded stupid and funny at the same time. Most of the foreign men in Shanghai had high salaries and nice apartments. This made them feel very comfortable and content to be here. And most of them, when they weren't busy making money here, were busily fucking Shanghainese girls. Most of these guys wouldn't have admitted that they had Shanghainese girlfriends, and they liked to say things like, Whatever you do, please don't fall in love with me; let's just be friends. What they wanted was that bit of skin, like silky yellow satin, and the helpless-looking face of their China doll.

How can friends sleep together? A lot of Shanghai girls couldn't even grasp this idea, or maybe it was just that they couldn't accept it. Most Shanghai girls liked men they could control; they coveted a man who would fall in love with them, and they used sex as a weapon. To them, Western men were the latest fad, a window that offered a glimpse of a new life.

Some Shanghai girls actually fell in love with foreigners, but these affairs didn't usually end well. They blamed the foreign men for being selfish, and simpleminded to boot. Sometimes, foreign men fell in love with Shanghai girls, and these affairs usually ended badly too, and they said that it was because Shanghai girls never told you how they really felt, and they were domineering besides.

There were also foreign men and Shanghai women who got along smoothly, because foreigners are expert at oral sex, Shanghai women have tiny asses, and so forth.

There were also some who fell in love with each other, but they rarely hung out together in public places.

And then there was that handful of lonely foreign men and lonely Shanghai girls. They didn't love anyone; they just got drunk and went home alone.

Whenever I went to DD's, I always sat in a high spot so I'd have a good view, and I watched the foreign men and the Shanghai girls, and there were also a lot of nice-looking Japanese exchange students. Everyone was pressed together and dancing. People who were tense about their jobs and people who were slackers all came here, and they all had empty, expressionless eyes, but the scent of semen was in the air. I rarely danced, since I had no feel for the music here. I liked underground music better — it could open up my body. The truth is that the Chinese acquire an underground sensibility while they're still in the womb, only nowadays everybody thinks they're white-collar workers.

Everywhere you look you see mirrors and red velvet. That night, Kiwi sat with me the whole time, watching. There were too many people, the air was terrible, and Kiwi kept on fanning me with a fan.

When it was time to go home, Kiwi said, Let's go to your place tonight!

We walked down the street, and Kiwi said, This town is too silly. At any hour of the day you can find all kinds of people in the street just doing their thing. I said, The Bund is nice, but there are so many homeless people hiding out there that it makes me feel funny.

I didn't have the kind of mirror he needed at my apartment, so we didn't make love. We just lay together, arms wrapped around each other, talking.

I said, You know, sweetie, you're like a novel, with all your plot twists, always leading me down some new path.

He said, That makes me feel good.

12.

Kiwi said that under most circumstances, when he's with a man who genuinely likes him, he can't think of anything but holding him in his arms. He said that if he could take Apple in his arms, the moment Apple smiled at him would definitely be the most wonderful moment.

Kiwi wanted something to happen between him and Apple. It even seemed to me that he couldn't let go of any of the old high school friends he was apt to run into. He'd changed.

The second time the three of us met was at my place. I was feeling low that night, and a little jealous, and I brewed pot after pot of coffee, popped batch after batch of popcorn. I couldn't get a word in, the two of them talked nonstop, and every word they said was sexually charged. I wondered what they would talk about if I weren't there. Would they sleep together? Women are soft, and men are hard, and Kiwi said that there was really no contradiction between these two pleasant sensations. When men got it on, it was definitely more like animals wrestling with each other. Men had to have a better idea of what felt good to other men.

I couldn't stop staring at Apple's hands. He was diminutive in every respect, except for his hands, which were rather large, with long, slender, pale fingers. I was entranced by those two massive hands, which had opened up in me a new lyrical world. At one time, all of my fantasies about men had been projected onto those hands. I was so young then. Many years later, Apple said to me, Do you know what makes us so beautiful? The fact that we've both been hurt very deeply, and neither of us trusts men. Both of us love men too much. We drift rootlessly like duckweed. But the most important thing we share in common is that we've both come back to life after being as good as dead. Life has been hard on us.

But now here he was, sitting in front of us and telling us precisely what kind of man he needed. He had to look piratical, with a pipe dangling from his lips, but God forbid Apple should ever smell tobacco on his breath. He should be extremely rational but have a good sense of humor, and he should be an older man, and so on. There was no mistaking the fact that the person Apple was describing had nothing in common with the mushily sentimental Kiwi. Apple explained to us that the kind of romance and madness he related to was bone dry.

Once again, Apple reminded us that we had to consider the legal issues that might affect our video project. He said, What I mean is, this is a problem we ought to be thinking about.

13.

Apple said that they had seen each other between our first and second meetings. They had embraced. Apple had been filled with excited anticipation, but much to his surprise, he'd felt calm the moment he put his arms around Kiwi. Everything suddenly felt very distant. Apple said to me, If I could ever be freed from my burdens, I know I'd finally be at peace!

Apple had definitely had a childish crush on Kiwi. He liked staring at Kiwi's shoulders, and for the longest time he hadn't wanted to get out of the bed where Kiwi was lying, and he'd placed Kiwi's undershorts beside his mouth. He'd felt that the moment Kiwi left him, the dark night would descend on him like a shroud.

They had gone to the Bund together that day, and Apple had brought along a bag full of kumquats, and the seventeen-year-old Kiwi was wearing a pair of coffee-colored shoes. Kiwi had said to him, Friends are one of the most important things in life, and you're one of my four closest friends. These words made Apple very happy.

The afternoon before Kiwi left for America, he casually dropped by to say good-bye to Apple, and for Apple the summer day seemed suddenly dark. As Kiwi descended the stairs, Apple felt an urge to be dramatic, and he stood by the window, watching Kiwi's receding form as if he were in a movie. And he willed a melancholy expression into his eyes, a look that was at once longing, distressed, faintly disappointed, and lost. And as if touched by telepathy, Kiwi did turn and look back at him. This proved to Apple that this was his first love. All of these years, Apple had never stopped thinking about Kiwi.

Kiwi said he didn't remember any of the things that had happened in the past. He only remembered that he and Apple had played a kind of game. He said, I felt as if we were acting like we were in love. He said, It was all a big joke. But now when he saw Apple, he felt excited.

This is basically what the two of them told me on the phone after our second meeting.

After I got off the phone with Kiwi, I went over to his place. In a flash we were caressing each other, but I started to feel bored because there was always something missing from the pleasure I got from sex.

I asked Kiwi, What is a climax?

Kiwi said, A climax is the climax you've never experienced.

14.

After his long separation and final reunion with Apple, Kiwi started calling me every night in the middle of the night and asking me to come over. So every night I found myself traversing those few broad midnight avenues to get to his apartment. I wanted to see how far, and how long, the two of us could walk together.

Kiwi liked to read magazines and drink endless cups of coffee. Every sculpture he made was spontaneous, a moment's inspiration. He didn't care about women's souls. When he made a woman's body, he created a perfect soul and a perfect life. I was mesmerized by the intensely focused expression in his eyes when he worked. He would always wear a little makeup, just to please himself, because although he was satisfied that he was quite handsome, he felt he needed just a few touches of the brush to make himself perfect. He was always making me up in new and different ways too, using every color trick of the makeup artist's trade. He burst into my life and became completely wrapped up in it. I was his Cinderella, and he was my glass slipper.

He seemed to need me more and more. He treated me with tenderness and sensitivity. I loved it, but it also worried me. I was afraid to bring up the subject of Apple, but at the same time I wished I could steal a glimpse of one of their assignations.

Ultimately I learned that Kiwi frequented certain discos and gay bars, although he sometimes went out of town to pick up a pretty boy, whom he would bring back with him. He would either pay the boy up front or else buy him things.

I felt as if I'd plunged into the ocean; I felt in constant danger. I started going to the supermarket to buy scotch, and I knew what I was doing was very risky, but I'd lost the desire to control myself. I spent the hours between midnight and four-thirty in the morning slowly drinking, and I was often touchy. I knew that what I was doing was extremely bad for me, but I had to answer some questions for myself, and this was the only way I could think to do it.

It became increasingly clear to me that Kiwi was much more interested in men than he was in women. There was nothing I could do about it; there was no way I could even begin to compete with those pretty boys with their tight little asses. But I can't describe the gay world with any authority. I said to myself, It's over; you're finished. The problem with you is that you're a woman.

Unlimited quantities of alcohol and chocolate put my blood sugar on a roller coaster, I got infections in my eyes and my tonsils, and my asthma came back to haunt me yet again. That's how things work: if you don't behave, you have to pay the price. I knew that another vicious circle had begun.

The day for the videotaping finally arrived. As Apple had wanted, we rented a hotel room. I felt that each of us knew that the filming could never actually take place, but it was as though we all felt compelled to take things to a certain point in order for it to be over.

I got there first. A little while later, the two of them arrived together.

The three of us sat on the big bed.

Kiwi upbraided me for drinking. He said, I haven't been drinking, and I don't particularly feel like drinking right now. But you had to go and get drunk, and now the two of us aren't on the same wavelength.

I said, I know what you're thinking right now. You're thinking you want this man to see the parts of you that you usually keep the most hidden; but that's not a desire I can satisfy. Do what you want. You're on your own! This video project is cancelled.

Neither of them said anything.

Who's responsible for this unhappy mess? We're all broken. I can't be with you anymore. I love you, Apple, and I used to love you — I know it. And maybe you loved Kiwi once, but he was in love with Lingzi, and maybe Lingzi was in love with Kiwi too, but she died, so who really knows? And what is love, anyway? None of us knows the answer to that question. What kind of passion do you think was in her eyes? Nobody knew but her, and she's dead. So no one will ever know. She wasn't crazy, I'm sure of it. She died of contentment; she felt that she had the power to attract you, that she had proof that you loved her. Her period was late, and she got upset because she was overexcited. Your bouquet of flowers didn't kill her; it was youth that killed her, it was fate that killed her, and no one else will ever be able to describe the happiness that she felt — I'm certain of this. In the end, will you ever be able to forget it, no matter how hard you try? I don't know. She died, and because of that, you'll always love her. You say you love me, but if I hadn't sat beside her in school, would you still love me? Don't answer! I don't want to know. What really happened when you went to see her? Why is it that the reflection of my back moves you so much? I don't know. Maybe you're in love with *him* now, and maybe you don't know. Apple knows, but he says he can't possibly be in love with you now, so who knows? What image is it that you want him to make for you? My back in the mirror, my back! What really happened in that bathroom? I don't know. And I don't want to know. What would have happened if you hadn't come out of the bathroom together? None of us knows. Apple, why did you kiss me back then? You say you don't know? Why can't you answer? I don't know the answer. And Kiwi, why am I always feeling miserable over you? Why don't I refuse you? Why are your tears so attractive to me? Why are you always teasing me and tasting me? If you didn't know how to make love to me so well, would I still be in love with you? You can't answer that. When do the words *I love you* become real? None of us knows.

I said I wanted to give Apple an introduction to female anatomy!

I cried, Men and women go together, like heaven and earth; it's heaven's will. But now I was surrounded by homosexuality, surrounded!

I started to take off my clothes. I said, These are my breasts, this is my vulva, and there are many parts, each with its own function. This is your chance, Apple, I said. So listen carefully to what I'm telling you. The world is like a garden filled with infinite variety, and you need to understand every blade of grass, every tree. I think that, like me, you sometimes make mistakes.

I hadn't planned any of this, but they seemed to have been expecting it. Neither of them appeared to be the least bit upset. Suddenly I felt that there was nothing to argue about. So I took a bath. When I came out of the bathroom, I said to them, We're always complaining about how unhappy our lives are, and now I know why. It's because what we ask of love has become increasingly technical. I've come to the conclusion that love is just a matter of personal preference.

We left the hotel together and went out for Hunanese food, and then we went together to that unbelievably stupid Hard Rock Cafe, where each of us ran into people we knew.

And suddenly I thought of Saining and a nightmare he'd once told me about, where he was on a bus, and everyone on the bus was wearing uniforms from McDonald's, KFC, TGI Friday's, or the Hard Rock Cafe.

That night, nobody got drunk. That night nobody called me. That night I fell quickly to sleep.

We are smoke, and smoke can only dissipate, but it cannot wither.

15.

When I'm feeling low, I almost always go to Tribes, this run-down club that's the only place in Shanghai where underground bands play live.

Today I didn't feel like listening to rock and roll, and today the songs I asked the DJ to play for me were songs like "Flowers for You," "The Street," "Whenever I Walk Past That Café," "Love Me Tender," "Running My Hands through Your Black Hair," "Blue Skies," "Applause," "A Small Town on Deer Harbor," "Winter Rain," "Heart of Glass," "Johnny Come Lately," "Sugar Pie Honeybunch," "A Kind of Moonlight," "Love in the Autumn," "Sergeant Pepper's Lonely Hearts Club Band," "Comrade Lover," "Clouds in My Hometown," and "Stormy Night."

These were the pop songs we'd listened to in the mid-1980s. A lot of them were from Taiwan, or oldies from the West. I would never have thought I'd hear them here in this rock and roll bar.

16.

I finally published my first story, in a literary magazine. I gave my first commission to my parents, and while it didn't even come close to covering the cost of one week's room and board, it made them very happy.

My story had been published, but there was already a pair of black scissors poised in my mind. I used to think that publication was power, you had to publish, you had to publish, and so I cut as I wrote.

As a result, the day my story came out, I was all fucked up because I couldn't get rid of that pair of black scissors.

Writing came to me on the doctor's orders. Really I was writing simply to gain a clearer understanding of myself. I wrote for myself, for my good friends, and sometimes for men with whom I'd once been close. As I wrote, I became more ambitious, and I wanted lots of people to read what I wrote — I wanted the whole world to see what I'd written. After the writing was done, I wanted to become famous, but was there really anything that great about being famous? I'd already imagined what that would be like. I'd set myself on this path, the path of a writer, and only now did I realize that it wasn't necessarily going to bring me peace.

If I died, where would my soul find a home? My soul is certain to remain after I've died, and the soul will follow the spider's web to heaven. But I used to think that writing was a ladder that would take me to heaven.

Lately I've been seized with the feeling that I'm going out of my mind, because I haven't been able to keep bringing the world a kind of heat, and I feel as though the writing I've done until now has already become meaningless. Without the warmth of the sun, how can I write? My phone is ringing, and I don't have the ability to become a professional writer, and I think that this is fate.

17.

Dusk, Kiwi's bedroom. Cold tones, his mirror, an oval on four wheels. We bared our upper bodies, his left hand grasping my shoulder, and we leaned into each other, squarely facing the mirror. The setting sun and the rising moon touched us with gray beams of light as we sat together in front of the mirror, naked from the waist up.

Our heads were the same size, our hair the same medium length, lustrous, perfectly straight, neither too thin nor too full. We had the same long, thin faces. The same large, shining eyes, the same unstable blood sugar, the same ugly nose, the same full lips, dry and curved. The same skin tone, the same height and weight, the same prominent collarbone, the same black hair.

We swayed together in the mirror, straining our necks and staring at our expressions in the mirror, until night fell, until we could no longer discern the expressions in our own eyes when we looked in the mirror.

The year before, red had been my key makeup color, and I blended together all kinds of reds. Red represented to me the confusion of youth; it represented extremity, desire, crazy love, menace, and romance. But what would today's theme be?

Kiwi was about to say good-bye to me. He wanted to go back to America to recharge, he said, and when he came back he'd bring some new work with him.

I said, I like you best when you're naked and wet, but I never want to be with you again. I don't ever want to feel that pressure and uncertainty again. So go. And I hope to God that everything will have changed by the time you get back.

We held each other. From the moment he'd first appeared, and then every time I saw him thereafter, I always had a strong desire to hold him. We often had our arms around each other. The rest of the world seemed to have gone into hiding, every pleasure seemed stale, and the two of us sat in the gloom, not speaking. I had the sense that he could see all of me, and I could see him in his beautiful but fatal flight. And it seemed that if we only held each other close, the rest of the world would be lost to us, but at least we would always have each other.

18.

I called Apple on the telephone. He said that he and Kiwi had gone back and taken a walk on that street. He said that the flower shop was no longer there, but that the little street itself was still there, and that things hadn't changed all that much.

Whenever any of the three of us got together, the conversation always took a beautiful but melancholy turn, as if everyone was a poet. Apple always said that I was beautiful, and having a beautiful man praise me as beautiful invariably gave my spirits a lift. He fed my narcissism, gave me a new persona. It was a wonderful feeling, like being onstage. I thought that the force of this dream could put me on playbills all over Shanghai. I thought that he could transform my life into something new and beautiful. He fixed my awful "heroin complexion," but he couldn't do anything about my mouthful of stained teeth. Saining said that he actually liked my tetracycline teeth because they let him know that I was still me. My new life had lost its freshness, and my body fell into an even worse state than before. My heart was burning hot but it was dark; my love was empty. I turned on all the lights, but I couldn't put the danger far enough away. I also wanted to get out of Shanghai for a while. What could be more wonderful than a change of scene? The day I left, I would try my best to leave my worries behind. Saining was in Japan visiting his mother, and I'd be able to stay at his little place. I wanted to go to Beijing. Shanghai was no fun anymore. Frankly, Shanghai had always been too phony, but Kiwi had a way of making pretentiousness something beautiful. My father agreed to give me money for the trip to Beijing. Maybe I would gain some new insight, and then again maybe every day would be the same. It didn't matter. I was a woman who could never decide what to wear to parties, which sometimes reduced me to hiding behind the door in tears. But I was unafraid.

Apple said, Don't be so depressed. As long as there is chaos, there will always be hope, hope for Truth and Beauty. We haven't reached that state yet, but that's only because our bodies are still here.

I said, I'm not depressed. It's just that there are so many ideas that I'm wrestling with in my mind, and I can't grasp them all at once. It's just a little vacation, but this trip will also be a kind of search.

Apple said, Don't let a man ruin your peace of mind. Unrequited love is always an illusion.

I said, I doubt it's really about men. Even though I matured early, I was very slow to grow up, and there are still lots of things I don't understand. The course of my growing up has been different from other people's, but I have to grow up, right? The future is always a kind of quest, and how things end up is always something new, isn't it?

Apple said, Be careful out there. I won't see you off, but people like us are never really apart.

K

I.

Saining came back. His complexion was muddy, he shook all over, and whenever I swore at him, he got a nosebleed. His black eyes were just as innocent as ever, which left me feeling confused.

I reflected ruefully that Valentine's Day and I weren't meant for each other. But I could still secretly imagine all sorts of things. Men treated me like shit; I couldn't think of myself as a piece of shit, though. I imagined an airplane parked in front of my house, and a man disembarked and said he would be a good friend to me, a lover.

It never crossed my mind that it was Saining I'd been waiting for! It was early in the morning, and it was raining. I opened the door as if in a dream, thinking back on those years between my nineteenth and twenty-fourth birthdays, and remembering the many rainy mornings when I would bitterly and plaintively sing an utterly ridiculous little song: "Come back, young Saining. Oh, when will you return? Dawn may never come; come back! Come back to me." Now, on the morning of Valentine's Day 1997, Saining was back again, clutching in his hand a bunch of wildflowers just picked from my garden.

Come in, I said. Come in. You look like a ghost standing there. If you have bad news, I don't want to hear about it. And if you're in some kind of trouble, don't expect me to help you. I can't sleep at night, and I've come down with a cough. Yesterday I even felt like jumping off a building. I'm not strong enough right now to share the burden of your sorrows with you.

He said, Don't send me away. I want to be with you. I've thought things through. I miss you.

I said, You've thought things through, have you? You asshole! I'm not your mother!

Saining said, My mother is dead.

And then a few tears fell from his eyes, rolling down his face, which was still wet from the rain. And then he started to weep out loud.

He said that his mother had died in Japan, of illness. While he was in Japan, he became addicted to cocaine, but he'd stopped. He wanted to be with me. That's what Saining was like — he did drugs whenever the opportunity presented itself. In addition to doing drugs, he also liked to take walks, and he walked all over town, walking and thinking. He lived in his own little world. He was his own best companion, and he always had been. From time to time he would think of me, need me. After all these years, his love for me was really quite simple — he always came back.

I felt like kicking this bad-luck, bad-news man right out of my life. The morning chill toyed with us. We were stuck in our own dead end. And then Saining's nose started bleeding. Whenever he got a nosebleed, I felt even more helpless.

I said, Why don't you lie down for a while. Let's sleep a little. We can talk later.

The wind started to blow, and the sound of rain falling outside made us feel empty, so empty that our lives seemed on the verge of being extinguished. A thin blanket covered Saining's lower body. He had grown much thinner. A couple of friends had been staying in my extra bedroom, so I had to sleep in the same bed as Saining. I didn't have a sofa.

How did you get here from the airport?

First I took a cab, then the subway, and then another cab.

Do you like the Shanghai subway?

Subways are all the same. Shanghai's is just newer, that's all. I like riding subways; everyone is themselves down there. There are lots of people from the countryside riding the subway here, and they stared at me. Their lips were cracked because the heat was turned up too high in the cars.

They come to Shanghai looking for work. They don't have lip balm.

The rain stopped, and somewhere outside, a crow cawed.

My father was a failure in real estate. I'm the only person living in this house now, but I like it here because it's so damn far from the center of town.

Saining's nosebleed stopped, but he kept fussing with his nose. I couldn't get to sleep. I had lain awake on so many mornings; Saining had gone missing on so many mornings. He'd last disappeared more than a year ago, and I'd almost gotten married in the interim. I'd hung on to the key to his little place, but he never called me, not even once. I respected his habit of wandering off, but I can't say that it didn't hurt me. I wished that I could just vanish with that kind of frequency too, but I wasn't able to. Saining's mother was always giving him money, and he had a British passport. He could go wherever he wanted.

2.

Whenever anything happened that had to do with Saining, Hong would call me. No matter where I was, she could always find me. Hong and Saining both loved to call people on the telephone; they both belonged to that category of people who will talk on the phone until their chins are bruised. Today when Hong called, I was in the middle of giving the dog a bath. Actually, the dog used to belong to her and Saining. I thought of this dog more as a movie camera: he'd filmed the whole Saining-and-Hong story, as well as the love story of me and my wife. Now my woman was gone, because I was bad, because I only made love to her a few times in an entire year. I loved her, but I didn't much feel like making love. I just didn't feel like it, and I'm not interested in why. What was the point of wondering? But she dumped me because I didn't spend any time thinking about it or trying to think of ways to solve the problem.

I'd been putting on weight, and Hong said to me, as a joke, You won't be able to make it as a sex symbol anymore. Now you're gonna have to learn to play.

Thank God we're still alive. Thank God I can still earn some bread playing in nightclubs. Thank God we've knocked music off its pedestal. That's what I told Saining that day.

Saining told me on the phone that he still loved that woman. He also said that he was absolutely positive he'd found the right woman. This got a rise out of me.

Many years ago, Saining and I had great ambitions and formed a band. But Hong just lolled around all day, living only for love. Now she's a writer, and her writing has become a kind of trend, spontaneous and of the moment. Hong the writer and her imitators were overnight sensations — at least their bullshit images were. If you browse the black-market bookstalls, you'll see pirated versions of their books displayed all together, right next to the cheap quartz watches. What I'm trying to say is that fame is a crock of shit! Other people pick out the most searing elements of Hong's writing and turn them into badges. Then they pin them onto their own crap, and it makes them rich and famous. The papers say this kind of writing "represents youth culture in transformation."

Representative, my ass! That's what Hong said. She said, I'm thrilled to death that I can't speak for anyone or anything. The window is open, and we can see the ocean outside, but our bodies are still here, inside. These times are witnessing the birth of many new things, people are abandoning the old rules, and everything's looser.

One night in 1994, I went over to Hong's place. I kept pounding on the door, but she didn't come to open it. I had a feeling she was there, so I used my identification booklet to pry open the door. Hong had overdosed. She lay barely conscious, soaked in her own drool, and her labored but agitated breathing sounded like the bleating of a sheep. She couldn't speak, but she told me with a gesture that she couldn't move, because movement would make her breathing dangerously hard. She signaled to me: Saining has gone and isn't coming back. What now? I don't want to die; I want to see Saining.

While waiting for the ambulance, we communicated with signs and gestures. I could have spoken but I used my hands instead. I may not look like much, I'm small, but I'm tough and I almost never cry; but that night I cried like a son of a bitch. I told her that I still had sixty *yuan* in my pocket. I'm feeling bad tonight too, I told her. I miss Saining as much as you do. I thought I'd come over so we could talk until dawn, and then I thought we'd go out for tea. We haven't gone out for tea in a long time. But I had no idea what you'd been up to until I showed up at your place tonight. I'm taking you back to Shanghai tomorrow.

I remember the way Hong's bloodless lips contorted as she mouthed: Don't cry. None of this will last. A new world is coming. All of our suffering and stupidity will be buried in the past.

I will never forget any of the gestures Hong made that night. Breathing raggedly, she faced the wall, signing with gestures that were at once sorrowful and fearless.

I think that that night was a turning point for Hong. She would have to write down everything about that time and place and turn it into a clear and simple story. I just hoped that she would have the strength. If she could do that, she would never have to feel afraid of her transformation into a writer.

So today I said to her, You have to keep writing! And whatever you do, make sure that what you write is close to your self, and follow your own lead.

3.

I'm as helpless as a child. I'm young and sincere and unlucky. My mom liked to say that a person can only be good at one thing in life. Even though my mom was incredibly mixed up about a lot of things, she was totally right about this. I began life as a broken piece of glass. My mother took the broken bits of glass and started gluing them together, piece by piece, and now I'm carrying on this work. I think that I have the perseverance it takes to keep going. Because my love is just this, a roomful of broken glass.

Hong's current hairstyle makes her look even more like a scarecrow. And me, I'm just a fainthearted little pigeon, flying into her open window at last. Right now she's sleeping beside me, with a thin blanket covering her lower body. She's become very thin. For as long as I've known her and been with her, I've felt as if I've had a new lover every year — but they've all been Hong. She was different every year. I barely had news of her for such a long time, but I still know that when we're together, every year it will be like meeting someone new.

Truly, I can find in her everything I might ever want. But I always want to be away from her. My world is a wound-up clock, but I don't know who it was that wound it. Maybe this is what fate is. Sometimes this clock of mine points toward Hong, and sometimes it points somewhere else. Sometimes it points toward the city; sometimes it points toward a village in the English countryside. Sometimes it points toward the eighty-eight-story Grand Hyatt Hotel; sometimes it points at a patch of flat ground. I'm exceptionally gutless. I often have to get away from the people I'm closest to, and I'll go off by myself to someplace I've never been before, and then I'll come back. This way, life is always fresh for me, because I know that there's always something new just waiting to be discovered. It's like gliding away, and for me it seems to be the answer to everything. Whenever I leave, I feel so real, and every time I come back I feel as though I've lost something.

Now, her cold, exhausted gaze chills me to the bone, and I'm afraid to take her in my arms. I don't know where I stand with her anymore, and this worries me. I couldn't take it if she didn't want to make love with me anymore. I just don't think there's any way I could handle that. She said, The truth is, you're not interested in me anymore. You need to go back to being like you used to, screwing around with other women. Then you'd be interested in me again.

But I can't do it, because love requires us to commit all of our feelings. And all of my feelings come back to her. Life is totally meaningless, we live out our lives for nothing, and the sole source of meaning in life is in feeling some sensation from time to time. That's all there is. That's why I'm attracted to drugs, and it's also the reason I love only her, because she's complicated. She's constantly changing, and she can always make me feel something.

And then all of a sudden there she was, telling me she didn't know what love was, that she used to know but that later she realized she didn't know anymore.

How could she not know what love is? She scares me.

Actually, seeing her now, I don't respond to her physically, and this is a blow to me. It used to be that if we spent the night together, we could do it lots of times, but what's happened? Seeing her body is just like looking at an ordinary pair of hands. My mother said that there was a limit to the number of times anyone could make love in his lifetime, and that once you used it up, it was gone. Even if what she said is true, I still don't think I've used up everything I have.

But when will we be able to start over again? Because I realize that I'm losing her right now. She's right beside me, and she's slipping away.

4.

A couple of my girlfriends have been staying at my place temporarily. They're lovers. At one point I told them about some meetings for lesbians, but they went only twice, and they never went back. They didn't think of themselves as lesbians. And someone at one of the meetings made a bizarre statement, that lesbians get together out of emptiness, unlike gay men, who are driven by intense suffering.

A. was androgynous. She was bright-eyed and had a generous mouth. She was short-statured and hunchbacked and walked duck-footed. When she was angry, she had a habit of beating her breast, but she said that her breasts didn't feel any pain. A. was attracted only to women, and she had a powerful sex drive. Her most cherished dream was to get a sex-change operation. She felt that if she could only be a man from the inside out, life would be a little easier. A. came from a small town in Henan and had studied *pipa* — the Chinese lute — and classical piano. She couldn't stand the prejudiced way that people in her hometown had always looked at her, so she traveled to one of the open cities in the hopes of making her career there.

B. was a dancer. She was half a head taller than A. She was brown-skinned, broad-shouldered, and thin-waisted and had a large ass. B. had been A.'s piano student and had been secretly in love with her from the time she was fourteen. B. was in love with A.'s talent and her melancholy character. They had run into each other a year earlier in a town in the South. A. had almost lost hope because she was always hungry. She'd worked in a hairpin factory, and she'd been a stylist's assistant, washing hair at a sidewalk haircutting stall. She'd been a waitress too.

B. thought of herself as heterosexual. She'd slept with men, and making love to a man was something that she understood. She didn't think of A. as a woman, but she didn't think of her as a man either. No man could give her seven or eight orgasms in a single day.

Bug had had a brainstorm. His idea was to hear how guitar and *pipa* sounded together. Sanmao had introduced us to A. Hearing her play "Surrounded on All Sides," I was moved by the strength and control of her fingers. We took her to the hospital for a complete physical, and after the examination we were told that she had a dark spot beneath her eighth rib. You could see her uterus, but it was extremely small. We asked how much it would cost for her to get a sex-change operation. Now A. lives in Shanghai and gives private piano lessons to children, and B. dances in the chorus behind a nightclub singer. B.'s dream is to introduce A. to her parents after the sex-change operation, and then they'll get married and live happily ever after.

I've heard that A. and B. drift off to sleep every night gazing into each other's eyes. Their lives are filled with hardship, but they're determined not to let anything stop them. This pair loves each other as much as life itself, and I see them swaying back and forth before my eyes. My apartment is badly soundproofed, and it seems as if they're always making love.

Saining and I spent the entire day in bed, asleep, but we were jolted awake by the sound of B.'s crying, followed by the sound of A. and B.'s arguing. We heard A. shouting, What woman would want me, with my looks? Why are you always so suspicious? Why are you always accusing me of things I didn't do? B. said, You know perfectly well how worried I am about you. It's not a joke. Silence followed, which in turn gave way to the sounds of their lovemaking.

I don't know exactly what they were doing, but there was no doubt that there were two women in there making love. Why didn't they think they were lesbians?

In any case, gay or straight, what did it matter, as long as you could love someone? And what about me? When was the last time I'd really been in love? It seemed a couple of years ago, at least.

Saining had just been relaxing with his eyes closed all along, and now he sat up and said, When two women are making love, can they do it without ever stopping?

And I was thinking that even though A. and B. lived exhaustingly difficult lives, they were happy because they loved each other. They worked hard every day for that sex-change operation. They were sharing in the labor, and they would share the fruits of that labor as well.

Saining and I each lit ourselves a cigarette, and we smoked and stared at the bedroom door in an uncomfortable silence. It was Saining who broke the silence, saying, How come all your music is dance music? What happened to all of our other records?

My face darkened. I didn't answer him.

5.

The two people on the other side of the wall climaxed simultaneously, and then we heard them singing. Later it grew quiet again, and I began to feel anxious. It was as if I could see them as they faced each other, their eyes locked, and I realized that Saining felt as agitated as I did. It had already grown dark outside, and although the sight of a loving couple on Valentine's Day is usually comforting, we were nagged by embarrassment. It was Valentine's Day, and maybe all they wanted was to spend the day in bed. For me and Saining to hang out with them like this had to be the height of stupidity.

I said, Let's get dressed. Let's go somewhere a little more festive.

And Saining said, Good idea! We gotta get out of here before they go at it again.

At dinner, Saining gave me three roses and a red plastic ring that looked like a giant cherry Life Saver.

What are these three roses for? I asked.

They stand for the words *I love you*.

How can you be so sure that's what they're saying? And I've got tons of rings at home, all from you. We used to be excited about each other and so sensitive to each other. I believe you love me, but you don't make me feel loved. You're hopeless.

After my mother died, I had a realization — that you were still mine! You have to understand that when you committed yourself, I was committed too. I've changed you, but you've changed me as well. You've brought me my greatest unhappiness and my greatest joy. I can't be without you. Do you really not love me anymore? I don't believe it. I'll never stop loving you.

When he got to the words "I'll never stop loving you," his voice was barely audible.

Saining, you just lost your mother. You're weak right now, so you need me. Don't be ridiculous! I've always been here for you; we're always together. Even when you're not around, I'm still on the same wavelength as you. My life and my writing are both stuck in a vicious circle. You're the creator of my lonely worldview. You can't possibly be saying that love is good, can you? Do you know what love is? I don't. Has it ever occurred to you that love has become a luxury for the two of us? We don't have the energy to be trapped into loving anyone anymore. God knows how this happened. We're burned out; we're used up. Don't you get it?

I have one more present for you. It's a song. It's called "All the Good Children Will Have Candy to Eat."

We're not good children. And I'm out of candy.

We are good children. Our candy is our stories.

I lost patience, and with a brusque wave of the hand, I said, Let's just eat, OK? Valentine's Day is just awkward for us.

He was still looking at me. His dark eyes and the dark circles under his eyes would always communicate to me the news of his madness. He said, You're really sexy when you're mad.

Sexy, my ass! I said. Pieces of shit like us don't know what sexy is.

I glanced at him as I spoke. He was wearing a black sweater. He had several others just like it, as well as several sets of identical coats, pants, and T-shirts. He once said that there was nothing more boring than clothing, that clothes didn't mean anything.

6.

We arrived at Tribes, where they were having a Valentine's Day party. A lot of our friends were there, broken people with broken hearts. Some of our friends who were in bands were there too, and seeing them was a rare treat.

There weren't as many live bands in Shanghai as in Beijing, so tonight was more like Beijing than Shanghai with all of the dance parties going on. Of course, most of the people at the parties in Shanghai were *laowai* — foreigners — or else Shanghai girls who wanted to snag a *laowai*. Everyone was so phony.

Saining said, I feel like getting up and playing guitar. I said, There are already a bunch of guitar players here. Why don't you play drums? Everybody can play together that way.

As he played, Saining dropped his head until the tips of his long hair brushed his knees. The drums in this bar had never been hit with such force, and he excited me. I hadn't felt that way in a long time.

A boy I didn't know approached Saining and spoke into his ear, and all at once Saining's face contorted into a grimace. He kept saying, I'm sorry, I'm sorry. Threading my way through the press of people, I caught sight of him looking at me with the tenderest expression imaginable. The look in his eyes took me back to the past, and I felt sad.

What happened? What did he say to you?

He said to me, "What do you think you're doing?" He said, "Who the hell are you? I'm a drummer too, and what matters around here is feeling, not just technique. You don't know shit about self-expression."

What? You've got to be kidding!

I think I'd better go home now!

What's wrong with you? You're good. You're better than you've ever been before. Everyone loved you.

Forget it. Maybe he was right.

Right about what? He wasn't speaking for anyone but himself. What's gotten into you? What made you apologize to him? Bug still wants to play guitar with you.

I'm too old.

I never thought I'd hear Saining say something like this.

He left, and I didn't try to stop him.

As soon as Saining walked out the door, I rushed up to that boy. I said, Who the hell are you to say that about him? I'm giving you two choices: you can apologize, or you can go up there right now and play for me. I'd like to hear for myself how much "feeling" you have.

To my surprise, the boy apologized to me on the spot, and he was sincere. He said, I was just joking with him. I didn't mean for him to take it so seriously. Please tell him how sorry I am.

After he'd said all that, there was nothing left for me to do, so I started drinking. When the fuck did this low-key little bar start attracting so many *laowai*-chasing college girls? It was disgusting!

I asked a Spaniard and a Hungarian to speak to me in their native languages at the same time, one in each ear. I said, You can say anything you want, but just start talking! Heads gracefully extended, and with serious expressions on their faces, they began speaking unbroken streams of words. One on my left, and one on my right.

7.

Hong stepped out of the bar. She'd had too much to drink, and whenever she drinks a lot she gets all soft and mushy, an innocent look comes over her face, and she gets glassy-eyed and starts blowing spit bubbles. She gazes at me as if from some distant place, and as I watch the cigarette in her hand, she says, Life is so short, but how short is it, really? Maybe you have to commit suicide to find out. But I'm not going to kill myself. Suicide is too damn extreme.

When I left her four years earlier, she'd become depressed. Now, no matter how hard I tried, I couldn't make her happy again. And if she was unhappy, how could I be happy? When I first met her she was still a virgin. She'd been so innocent and full of life. Today was Valentine's Day, and I wanted her to be happy, but she was despondent. I would have been better off just buying her a nice pair of sunglasses! It would have been so easy. A cheap pair of sunglasses with big lenses would've kept her happy for days!

She walked over and looked at me. She said, I knew you'd be waiting for me out here. I know your habits. But you can't get to me anymore. The first time I met you, you said you were looking for bars that had stages. You wanted to play your heart out, until you ran out of songs to sing or until they kicked you out. You said your motto was "Die young and leave a beautiful corpse." You said you thought that was your destiny. I asked you where those bars were, and you said you didn't know, but that you were going to find them. With those full lips, big eyes, and long hair, and your love of chocolate, and your guitar playing — I was crazy about you! Do you know why your eyes always look so beautiful?

Because you're so lonely, and you speak with your eyes. What's it going to take to get you out of your loneliness? I didn't think you could be lonely tonight. You like places like this, don't you? Shanghai is full of clubs now. See that young girl there? The one who looks like a little cookie? She lives in a damp basement room, and lately she's been practicing Joy Division tunes as a way to find her own sound. But you sit outside apologizing for yourself. What are you doing waiting for me, anyway? I love you, or maybe I just love your asthma. Asthma is such a fucking nightmare.

I couldn't figure out why she was so sensitive. Coming back this time, I found her constantly on edge. Was it because she had no sex life? Or was it because she'd become a writer? Or because she'd once predicted that she was going to die at twenty-seven? I wanted to play the violin for her. I thought it might soothe her. We needed to build a new love together.

I came outside because it just wasn't my scene in there. And I was waiting for you because I don't know the way back to your place. I thought we could share a cab and save some money.

My nose started bleeding. It was an old problem of mine, that whenever I got anxious or upset I'd get a nosebleed. Hong looked at me with disgust. She said, I'm not taking care of you anymore. You don't care about anyone except yourself. You left me just so you could go and mess around with drugs. You left me in that horrible city, and you blew your inheritance on drugs. You hurt everyone!

Hearing these words directed at me, and seeing them coming from such a sweet face, was more than I could bear. I figured I'd lost her. I took her in my arms, and she was so light that she felt nearly weightless. She looked up at the sky, her eyes motionless as a cat's. Those dark eyes of hers would never again express to me that sense of her madness. It was as if I wasn't strong enough to love her anymore. We were never going to experience feelings of love again. I was going to have to accept that fact. Our bodies, our bodies had left us long ago. We had no bodies. And our lips were too dry for kissing, and our desire had burned out, but it didn't matter! What mattered was that we were family, companions. We had come from the same place, we were still alive, and we were going to go on living. Who says that isn't love? I couldn't leave her again. I wanted to be with her all the time, that was all I wanted, and I wasn't going to make her miserable anymore. I would do whatever she asked, if only I could see her every day, if only she would smile at me again. For this tatter of hope, I was willing to jump into it again with her, despair and all. I had to have her in my life. If she ever decided to get married to someone, I wanted it to be me.

I thought these plans over, but I didn't say anything. I didn't dare. I would talk about it the next morning, over coffee.

L

I.

Outside my window, the sky. Two black birds halt in midair, one on top of the other. After this collision they fly away, and then they crash into each other again before flying off. A while later, one of the birds begins to get agitated. First the feathers on its neck stand out, and then all of the feathers on its body puff out, and when they're standing on end like this, the feathers are half white and half black. The crest on its head also stands straight up, and it starts poking with its crest at the other bird. Seen from the front, these are just a pair of courting birds, a pair of white dots inside a pair of white circles. But from the other side, they're a pair of black dots inside a pair of black circles. In the tree outside the window, a gray bird is constructing a little house. It will put leaves on one wall inside its little house, red berries on another wall, green seeds on another wall, and cow manure on the remaining wall. Then it will wait for its mate to come. Sometimes it will build a pagoda out of a big pile of twigs, and it will stand on top of that and wait. Sometimes it sweeps the level, grassy surface by the door of its little house clean. If another bird happens to fly past but stops to place a leaf or a feather there, and if the gray bird takes the offering in its beak, that proves that it loves the bird that flew by. And if the second bird flies back and keeps setting down leaves or feathers, then the gray one will keep on taking them in its mouth, and in the end the two birds will make love on the grassy, level spot by the nest.

Just now a bird has flown over. There are markings by its mouth, a large fire-red circle, with fire red in the center, and three little yellow spots forming a triangle, so that the whole thing looks like a red face with yellow eyes and mouth, like the face of a child. This bird's body is solid sapphire blue, and its tail is silvery white, with a split in the middle. The two sides are very slender, and from where I'm sitting it looks like two white ribbons fluttering behind the bird's body. The pair of birds has found a slightly longer branch, and one of them perches at one end, while the other one perches at the other. They start pecking rapidly at the branch, moving along its length, until their beaks meet up, and then they separate again and peck back to their original place. They go through the whole process again and again, repeating the same motions over and over.

The wind has come up, and all of the leaves are blowing down from the trees. There are many trees outside, but it's only in that one tree that I love that I can see so many birds. It's the weekend. Could it be that birds have weekends too? Is this tree a weekend playground? Why have they all chosen this very same tree?

Sometimes I need to leave the surface of the earth; sometimes I need to be full of love for the entire world, I need some ecstasy; sometimes I need to nourish my brain. When there's nothing else but me and the starry sky, and the moon looks like a child's face, I don't dare smile at it. It seems as if maybe I'm a child too. Children are the true observers in this world.

2.

This candy-coated city, blurred but seductive, where the speed of the car controls my mood and heartbeat. When he speeds up, I feel good, but when it's more than I can take, he slows down. The taxi driver puts on the music I brought with me, the elevated highway becomes soft, and my eyes stand up, and my eyes lie down. Warm and gentle sparks embrace the emptiness; when the music plays and the bloodred pipes in my head begin to melt, I feel myself stepping into another skin.

I've decided to go to China Groove on weekend nights. The first floor is like an aquarium, and they usually play ambient music there. Outside, there's a big garden, where they play drum and bass. The second floor has several red velvet booths, and they play hard house and trance there. There are a couple of twenty-something Shanghainese DJs there, and they're always going through amazing contortions to procure records and marijuana, and sometimes they can get a little E from the prostitutes they know. On weekends, Bug, Nunu, Cocoa, and I go and hang out with them.

When the music is empty enough that I can put myself inside it, taking it in on every level, and the air is charged with electricity, I can achieve a dream state, and like a dream, there are no words to describe it. The music is moving me; I don't need to move on my own. Sometimes the moon appears in the room, bringing this news: all the news that terrifies me to the depths of my soul, all the people who make me their clown. We will never be parted; we will always be this perfect, this complete.

DJ King's music is a kind of psychoanalysis. He gets deep inside you, he doesn't wait on you, his mood decides everything, and you have no choice but to follow him. And even though you might catch up with him at some particular point, you won't be able to stop there — you can't stop. The King tilts his head, auto-cratically, mysteriously. For some people, DJ King is as dangerous as his name.

I like clubs best in the early morning because all of the boring people have gone and only the truly boring people are still there. Chinese and *laowai*, phony artists and real ones, prostitutes, local slackers, dumb-ass white-collar types. It doesn't matter who they are; it's too late, and none of the men are likely to pick up a woman, and none of the women are likely to pick up a guy. Nobody is going to pick anybody up; they're all fucked. A few cold rays of early-morning light pierce the room, and we sway inside the music. Everyone has a language that belongs to his own body. After hours is the most real time of all.

3.

The night is my lover, my sweetheart, and if I go out at night, I want my night to have all of these things at once: a sense of occasion, a dramatic plotline, and someone else with whom I can share an exquisitely beautiful understanding. But in fact, none of my nights out has ever possessed all three of these qualities. I know that somewhere along the line I get lost.

That's why every night when I get home I check my E-mail. E-mail begins at the vanishing point of you, me, and the night. My mailbox exists within a fixed protocol, and I know that as long as I don't make a mistake, as long as I hit the right keys, the messages I write will be sent out. I can feel reasonably certain of this, and I find it deeply satisfying.

I like to tell stories in my E-mails. If a plot that has me in it is unfinished and has lots of loose ends, I'll add on to it. If none of the stories I'm in are ever beautiful or moving, I'll still go on telling them. If none of the people in my life are ever adequate or ideal, I still won't give up my search, even if the best I can do merely is to find something that resembles those people.

When I transmit a story electronically, I'm weaving memories together between my fingers. If the recipient has come into my thoughts, he will learn what he means to me. Even though I may be rather scattered, I still think there's nothing more important than stories. Every detail in a story dances because every detail is a fragment. Perhaps nothing has been set into motion yet today, but that isn't going to knock me down.

M

Ninety-nine percent of the men I know are boring, and of the 1 percent who aren't boring, 99 percent of them have girlfriends. A lot of men want to fool around with me, but they all have girlfriends. That kind of arrangement isn't acceptable to me. I can't believe that accepting that kind of offer could make me happy.

I've been feeling more and more dismal all the time. Clouds are darkening my skies and I'm sinking into gloom, and my hopes are fading. I'm yearning for a day when I'll walk into some situation and suddenly something there will set me free.

A month ago I started running twenty minutes a day. Working hard to maintain a graceful and balanced posture and keeping my head lifted as I jogged along, after three days I realized that the swaying motion of my body was real exercise.

Maybe I'd overlooked a lot of finer points before, but physical activity brought on some changes, and I decided that it was high time for me to have a sex life again.

I got in touch with all of the men who were potential partners, and I settled on someone who definitely didn't love me and whom I was sure I didn't love either. Our first night was a bit depressing. Sweetness was elusive, always a step or two ahead of me, there were spooky-looking green roses in the garden, and I'd all but forgotten how to touch a man's face. I needed opening up. When I'd opened myself up, my life would be so much happier. My efforts left me feeling stupid, and I felt that life wasn't treating me fairly at all. Why would life put me in this kind of position?

Bug said, You're going about it all wrong. You should try to find someone you honestly like.

I said, I've wasted too many kisses already! Lovers don't come to us unless they want to, but happiness is something we can go out and look for. At least this guy makes me feel relaxed, and when I make love with him I can forget myself for a while. Plus I like him a lot, he's sweet, and he's a friend. Right now I'm trying to learn how to tell the difference between love, and lovers, and friends, and friends you have a sexual relationship with. I think it's important to have a clear sense of the distinctions between these things. And anyway, condoms are always faithful to one lover — that's one thing in life that can't change.

Bug looked at me for a moment, and then he said, Even if you reach a point where love can't touch you, I hope you won't stop yearning for it anyway.

One day I had my first orgasm. All I can say is that I experienced it, and that's how I know. There had still been some traces of opium in his bong. I was completely unaware that I was nearing orgasm, and it came in a flash, nakedly simple, unbidden by my thoughts or spirit.

I finally understood why I had always been so uptight. I had never allowed myself to relax and let go and experience pleasure.

I thought about it all the next day, although my joy was mixed with grief. Now that I'd achieved one kind of climax, I wanted to have the other kind. People said that the two kinds of orgasm were very different. I recalled those long-ago pleasurable spasms of my girlhood, and I began to sleep with him frequently. It was always at his place, where there was music, and a big bed, and afterward I would always smoke a cigarette. Then I'd go home and take a bath.

It seemed as if orgasms were hard for me to achieve. The next time I was with him, it took a lot of work to get me to come, and afterward I spent the night at his place for the first time. I had a nightmare there. I woke up in the middle of it, and I told him, I'm having a nightmare. He glared at me coldly, and without saying a word, he went back to sleep. This hurt me deeply. I felt so pathetic. I felt as though I needed tenderness and sweet words too. Language had hurt me again! I knew that I'd probably never be able to open myself up to him in bed again.

Apple said, If you have it in you to screw someone and then kick him out the door as soon as you're done, then go ahead, be my guest. But if you can't do that, and if you can't stop thinking about it all the time, just do me one favor. Please, please, stop hurting yourself.

I said, But when I don't have a man, my body turns to ice. What am I supposed to do?

Apple said, I guess you're getting what you deserve.

I decided I would need to solve this myself. Life is a big experiment, and we have to keep trying new things, learning new lessons. This was a sort of lesson.

I had come down with a very pathetic kind of sickness: I didn't think that there was a man anywhere in the world who could love me. I was ill-fated.

The moon is my sun; its rays penetrate my room, making me realize how depressed I am. When I lay my body down, I can hear the sound of my blood flowing. It's a feeling that's both inspiring and oppressive. So many tedious efforts, my body is cold and frail. In my own bathtub, it's me and my body together under the moonlight. And when we're alone together like this, it's as if we've lost the entire world, but at least we'll always have each other. To hell with language! To hell with orgasms! To hell with whores! To hell with love! My body and I just want to throw up! If there ever comes a day when I can have an orgasm without having to depend on a man, I will lie down in front of the moon and have a good cry.

Saining was back in Shanghai again. He said he wanted to open a little bookstore there.

He had found a huge plot of marijuana growing in the Beijing suburbs. A lot of people had found similar places. Everyone smoked as much as they wanted and then harvested a bit to take home. Nobody knew how it had happened; just like those hole-punched records, it was a gift from heaven.

We'd never talked about our orgasms. He slept beside me every day. Looking at him, I found myself thinking that it didn't matter whether or not we came. I felt that the weak were finally getting some muscles, that the bored had finally reached orgasm, and that the stupid assholes had finally seen the big picture.

But I was still ashamed, ashamed of our relationship.

N

Maybe you think there's something noble about doing heroin, as if it's some sort of journey to self-realization. Junkies' souls are richer than ordinary people's, and their aesthetic needs are even higher. Even if you recognize that it's an illusion, you will still experience many revelations and become aware of many new things, as if you had thought of all the things you'd never thought of before. Your metabolism speeds up, you experience the drug, and the drug is good to you. Your sense of safety is enhanced because you are transparent and others are unaware of your sharpness. Because you are so self-realized, your entire being is like a thief. You think it's a gift from heaven, it's impossible to feel guilty, and because you feel it is so pure, it's the key to your soul, and all of your inhibitions and self-doubts vanish into thin air.

But if you want to be a "flight commander," I'm going to give you some advice. You need to be extremely cautious around chemicals, even a three-*yuan* bottle of pills. Because, as you'll discover very quickly, you're constantly going to have to increase your dosage, and it will never end. Everything will start to seem boring to you, until finally it will have stolen away your entire self. My lungs are shot full of holes, and my vocal cords have been ruined by heroin; I'll never be able to get onstage again. My brain is like a sieve — I have no memory — and there are a number of other heroin-related traits that will always be with me. If you want to get high, there are plenty of ways to do it, but don't go using just any old drug without thinking about it. For instance, you can put Fisherman's Friend in your espresso. This is a trick we impoverished Chinese kids came up with. You have to do it regularly, but it can throw you into the realm of the imagination in a hurry.

Don't be so serious! I just happened to come into the pharmacy to buy some medicine, that's all. I need the warmth; I'm one of those people who always need to be high.

Let me tell you something. If you were to give me your drugs and I took them now, and if we were in a high-rise right now, and if what we saw before us right now was a smooth and shiny plate-glass window and you said you wanted to jump, I would want to see how you looked as you jumped. You're my best friend, but I would want to watch it happen, because if I couldn't see it happen, it couldn't touch me, and I wouldn't be able to respond. Because I'm your friend, I wouldn't try to pull you back.

That's you. You're low, and I'm high. We're not the same. Your heart is sad and dark.

Bug had used Special K a few times lately, and he'd changed. He was looking for ways to get high every day. It didn't take him long to discover at the pharmacy a kind of pill that cost only three *yuan* a bottle (and because I don't want anyone else to go try it, I'm not going to say what it was), but the effect of this medicine was a lot like speed, and after he'd taken some, he felt energized. The first day, he took three pills, and he was euphoric. The second day, he took five pills. The third day, he didn't take any, but on the fifth day he took seven, and that's when he discovered that his genitals were starting to shrink. Nothing frightened him more than that.

So he came and told me. That's how he is — whenever anything happens that makes him upset, he runs and tells me right away. He looked as if he'd been up all night partying, and in fact he hadn't eaten or slept in days. His face had a green-gray pallor, his breath was foul, his eyes were sunken and often crossed, his face was covered with fresh acne, and the skin just below the corners of his mouth was a mess.

That's how chemicals are. You feel great for a while, but afterward all the bullshit that's been troubling you comes back in full force, and you find yourself in even deeper shit than before.

He soon quit taking that stuff, telling me that he thought his old life was better for him. It was more solid.

The night he told me that, I lit all the candles in the house and brewed a pot of oolong tea. I said, Let's pretend it's a pot of magic-mushroom tea. That night I played DJ and played him some music, and for a long time we watched the shapes of the candle-light flickering to the music, and we talked about silly things, and once again we had the sensation that we were being lifted up together, in one of those rare peaks of experience you have from time to time. Bug was like Saining, one of those hard-to-find people who always understood me, no matter what nonsense I was talking. The more off-the-wall I got, the better they understood. Conversations like those were my favorite kind because they had nothing to do with everyday life. Some weekends, Saining, Bug, and I would get together, along with a few others we didn't pay much attention to because they were just hangers-on. If we'd eaten E, we would emerge from a club on a weekend morning, sure to be bound for the café in the eighty-eight-story Grand Hyatt Hotel, where we could continue our bullshit session. Places like the Grand Hyatt didn't feel so over-the-top if you went there with your closest friends. Saining said that the Grand Hyatt building was the only place he liked in Shanghai, and aside from wanting to be a fireman, he had another fantasy, which was to be a window washer at the Grand Hyatt and to hang by a safety rope. We always left the Grand Hyatt with black circles under our eyes because we always sat there for at least ten hours, blabbing about everything and nothing and gazing out the windows.

A month later, Bug told me that he'd been running a low-grade fever for two weeks, and he had had diarrhea. And there were other symptoms that were more serious. I said, What are you trying to tell me? He said, Can I show you something? He led me into the bathroom and took off his pants. He wasn't wearing any underwear. He took my hand and said, Feel this. I said, What are you doing? He touched my hand to his inner thigh, and it felt as though there was something hard inside the muscle of his inner thigh, something rock-hard.

I said, I think this is where your lymph glands are. They seem to be swollen.

Bug stood there without moving. I looked between his legs and then back at his face. He was holding his neck very straight, with his head tilted up, but his eyes were looking down at me, and his gaze seemed to bore right through me. Then he looked away from me, straight ahead, and he said, I've been thinking about it a lot, and I've gone through all the possibilities. I think I have AIDS.

I had a lot of friends with AIDS when I was in America, and I remember thinking that if my neck ever started to swell up, it would mean that I was going to die.

Just then, Bug's beeper went off, and he started hunting around for it.

I said, Who paged you?

He said, It isn't mine; I don't wear a beeper.

I said, Then what was that sound we just heard?

He thought for a moment and then said, Oh, yeah! That's right! Now, where did I leave it?

I said, Getting high all the time has really messed you up!

It's not the drugs; it's AIDS.

What are you talking about? How could you have AIDS? That's impossible.

Why is it impossible?

Well, in the first place, you've always used a condom.

I've never used a condom.

For God's sake! That's not what you told me before! Put your pants back on. Let's not panic; let's discuss this rationally. How could you not use a condom?

I don't like them.

Who does? That's not the point.

I'm not promiscuous.

How many people have you slept with?

Not that many.

Yes, but how many people had they slept with?

They were all nice, unsophisticated girls.

Nice, unsophisticated people are the most dangerous. The vast majority of what you call "nice girls" are incredibly ignorant. I don't want you to get mad at me, but —

They were perfectly healthy. The problem is that I slept with *laowai*.

The problem isn't foreigners. It's not who you screw; it's how you do it.

You're starting to scare me.

I doubt that you have AIDS. You probably haven't been exposed to it.

What makes you think that?

Nothing in particular. It's just a feeling.

But how do you explain all these symptoms? I want to get tested.

Where do you want to go?

A hospital.

Which hospitals do AIDS testing?

I don't know. We can ask around.

Who are we going to ask? This isn't an ordinary STD. I've been tested for HIV twice, but that was in rehab.

Bug sat down on the sofa, sucking nonstop on breath mints. He said, Why did this have to happen to me? Why me?

I said, Let's not talk about that for now. First we get you tested. Then we'll see about the next step.

Bug didn't want to go home, so he stayed at my place. Every day I gave him all kinds of cold medicines, as well as medicine for diarrhea, and every day I checked his forehead repeatedly, hoping to find that his fever had subsided. But what I found troubled me. I couldn't understand why things had to be this way. Every time he came out of the bathroom, he would stare at me inconsolably, and then he would say, I had diarrhea again. We spent our days in an ignorant haze, watching pirated VCDs. We would watch any pirated movie we could get our hands on. But finally I said, I can't stand it any longer. Why don't we get on the Internet and see what we can find out?

We visited every HIV Web site, but aside from having information about the history and medical aspects of HIV, they didn't provide any detailed descriptions of the symptoms, beyond a slightly elevated temperature, diarrhea, swollen lymph glands, and a spotty red skin rash. That's as far as it went. There were, however, a lot of phone numbers. I figured that this was because they didn't want to encourage people who didn't know what they were doing to sit at home and diagnose themselves. But all of the telephone numbers were for hot lines overseas, and we couldn't call them from here. What's more, neither of us spoke very good English. As it was, we'd had a hard enough time trying to decipher what we saw on the Web.

We got in touch with our mutual friends Xiaochun and Xiaohua.

I said, We have a serious problem. I think you may have guessed what I'm talking about. What should we do?

Xiaochun said, You can't go just anywhere for testing. If you're positive, they'll haul you off and banish you to some deserted island, and they'll never let you go. This scared us. Xiaochun was one of those people who spent the whole day sitting in an office reading the newspaper, so we figured she knew what she was talking about. Xiaohua said, Don't get tested in China. She also didn't think that the tests in China were reliable. She said that the last time she'd come back from abroad, they'd demanded at the airport that she be tested for HIV, and they took blood from lots of people and then put it all in different squares of a gridlike frame. They shook the whole thing several times, back and forth, and up and down, and then they pronounced everyone OK. She concluded from this that the greatest danger in China wasn't from *laowai* at all, but from all of the Chinese who regularly traveled abroad.

We tried to imagine that "deserted island," but we couldn't exactly picture what it would be like. And because we couldn't picture it, we felt even more afraid.

We thought about all of those Chinese people who frequently travel outside China. When they're overseas, they sleep around. They're careless, they don't use condoms, and when they come home, they pass through immigration wearing dark glasses before vanishing into the crowd. And then they fuck around some more. Afterward the people they fucked go and fuck a bunch of other people. It's terrifying, this promiscuous world we live in.

Bug launched into a silly chant: I'm tired, I'm wired, I'm tired, I'm wired.

He stripped off all his clothing and inspected every square inch of his body, and he found a couple of little red spots on his calves. He said, Hey, look at this. Can you see them? He was blinking hard as he spoke. A few days later, he discovered a gray stripe on his tongue, and this was followed by alternating sieges of diarrhea and low fever.

Every day saw new developments. It was always something, as if he'd been possessed by evil spirits and the wheel of life was spinning rapidly into the darkness. The whole situation just made us want to get high every day. We weren't doing much of anything, but our appetites suddenly improved, and our metabolism sped up, and every day we devoured lots of different flavors of instant ramen like a pair of hungry ghosts. When we weren't eating or sleeping, we were thinking about HIV, but we couldn't think of a solution.

Xiaohua phoned. She said she'd gotten on the Internet. Her tone was grief-stricken as she announced, It doesn't look good. What he's got sounds pretty similar.

I called Kiwi in the United States, and he called a hot line over there. When he got back to me, he was using the same tone of voice that Xiaohua had. It's not good, he said. It sure looks like that's what he's got. He concluded, Whatever you do, don't treat him like a pariah. What he needs more than anything right now is understanding and comfort.

I couldn't take it all in. How had words become reality in such a short time?

We started analyzing in detail each and every girl that Bug had ever slept with.

We soon realized that all of the girls he'd been with had at least two things in common. One, none of them had insisted that Bug use a condom. Two, Bug always knew at least one of the other guys these girls had slept with. But what other girls had those guys slept with? What were they like? Bug could always find at least one other girl that he knew. Following this information to its logical conclusion, we became increasingly alarmed. The more we knew, the more worried we became. Ultimately we estimated that Bug had, in effect, made love with hundreds of thousands of people (and because Bug and I were such close friends, I was soon infected with the same panic). As I multiplied all these numbers in my head, it started to seem likely that everyone was in trouble.

The next morning, I came upon Bug in the bathroom. He was staring into the mirror with a dazed expression on his face, and he asked, Is it OK if I brush my teeth? The vulnerable look in his eyes made me feel sad, and I said, Of course you can brush your teeth here. Please just don't use my cup, because both of us have bleeding gums. Bug blanched. He said, It just hit me. I know how I got it. When I was in America, I used more than three different people's razors. I said, Why would anybody let you do a thing like that? He said, They didn't know.

This got us thinking about all of the potential hazards associated with our daily routines. Bug had borrowed people's toothbrushes before, and even though they'd belonged to his lovers, it was still risky. And there was one time when Bug was making love and somebody's skin had broken. He wasn't sure who had bled, but it had been painful, and afterward he'd seen blood on his toilet paper.

My best friend Bug's private life was bit by bit being exposed to the light. Things I hadn't understood before were becoming clear. After he'd told me everything about himself, I started thinking about my own history. Life is hard to pin down that way. How can people be certain they know the truth? I didn't feel I could trust anybody anymore.

Saining was in Japan on business, and I called him on the phone. He said, I can come back early. I know there's a hospital in Shanghai for foreigners, and since I have a foreign passport, I can be seen there. We can go there and talk with one of the foreign doctors and get the doctor to agree to test Bug. Or maybe they'd be willing to put my name on Bug's blood sample. I said, There's no way anyone would agree to something that serious. Bug sat down next to me, his head hanging and his eyes riveted to some spot on the floor. I said, Why not send him to Japan for testing? Saining said, Getting a Japanese visa is too much trouble. He'd be better off going to Hong Kong to get tested! I said, But Hong Kong is China too. Wouldn't they arrest him there as well? Saining said, I've been tested there — they don't even ask for your name. I said, You've been tested in Hong Kong? Oh, so that's what you do in your spare time. Why do you need to get tested all the time? You're supposed to wear a condom when you sleep with girls! Although Saining and I were still living together, we hadn't had a physical relationship in a long time. I slept with other men, so I didn't think I had the right to criticize him. It was a sensitive subject. Finally, Saining asked me again, Are you absolutely sure that there's nowhere in Shanghai where he can get tested? I said, Don't even suggest it. Xiaochun said that he could get arrested, and everybody who gets tested is a junkie or a prostitute. We can't send Bug into a place like that all by himself; we just can't.

So we set about arranging a Hong Kong visa for Bug. Since he was broke, I didn't have any choice but to lend him some money, although I didn't expect that he'd be able to pay me back. That was when the reality of AIDS finally sank in. I was certain that my dear friend Bug had AIDS. I thought about how his sparkling Chinese eyes would soon be dull, about how his long, beautiful hair would be shaved off, leaving him bald. I thought about how his fingers would bleed when he played guitar, about how this talented guitar player was going to die of AIDS, and about the fact that he'd always dreamed of making his own record. I thought about how I'd never have to worry about his coming over and messing up my place anymore, or eating all my food, and as I walked down the street, I thought about how Bug wasn't going to be bouncing along beside me anymore. I thought about all of the things we would have to face in the future, but how could we face them? We'd been left empty-handed. Sometimes I would break into tears and I wouldn't be able to stop. It could happen anywhere, and I could be doing anything. If I thought about it, I would start to cry in fitful, choking sobs, and sometimes I cried so hard I couldn't breathe.

I got Xiaochun to spend a lot of time with us. I was afraid of the night, afraid of the day, afraid of thinking, because whenever my thoughts turned to this close companion of mine and how he was about to slide into a pitch-black hole where he couldn't feel the ground beneath his feet, my every breath became fraught with a sense of crisis. Xiaochun was sitting with me. She said, Everyone has his own fate. If heaven wants to take him away, that means his time has come. Maybe it's because he doesn't really want to grow old. You know how he's always been so innocent, so pretty. Have you ever tried to imagine what he might look like when he gets older?

I hadn't. But that's nothing more than guesswork anyway. Finally she said, Here's what I think we should do. First, let's have him get checked for ordinary diseases by, say, an internist and a dermatologist. I said, No. I don't want to put him through all that. If he's going to die, I want him to die a beautiful death. Xiaochun said, Nobody knows for sure if he's really sick, right? He needs to see a doctor. I said, His Hong Kong visa is going to be ready any day now. It'll be better if he gets checked out in Hong Kong.

Xiaohua had stopped calling, so I called her up. I said, When something as serious as this happens to a friend, you're supposed to show even more concern for him than usual. Xiaohua said, I need to know the results of his examinations. It's confusing for me, not knowing what he has. I don't know how to treat him. If you need money, I can give you as much as you need. But please don't come over to my house. I can't have him touching my things.

I said, What if he is sick? Do you think you're going to get infected just by talking to him? Do you think if he touches your things you're going to get infected? You two are close friends.

Xiaohua said, It has nothing to do with whether or not we're good friends. The point is that you're going to go get him checked out. You want to know if it's AIDS. Now, one of the early symptoms of AIDS is hepatitis, and hepatitis is supercontagious. I can't afford to get hepatitis. I need to work.

I said, Hepatitis? Who the hell told you that? How can you think about yourself at a time like this? You should be thinking about him!

Xiaohua said, Why don't you mind your own business? It's not as if we aren't doing anything for him.

This conversation felt like a death sentence. Once again we felt it had been confirmed beyond any doubt: Bug clearly had AIDS. And the worst thing was that when I was making the call, I'd accidentally pressed the speakerphone button, so that Bug had heard every word Xiaohua said. Bug looked stricken. He said to me, Take me to the hospital. That's where I belong. And then he started to cry. I'd never seen him sob like that before, and I was struck by how ugly my cute, gangly Big Bird of a sweet-voiced pal looked when he cried. He was shaking all over, and his entire face was twisted into a knot, and I felt acutely uncomfortable. I was used to looking at a pretty face.

I said, Would you stop complaining! Nobody else is complaining.

Bug said, I'm not complaining. My past has caught up with me. But why did it have to happen to me?

I said, Just stop crying, OK? If you die, my life will be over too. I'm your bosom buddy. We're always hanging out together, and aside from the fact that you never told me you didn't use condoms, we didn't have any secrets. Anyway, I've lived long enough. I mean, I don't think I'll be able to get used to not having you around. We're going to have to die together.

Bug said, You've answered my prayers. But if you don't die with me, I'll end up like that girl in *Rouge* and I'll come back to find you.

I said, It's a deal.

At the same time, though, I wondered what my mother would do. How she would feel if I went through with it? My dad was really strong, but would my mom be able to manage? Just thinking about losing my friend had plunged me into depression, and if that could make me feel this sad, how would my mother feel without me? I couldn't bear to think about it. I remembered something my mother had said to me when I was back in rehab: If I thought it would ease even a little bit of your pain, I would gladly give my life. I wondered if I was really willing to die for Bug. I didn't know. I only knew that I didn't want anybody to get AIDS. Not anybody.

Xiaohua called up to say she wanted to pay my way so that I could go to Hong Kong with Bug. She said, Think about it. We can't let him go off on such terrifying business all by himself. He'd probably crash his car as soon as he found out his results. But then

Xiaochun said, I don't want you to take this wrong, but I mean, if he really does have it, it would be better for him if he did what Xiaohua just mentioned! When we talked about AIDS, we never actually used the word. It was as though we were afraid even to mention it, and so we always said things like "has it" or "doesn't have it."

Bug said, I don't want Xiaohua's help. He said he didn't want to see her, because whenever one of her friends got into dire straits, she treated it like a math problem; it was just about numbers. What he really needed now was his friends and his mother, because when he went to bed each night, he never knew where he was going to be when he woke up. He knew it was stupid for him to think this way — things wouldn't happen that fast — but he couldn't help worrying. He said, You can't understand what it's like unless you've been there. Words just can't describe it. He said, I don't need any drugs anymore. I feel high every day. And I've concluded that I'm an idiot, because there are so many things that I don't understand. I feel as blissfully ignorant as that little dog of yours.

Sometimes Bug was able to forget all about it. He would preen in front of the mirror, just as he always had, and he'd sing and play guitar. But these were the times that left me feeling the most despair. I thought that since I was his best friend, it was my responsibility to make arrangements for him to go get tested. But I also had to think about what I was going to do if he turned out to be positive.

I felt I had to find a way to help him record his own album. He'd always wanted to turn "Surrounded on All Sides," the general's

swan song from *Farewell My Concubine,* into a rock opera, and he'd
even lined up most of the instruments. He could play drums, guitar,
and bass, and we had *pipa* players too. The only studio that Bug had
ever set foot in was the one I had at home. Saining had set up a
recording studio in my apartment, but I was sure it wasn't well-
enough equipped for a project like "Surrounded on All Sides."

I got in touch with Xiao'er. Xiao'er had a pretty decent recording studio of his own, and even though he was a lousy recording
engineer, he was a great guy. When I told him solemnly that Bug
was terminally ill and that we all had to help him, the first thing he
said was, Is it AIDS? I said, What makes you think that? He said,
The crowd you hang out with is pretty high risk, y'know? I said,
Will you help him or not? He said, As long as the studio is free, it's
all the same to me. The only thing is that making recordings isn't
easy, y'know? I said, What are you trying to say? Are you going to
help or not? He said, What I'm trying to say is this: Are you trying to kill him? How can you think about music at a time like this?
You ought to be thinking about getting him treated. Or sending
him overseas and marrying him off to a foreigner so that he can
get foreign residence and get cured over there. That's what you
should be thinking about. If you were sick, would you sit around
dreaming about making fucking records? You must be out of your
mind! Out of your fucking mind. At one point I thought I had
AIDS, and I just wanted to go away to a beautiful little island
somewhere and wait to die. But later on I found out I wasn't sick
after all. I said, How did you know you didn't have it? He said, It
turned out I had an allergy that made me break out in a rash.
That's all it was. It was easy to treat, and it definitely wasn't AIDS.

What Xiao'er said made sense to me, and I started racking my brains trying to think of ways to get Bug out of the country, but how could we do it without money? We couldn't even afford to buy new CDs, so how were we going to go overseas? It occurred to me that maybe I should do something with the stories I'd written. I'd never thought about making a lot of money off my writing, but the time had come to start thinking about it. I'd gone over all kinds of possibilities, and the most you could make from a story was a thousand *yuan,* and after a book came out, it was only good for a few thousand more because it would soon be pirated. In my entire life, I'd written only a dozen or so stories, and I couldn't possibly write a dozen more in a short time just to cure Bug. I couldn't crank them out like that. In short, we couldn't afford to go overseas.

We didn't have money now, and we never had any money. I bought all my lingerie on Huating Road, where you could buy cheap but pretty things and counterfeit designer clothes. I bought thongs and bikinis two for ten *yuan,* but on me they looked like fifty *yuan.* I had a knack for it.

It was these thoughts that emboldened me. A friend of mine once said that people who don't have shoes aren't afraid of the well-heeled, and I saw a lot of wisdom in this. We'd grown up on movies from the Soviet Union and North Korea, but now we listened to music from England and sat in our kitchens eating instant noodles, wondering if we had AIDS. We smoked marijuana from Xinjiang, popped three-*yuan*-a-bottle pills, and once we got high, we could listen to punk rock and tell ourselves it was a rave. What did we care? We were so sick of waiting. Sometimes if we waited around long enough there would be some E for us, and you couldn't waste free drugs. After eating E, I felt euphoric, and it reminded me of a line from "Howl." But that doesn't mean that Allen Ginsberg and I have anything in common, much less that I understand him.

Never forget who you are (even if you end up having a lot of money someday). This is very important. We're poor, so at least we can't stand around in record stores, chewing gum and picking out whatever records we want. A lot of those records would drive us crazy, anyway. Remember this: always stand in a poor man's shoes, because if you do, you'll always be yourself. And keep those bourgeois like Saining and Xiaohua far away from us! We're not like them at all!

Of course, I still have to go to Saining to borrow money, although I've never actually returned any of the money I've "borrowed" from him. This time, I'm going to need more than usual. I have to go to the limit for Bug's AIDS.

I'm also afraid of hepatitis. I think I can stand the thought of dying, but I've never wanted to get hepatitis. It got so that I became afraid to go to anyone's house because I was worried that I had hepatitis.

Apple gave us the name of an AIDS specialist in Beijing. He said, You can call him directly. So I called him immediately, and, using a false name, I described Bug's situation. Bug was squatting down next to me, and he kept his eyes fixed on me the whole time. The doctor said that from the sound of it, Bug was probably HIV-negative, but he said that Bug might have leukemia or possibly syphilis. The doctor said, If he does have AIDS, then his present symptoms suggest that he would have been infected at least five years ago.

I hastily wrote down "syphilis or leukemia" on a piece of paper, and I held it up for Bug to read. Bug's face lit up as if he'd just had some kind of epiphany. The doctor said that he would still have to go to the hospital and be examined. I said, We're afraid of being arrested. The doctor said, That's ridiculous. Come to Beijing, and come to my hospital. Everyone who comes to me is an AIDS patient. They're just like anyone else who's ill: they have a disease. I said, Is it really safe? He said, Of course it is. You can trust me on this. Your friend won't be arrested.

After I hung up, we collapsed on the bed. I said, Fuck! There was never any danger of your being arrested. That Xiaochun is a real piece of work. Then I said, If you have syphilis, how come you're so healthy?

I called up Xiaochun, and I said, You're really something! People don't get thrown in jail for that. But you almost scared him to death; do you realize that? Xiaochun said, I saw a documentary where that happened, and if you looked at the people in our crowd, you'd realize that anyone who's ever gotten AIDS has been hauled away. Anyone could have made the same mistake I did. But I guess this time I was wrong.

It was too good to be true. Leukemia was scary, but at least Bug would be spared the extra psychological torment. We decided to go get Bug tested straightaway and made an appointment with a specialist in STDs at Huashan Hospital.

That evening, when I was going to the bathroom, some liquid splashed up onto my vulva. I figured that it was probably full of deadly bacteria, so I decided to disinfect myself with Dettol. It worked on cuts, so I figured it would be good enough. I pulled up my pants and started hunting for the Dettol, cursing all the while: You and your stupid Mr. Syphilis, look what you've done to me. AIDS, hepatitis, syphilis! Bug said, What are you doing in there? I said, I'm looking for the Dettol so that I can disinfect my private parts where the water from the toilet got me all filthy. Bug said, For God's sake, don't use Dettol on yourself! If you use that stuff, you're gonna have the face of an eighteen-year-old and the genitals of an eighty-year-old! It'll turn them black. It has the same effect on women and men. He said he learned this from a hooker, whom he referred to as a chicken. I said, What? You fuck prostitutes? He said, What's wrong with that? They're a lot more genuine than you writers! I said, Fuck you! What's wrong with writers? He said, Don't go getting angry at me. I was just giving you an honest opinion, but I could be wrong.

The next morning, I helped Bug find some sweatpants and a sweatshirt. I told him, Put these on, and we'll get a hat to hide your hair. Don't worry; I'll talk to the doctors for you. You don't have to say a word.

We arrived at Huashan Hospital. The Department of Venereal Diseases was full of zigzagging corridors. The large rooms had been divided into lots of smaller rooms, and the little rooms in turn defined a network of twisting and turning passageways. Bug and I got dizzy from going around so many corners, and we lost track of each other and had to call out each other's names. The more I called, the more hopeless I felt. We'd finally made it to the place where Bug could get tested for AIDS, only to lose each other.

At last the two of us found the room where AIDS testing took place. I saw several girls there getting their blood drawn, and a nurse asked me, Is your friend a man or a woman? I said, A man.

She asked me who I was, and I told her I was his sister. I said, He's been overseas, and he's been careless. I thought he should come in and get checked out. I forced myself to speak loudly in an effort to conceal my panic.

The doctor said, What do you want him to get tested for? I said, He has diarrhea and a fever. The doctor said, I see. You want him checked for HIV, right? I said, Can you test him for syphilis too? The doctor glanced at Bug, who sat facing him with an idiotic grin on his face. The doctor gave me the bill, and while I was going to pay, I couldn't stop worrying that I didn't have enough money. Even though I'd borrowed a thick wad of bills, I was still afraid it wasn't going to be enough. That's how it is when you're poor. I said to myself, We're here; we've finally made it. Please, please don't let me get caught short. In the end, the total bill came to only seventy-two *yuan*, and I wondered why it had cost eighty in the rehab clinic.

Before they drew his blood, Bug had to fill out a form with detailed personal information. The nurse said, Don't worry; the form is just to help with the diagnosis. There was a question on the form that Bug didn't know how to answer: What kinds of sexual acts have you engaged in? Bug looked at me and said, How am I supposed to answer that? Don't ask me, I said. He said, Then I'll just write that I haven't. I said, What do you mean, you haven't? Are you a virgin? You can't be that stupid! I was talking too loudly, and everyone in the room turned to look at me and then at Bug. He lowered his head as if he was giving the question some considera- tion, and then he wrote: "Heterosexual, never used a condom."

The future hung in the balance, a mystery we could never touch. We waited for the report, and I held Bug's hand, saying, Don't worry. If something is wrong, you're so young and so beautiful that it wouldn't be so bad to die now. We can all learn from you. Bug said, If there really is something wrong with me, please promise me one thing. I said, What? He said, I want to tell you the story of my life, from childhood to adulthood. I want to tell you about my experiences and my impressions, and I want you to write it all down and turn it into a book. And give any money from the book to my mom, OK? Because I don't have anything to give her. Don't feel sad for me. At least I can die in my own country. I wouldn't want to leave China.

The results came back quickly. Bug didn't have syphilis, and he didn't have AIDS. I couldn't believe it. I said, Can you run these tests again? The doctor said, If he didn't do anything bad, why are you so frantic? We use a rapid test, but if there had been anything there, we would have picked it up. This is one of the best hospitals in the country, and if you don't trust our results, there's nothing I can do for you. I said, I'm sorry. It's not that I don't believe you; it's just that I'm still worried. Do you think he's healthy? I asked. Can you examine him some more, run some more tests? The doctor said, All right! Come with me. As I followed Bug and the doctor into a small room, the nurse shouted out behind me, Where do you think you're going? I said, I'm his sister. She said, Even his sister can't go in there with him. He's being examined for STDs.

The doctor and Bug came out soon after, and the doctor said, He's fine. There's nothing wrong with him.

I still couldn't believe it. Bug and I stood there staring at the VCR, watching information programs about all kinds of STDs. We saw red genitals, yellow genitals, and black genitals, and I found myself thinking that even if I didn't care about this stuff right now, it was still worth my while to look at it. Looking didn't hurt.

We asked the doctor, So, what do you think is causing his symptoms? The doctor said, He'll have to see an internist. We can run some more tests on the blood we drew, and we can let you know in three weeks if anything turned up.

We went to Internal Medicine, and they drew some more blood. The doctor there said, There's nothing wrong with him.

We walked out of the hospital in a daze. We felt as if we were floating between heaven and earth, but I was still wondering: Did we still need to disinfect our apartment?

As soon as we got home, we phoned the specialist in Beijing, who told us that we could absolutely trust the results of tests from Huashan Hospital. He said that there are instruments that are used to get quick lab results. He said, China takes AIDS very seriously. We don't fool around with things like that. I thought, Seriously, my ass! We had to go all over the place before we could find a hospital where he could even get tested.

The next day, Bug's swollen lymph glands suddenly went down, and his temperature was back to normal. I thought the whole thing was too hysterical.

But the cause of Bug's illness remained a mystery to us.

Then Xiaochun asked pointedly, Has it ever occurred to you that it might have something to do with those three-*yuan*-a-bottle pills? There might be something wrong with Bug's nervous system, or maybe he's just extremely sensitive to certain chemicals.

We dropped everything and rushed over to the pharmacy to buy some of those pills. Bug, I said, take a few of these. Let's see what happens.

Sure enough, all of his symptoms came right back.

We'd finally got to the bottom of it. Why hadn't we thought of that sooner?

Xiaochun said, God was testing your friendship. It was a warning from God. That's the only possible explanation.

I said, It's like some kind of sick joke. How could we have been so blind? We had such one-track minds. I can't believe we were so fixated on AIDS!

I thought about all the days I'd had to put ice packs on my eyes because they were so swollen from crying. We'd gone through such torture, spending every hour of the day trying to figure out how to borrow money from everyone we knew.

Xiaochun said, It was God's way of waking us up.

This particular AIDS scare was over, but the nightmare of AIDS hadn't been banished from our lives. Far from it.

Xiao'er had been petrified and he'd told a good friend of his. He said he'd just wanted to get all of his fears out in the open, but this good friend had told everyone in town. Everyone knew about it, but nobody bothered to ask us about it or to express any kind of genuine concern for Bug. Instead, the story kept making the rounds, and the more it circulated, the more outlandish it became.

I had a strong desire to take copies of Bug's lab report and plaster them all over town.

But in the end, Bug decided to tack the report up by his bed, as a reminder to himself to be more careful.

Whenever anyone asked me how Bug was doing lately, I would always answer, Why do you ask? Have you heard something?

Xiaohua still didn't trust Chinese hospitals, and she said she still wanted to pay our way to Hong Kong so that Bug could get tested there. She never stopped offering, and every time I ran into her, she would always say the same thing.

Bug had changed. He pasted up slogans like this on the wall of his room: "Treat your friends as gently as the spring, and treat your enemies with the harshness of winter — Lei Feng."

I said, That Lei Feng was pretty amazing. There's a lot of truth in that.

Even Bug's guitar playing seemed to have taken on a new tone. He said, Being a good person is a complicated thing. I've finally come to understand this, but I wish I didn't. I've been trying to avoid people as best I can, so I go out as little as possible.

We returned our Hong Kong plane tickets, but I was still broke.

Since he'd thought he was going to die soon, that bastard Bug had made a ton of overseas phone calls to his lover in the Netherlands. He'd run up a six-thousand-*yuan* phone bill, and he promised to pay me back, now that he understood the importance of money.

I told him sternly, I understand what you were going through. The trouble that you brought on yourself with chemicals, and the panic that consumed you because of sex, all revealed that people who call themselves friends don't always feel that close to you. But we aren't friends; we're family, you and I. You mustn't forget any of what happened. And remember the mistakes you made.

I had faith that he was going to repay me the money he owed me, but what was I going to do in the meantime? My dad had given me that money to live on. In the past week alone, three pairs of my pants had fallen apart. The crotch tore on one pair, the zipper got stuck open on a second pair, and a third pair was ruined when I was disinfecting my bathroom and splashed disinfectant on them, which destroyed the color. Whenever I was broke, my thoughts turned to my teeth. Three of my teeth were missing, and I was afraid that if I didn't get them replaced all of my teeth would become loose. I'd run out of cleansing cream for my face, and my electricity bill had come. It was for six months' worth of electricity, and if I didn't pay it on time, I was going to end up like Mozart, writing by candlelight.

I sat on my bed, wishing I could just grow old now! If I were old, at least I wouldn't have to worry about my teeth, or new pants, or cleansing cream anymore.

As luck would have it, Saining came back. Saining and I were both nearly thirty years old, but we were still living off other people's money, just as we always had. It was a scary thought.

Saining said he could cover all of the bills, and he also offered to buy me some new pants and cleansing cream. Thank God, he'd rescued me again. Saining said, You have to tell Bug to get himself tested regularly, like me. I get myself checked twice a year. We should all do that. You too.

I said, You're absolutely right. But what's this about your getting tested twice a year — is there something you haven't told me?

O

I.

Every weekend is the same to me. The locations change, but it's still the same old bullshit. Shanghai nightlife is hopeless. But we go out on weekends anyway. Weekend nights are like a stage, and we're the performers, only we've started to forget our lines. We wander down South Maoming Road, thinking we'll go barhopping. Groove is gone, permanently shut down, and in its place there's a teahouse. YY's is empty, and with no one there, we don't want to be there either. We're hopelessly boring, ourselves. DD's has moved, and it's completely changed. DKD is still pretty good. But could a little place run by purists really survive in Shanghai? There's always DKD, but it's too dark inside, and we're reluctant to spend a long time in a place that's so dark. Maybe a fantastic new club owner is about to be born. But for now, all we have is the phoniness of South Maoming Road. There is one other kind of club — the places where "head-rockers" go. Green CUs, yellow CKs, red Ps, green Ps, pink JJs, white Mitsubishis, green butterflies, oblong CCs, those scary K-holes. Drugs are like vacations. Sometimes they're good, and sometimes they're bad. Some people remember the good times, but I always remember the bad times.

2.

She walks beside me in a red overcoat, something unfocused about her expression. When the cold descended, all of our combined umbrellas, gloves, and scarves couldn't bring us enough warmth, so we went out looking for whatever little bit of fun might materialize. I imagined how, when that little bit of joy slowly began to spread, the space between my feet would grow wider. And there would be a passage leading me to this place and lending me an absolute balance. But certainty is always found south of the South. It's already time for counting sheep as we walk along this street. We can buy some scotch to drink at home, but she says, If we do that, we'll turn into a couple of drunks again. I say, We can't be drunks anymore. But she said, Oh yes, we can. Which is why when we feel like drinking, we need to go out.

3.

The lights on this street are so bourgeois. Withered parasol trees transform the lights into countless little black spots that tremble before my eyes. When I'm drunk, I only need one of my eyes. I listen to his breathing. He came back, but nothing else came back with him. He can't control the weather, and in the night his hands find my breasts, but that nameless joy has already vanished without a trace. And memory is like two pieces of glass placed on a dusky nose bridge.

4.

Terror and joy have bred a dangerous lifestyle, and we are doomed to suffer bizarre deaths. She says, We're still young. She says, Everything will turn out fine. I like hearing this. She always brings me hope. I don't know if she's still worrying about trying to solve her "writer's problem." I know that changing ourselves is always a headache; we can't completely escape who we are. I don't know why people always have to get themselves all worked up about things. You should just be happy in your work, although I think it's also important to give some thought to what lies ahead. She might say that I think too far into the future, but you can't wait until the last minute to fix your problems. But there are still some mysteries I don't understand. We've heard the story of how three fools together made one wise man, but the truth is that in the end their efforts were wasted. Some people say that when this world comes to an end, everyone will find his own way out, but in any case I'm going to keep trying to understand this transformation into a "writer." If I make any progress, I'll let her know.

5.

Moonlight sets the road atilt. Our luck is holding. We can see the moon, and we can see that there will always be hope for the children of the moon. Sometimes we see a huge billboard, and it directs us to the next whiskey bar: Manhattan. A place where foreign men and longhaired Shanghai girls come to pick one another up. I think I'd rather go to Goya. The moody woman who ran the place was a bit nasty, and the chemical music there inspired fantasies. When you'd had just about enough to drink, she was sure to give you drinks on the house. In other words, she liked to see you stumble out of the place blind-drunk. But drinking till you're falling-down drunk is a waste of time. Goya is a dangerous place, and new kinds of dangers are constantly proliferating there. And now even that proprietress is gone. Interesting people never stay in Shanghai for long, or maybe it's just that the longer they stay, the stupider and uglier they become. The woman who ran Goya went to Beijing, and she says that now just thinking of Shanghai makes her want to throw up. I think that the problem is hers, not Shanghai's. Shanghai at night is like a beautiful but frigid woman. My Shanghai is always grieving; it's a city without men. On the way from one party to yet another party, riding in a taxi, we talk about men: as soon as men get hard, they get stupid. Hard men are softhearted, and soft men are hard-hearted. We're unhappy all the time. The only genuine moments we experience at clubs are when we go to the toilet. In other words, the most trivial thing is the most real. Whatever you say.

6.

Her gravelly laugh is warm and freewheeling. How I want to find a new place so we can have another drink! We're tasting the same old ennui, as if we were living on the last day of the world. As I watch that guy pacing back and forth over there, I feel certain he's not there because of some woman. From the looks of him, I'd say he's looking for drugs. Because we've been there ourselves. We too used to spend the whole week waiting for Friday. On Friday we'd go out looking for drugs, and once we got them, we took them right away. And we'd feel happy, and then we'd wax sentimental, and after that we'd talk about nothing, and then we'd come down. On the way home we'd start to feel afraid, and when we got home, the sounds we heard inside our ears left us speechless. For the next three days we'd tell everyone we saw that we'd never take drugs again. We weren't going to touch any of it, ever again. I mean, when did it all start — that whenever you ran into someone, you'd ask them, What colors have you eaten lately? I don't want to take any more drugs unless there's a really big party. This town is all wrong. It's no fun. I want my violin. But I still have to pass through the next whiskey bar before I can go home. My violin is at home waiting for me. A cuckoo clock echoes, and an indescribable fragrance encircles me. When my torments have come to an end, it will be just me and my violin. But first I have to say good night to this lady in red. Good night. And so ends another day.

7.

One day I lost faith in myself. I didn't understand my body or its mood swings, and I was always making a complete mess of things. What lessons does life hold for us? By all rights, this man ought to vanish into my embrace in some impossibly beautiful way. It's been ten years, and that's what he should do, but there's no way to slash open this black sky, and extremely beautiful ways of doing things have always been difficult to find. The city is growing up, and we're growing up with it. Standards are constantly changing. There's a car in front of us, and another car behind us, and the people in both of these cars have taken head-rocking pills. I don't know if they've been listening to music, because the cars are taxis. Is it even possible for people to bob their heads without that head-rocking music? Left, right, right, left, the left side has forgotten all about the right side, and that old guy has taken off his jacket, and he's rocking his head back and forth. He's naked — we can even see his fat belly. He has such an ordinary face, so he must have some dirty secrets. I bet he's committed some serious transgressions in his life. Maybe, starting in childhood, everyone does the same things, which is why everyone wants to stick together now, more than ever. In this age of vast and sweeping changes, in this fucked-up head-rocking culture, we don't have any tomorrow. They shake their heads; I shake my ass. We're all the same. So I've sworn off all drugs. I just drink vodka and tonic. And when I go out, I feel compelled to drink until I'm totally fucked up before I can go home — even if I end up drinking myself to death in some wretched little bar.

8.

Maybe the process we're engaged in counts as some kind of progress. Maybe things are about to start looking up. A pair of big shoes tromping down the street like a couple of mountain goats. Everything is moving forward, toward another world. This poor girl, she's never been abroad. I have to take her somewhere beautiful, where there are animals, and music, and friends, and a bed, and the purest drugs. When we look out at those mountains and rivers, conceptions of purity will come to us as a matter of course. We have to go away. She said we had to find the way to the nearest whiskey bar.

9.

Maybe you think that there's something wrong with my language, but problematic situations are the most worthy of analysis. All I want is for the two of us to find a sign, some newly created symbol. Or maybe what I want is to let myself go with you. Let's just let ourselves go! That's an exciting thought. Every time I hit the street, I feel as though I've lost everything and that I'm about to be reborn. And here we are, back on the street, "troubled youths" who grew up on the street. But what is "youth culture" anyway? We're looking for a sign, but this street can't give us an answer. It never could.

10.

We need to give ourselves a dream, an entirely new dream. Her fingers are on the keyboard in a dull-witted and hopeless search. Blindness has guided our blood all along, and my patience is gradually spilling over. I'm mixed up; I know that the grass is always greener on the other side, and maybe that's nothing more than a street corner. She just keeps on typing, tirelessly, gently striking the keyboard. Floating on Shanghai's sweet water lilies because the leaves have all been eaten by frogs. Toes are sinking deep into the mud, and it has everything to do with her. Where will she go at the end of 1999? That frog has gone crazy tonight, leaping free and out of the line of sight. Tonight is my best chance to lock myself up.

11.

There are always bits of news flapping along the street on the
evening breeze. This never fails to remind me of the bad things
I've done. This little bird that only knows how to sing, her innocence flickering in and out of view, her dull eyes shot with anxiety.
She suddenly says, I will always love you. She says, If I give up
this right, then even the little bit of sweetness that remains will also
disappear. I know that there are things that have left her feeling
confused, just as I've always felt confused. A cat rolls off the win-
dowsill, its eyes moving, like a big stack of data. People walk by,
and we'll never see them again. Life has always been this way.

12.

Night comes to my spirit. When a tattered cloud causes me to lose
my vision, when my fingers touch my violin but have no strength,
she will take away all of her clothing. She's always been this way:
She told me a bunch of pure stories and turned me inside out, but
I didn't even realize it. She made me believe that if I stood by her, I
wouldn't need heaven's holy waters anymore. This was how she
made a fool of me, but I think she's just as mixed up as I am. I feel
like this confusion will never end. We've dragged ourselves ashore,
and while we're nostalgic for the pain of the past, our bodies no
longer supply us with the necessary breath. It's hard to respond in
a situation like this. Of course there are other problems, like the
fact that people have begun calling her a writer. Like the fact that
our finances are getting shaky. Like the fact that she often goes out
to pick up men. I haven't been seeing any other women, and I

haven't become a writer, either, but we carry in our hearts the same terror — I know it. But what I'm really trying to say here is this: I'm all mixed up.

13.

There's another kind of music here that we can breathe. Little insects, little plants, filthy air, arrogant cars, enticing boulevards, houses with stories to tell — we have an unspoken understanding. This is our music for tonight. The ears that can hear this music have been opened by this man. But he stole all my shoes. My shoes were the eyes of the night, and now the night has no eyes. His curving, mobile lips can no longer bear witness to the worlds of my dreams. So why are we still together? Because we don't have anything else. Isn't that right? This is a mistake that anyone could have made.

14.

She said she wanted some ice cream. We walked into the super-market, and she rushed to open up the freezer. She looked over all the cartons until she finally picked out a brand she really didn't like. Neither of us liked that brand, but she said, It's cheap, and it doesn't taste too bad either. I said, You can pick out something you actually like. No! she insisted. I want this one. In the past, as long as she had enough money in her pockets, she would never have bought a brand of ice cream she didn't like. She used to think of herself as a rich girl who was just temporarily out of money, but only last week she began to realize that she was poor. She said the truth was that she'd always been poor, and she told me that this knowledge had given her a new perspective and that she was going to have to change her lifestyle as a consequence. No wonder she felt compelled to pick out a kind of ice cream that she didn't even like. In any event, she'd got me all mixed up again. She told me that she despised intellectuals, but it seemed to me that she was becoming more of an intellectual herself all the time.

15.

He suggested that we buy some whiskey to drink at home, but I said, Tonight we're going out to drink. He said, But what if we can't find an interesting spot? I said, If I were you, I wouldn't expect too much. But I want to find a bar tonight, even if it kills me. He laughed. He started calling me sweetheart. Whenever he calls me sweetheart, I get thrown off balance. It makes me think that when other people call me baby, they don't really mean it. I think that this is love.

16.

She came to understand even more completely that nothing was going to happen. Because we both knew it, the Shanghai nights no longer belonged to us. Because we'd grown up and had had some wonderful nights out together, we were getting harder and harder to please. So why did we still want to go out? Where could we go? Seeing all of those head-rockers had given her a fear of the dark. Of course, there were plenty of people who took drugs and didn't loll their heads around, and they were happy; but whenever she popped one of those pills, she started thinking about those head-rockers, and she was afraid. She was constantly on edge, fearful that she might accidentally hear a snatch of head-rocking music as she browsed in a store. And because she was also afraid of the dark, she couldn't stay for long in a dark room, and at night she had to sleep with the lights on. Every day we swore we were going to quit taking drugs. We hated trendiness, and we still felt a need to put on a show of being cool. But the truth was that the streets were full of happy people and she was simply being much too neurotic — because the streets should be full of happy people. The desert inside a glass of alcohol crumbles ahead of us, and my nerves are scattered to the winds. We need to think of some way to have a party somewhere outdoors. How I want to see mountains, rivers, sunshine, and ruined fortresses! Let the wind course over us until we become beautiful. A lot of world-class DJs have come to Shanghai, but they haven't changed a thing. We have to have our own party. She's DJ No Mix, and I'm DJ Good Music, and we'll play some nice hard house. We'll get China's youth to dance and wave their arms in the beautiful outdoors.

17.

He said that we could buy a bottle of Black Label and drink it under a tree, just as in the old days. I said, We've already drunk beneath the trees. We should find someplace new. He said, Has it ever crossed your mind that we don't have to drink? Seriously, we don't have to drink. Like right now, you're eating ice cream. Therefore, I conclude that drinking isn't strictly necessary. I said, Please shut up. Or else think of a way to get me to shut up. Let's talk about not talking.

18.

I love all the service workers in this town. They're the prettiest anywhere. There's one girl I absolutely adore, the provincial girl who washes my hair. She lets her gentle fingertips roam around my head just so she can earn a few coins. And then there's the woman beside me. One day she wore all black, from the inside out and from head to toe. Except for her socks. They had a multicolored print on a white background. She always made it easy for me to find her flaws. I think about how she was, ten years ago, when she was a virgin, and how she didn't know where to put her legs. She was a cookie laced with poison. Dressed in a borrowed overcoat, she slept beside me in the early morning. We gazed at each other, and I thought it was love.

19.

A nine-headed bird is circling in my head, descending, descending, descending. This is how I fall into depression. He wants me to see a psychiatrist. I say, I despise bourgeois charades. Sinking down, down, down. I have sunk into a depression. I think that the music at my funeral should be that song by Teresa Teng that goes, "If flowing water can look back, / Please, take me with you."

20.

Every day when he wakes up, he takes a shit. Then he bathes, and then he combs his hair, and then he has some coffee. All day long, caffeine courses through his clean body. He's so beautiful (I say he's beautiful because I love him, I suppose). He lightly touches the coffee foam to his lips, and one of his eyes is swollen. It's like that every day. I want to make him disappear, and he knows it. He's a useless diamond. I can't explain his radiance. But I can't say no to him, because neither of us has anything else.

21.

We went to YY's, and I rolled a joint, but she doesn't even smoke grass anymore. She says that even one puff makes her emotionally hypersensitive, and her thoughts run away from her. I say, If you smoke just a little more, you won't feel afraid anymore. She says, When I smoke too much, I get close to the truth. I'm afraid. I said, What is Truth? Do you think it's that easy to get close to the truth? Rolling a joint, now that's Truth. Cocoa came in. He played the piano and sang "Good-Bye, My Love." Last year there always used to be a group of people who didn't want to leave, and just as it was about to get light, Kenny, the boss, would say, Coffee, tea, or me? But now we're in a hurry to get back out to the street. Kenny says, Shanghai is *fadaga*. Shanghai is over.

22.

Without the warmth of the sun, how can we play our music? And if we can't see the moon, how can we keep this strangeness under control? The moonlight is well versed in the art of the caress. It lingers over her body, illuminating her interior structure. A lock of hair still hangs over her forehead. We'll press our black lips too close to the street, but whose creation is this? I cried. I love her. I can't stop thinking about it. Looking at her breasts, I'm at a loss for words. I don't even belong to myself. But I imagine that we've embarked on some kind of task and that we're making progress. One day I'll kiss her, and it will be like falling in love for the first time. Or perhaps sometime before we die, we're destined to meet that someone again. Life is more mysterious than we can imagine. And then again, maybe we should just drop everything and go engage in some hard physical labor. Her father says labor makes people strong.

23.

A dark red sky — already it has the luster of velvet. Beloved brothers, beloved sisters: we are defeated, and the whole world knows it.

After Saining came back from Japan, he didn't fall back into his old slacker ways. Instead he moved his book-and-record store from Beijing to Shanghai. The store was full of his paintings and the records he'd collected, and customers could come to the store to read, drink tea, and listen to music. Although the store didn't make any money, it didn't lose money either. But arranging for licenses and moving around like that did burn up a lot of cash. He couldn't just pick up and go whenever he pleased anymore. He had to watch his money.

It's 1999, and we still share a bed every night, and we share a headset as we drift off to sleep. Occasionally he masturbates in the morning, while looking at a cartoon drawing of a Japanese middle school girl. He calls her his girlfriend. This is what he tells me, anyway. I've never actually seen it.

My writing has placed me in an extremely messy and confusing situation. I'm hot right now, but not because of my writing. All I did was write about a bunch of kids from a socialist country who took a lot of drugs, but God only knows what was really in the stuff they took, because they didn't get off at all. Instead they were totally fucked up. Our idiotic drug experiences were completely determined by our education. Our minds were empty, but drugs couldn't give us imagination. We didn't know what it was to feel pleasure, so all we had was our collective destruction. I am the one who has written these stories, but everything that is to come will seem like an even more pointless ritual. A lot of crazy things have happened. This world is full of con artists and charlatans. It's a pathetic, materialistic age, and I've been asking myself, Why do you want to write?

I've begun planning all kinds of huge dance parties. I want to see a thousand lonely strangers dancing happily at my party. This feels more real to me than writing, because I think that the Chinese people need to dance — they need to open up their bodies. I want to make everyone dance, and if they won't dance, I'll trick them into dancing.

On weekend nights, Saining and I are a couple of "hunting buddies." Bearing our common illusions, we always go out together on weekends. After we heard some rumors that police from the provinces were going to raid the clubs and give all the Chinese there urine tests, we were afraid to take E anymore.

But we still get fucked up every Friday and Saturday night, sleeping and not eating all day Sunday, dumbstruck on Monday, sad on Tuesday, better by Wednesday, and starting to think about Friday when Thursday rolls around. Talking a lot of bullshit to Saining after getting fucked up is a lot of fun. Sometimes we play guitar together into the tape recorder. All these random fragments you've just read are something Saining and I created together — that's how they came out on the tape.

P

If you knew my friend Apple, please listen to some Chopin. If you liked him, please don't use a candle to light a cigarette ever again. If you loved him, please leave the door open when you bathe, and let in some fresh air.

It doesn't matter, but he left with a calm expression. It doesn't matter, but soaking in the bathtub was his favorite thing. It doesn't matter, but when he smoked those cheap, lousy cigarettes of his, he would often say, What's the point of worrying? We all have to die sometime.

He once said, Human life is suffering, and once you understand this, you will be completely free.

He once said, If you can love with abandon, then you can relax and stop worrying.

He said, Love should be an incomparable radiance.

Once he'd come to these realizations, he left us. It doesn't matter, but he went in his favorite bathtub. His lover was in another room, talking on the phone, and by the time the two-hour conversation was over, my friend Apple was already in another place. It doesn't matter, but he loved his lover. We know that, and that's enough. Apple was the person who took me to my first café, when a cup of coffee cost five *yuan* in Shanghai. That sidewalk café was called Little Brocade River. Shanghai was like his lover. He took me to so many streets and boulevards. He said that Shanghai's four seasons were so distinct, and that this had always kept his senses sharp. He said, Especially in the winter. In the winter I feel a strange kind of excitement when I'm wandering through the little alleys and lanes. He'd always wanted a comfortable bathtub; the one he had now was his first. The bathroom was too small, but he insisted on putting a child's bathtub in there. The bathroom really was much too small, and there was no ventilation. He didn't die because of fate; he died because of an accident, and he died because of his standard of living. He died in the cold and cloudy Shanghai winter. It's not important, but he was beautiful, and he always had been beautiful. He knew more than any of us about how to enjoy life, and he would walk for hours just to get a good price on some high-quality goods — that's how he was. He died in the first bathtub he'd ever owned. It doesn't matter, but he'd already possessed countless bathtubs — in the magazines he saved, and in his mind. The world is so big, but he never even went to Hong Kong. He always said, I really just want to go abroad to see what it's like. He didn't even have a computer, but it didn't matter, because he had been everywhere and seen everything in his mind, through information he'd come by in every way imaginable, and through his eyes.

I held Apple. His body was full of water. His expression was so peaceful, but I suddenly felt overwhelmed by countless regrets. I felt I hadn't really understood him. The air always carries the scent of souls, a scent that is always sweet, but where do our spirits go in the end? We don't understand death, nor do we understand ourselves. Nor do we understand even our lovers, or our friends of many years — no matter how close we might become, we can never really grasp the truth about one another. We are condemned to solitude, doomed to live in confusion, and nothing we've done so far has been able to resolve our yearning.

Apple once said to me, We should go to Thailand together and go sit at that temple, where we can keep vigil over the body of an eighteen-year-old. We'll watch over his beauty, his youth, and his decay, until finally there is nothing left of him.

Apple once said to me, Life is like a bridge that connects what's gone before with what is to come. Everything will become more pure and precious and ultimately clearer in its own time.

Apple once said to me, As long as there is chaos, there will always be hope for Truth and Beauty. And what's kept us from attaining these things is our bodies.

It doesn't matter, because some people can never really be separated.

There's just one thing, though. What about all of the clothing he picked out with such care, all of the shoes and the jewelry — didn't he want them anymore?

Whenever I think of him, I listen to Chopin. Not that I know whether or not Apple liked Chopin. We never discussed it.

Death gave my friend Apple the wings of an angel, and he'll wear them to all of his friends' banquets.

I didn't go to Apple's funeral. I took him a note instead: "No one can ever take your place, spending time with me, sharing all of my toys with me!"

Apple, we didn't wear black armbands, because wearing black armbands is too conventional, and you'd like us to look pretty.

Apple, I'm glad that I knew you.

Q

I sleep in the ruins, in splinters and ash.
What died was your beauty.
That window on your soul
Changed, became earnestly transparent.
You will never return.
You will never return.
But who says?

— MIAN MIAN

I felt black eyes boring into the back of my head through a part in hair blown about wildly by the wind, and then there was his breathing, rendered harsh by his illness. When I turned around, his last footfall settled like ash before my eyes. Kiwi was wearing a long black leather kilt. It dragged on the floor, looking like a big black fan, the dark fan of the night.

I caught a whiff of Kiwi's cologne, and I touched him, as if my sorrow had lost its strength.

I said, Our Apple is gone! The moon looks like a child's face!

He embraced me, and we went somewhere. I wanted to talk, but he couldn't wait to screw my ass again, and this time the pain touched my heart.

We didn't talk on the phone anymore.

Once, I had wanted to pass all of my craziness and confusion on to this man, which was why I'd desperately wanted to be controlled. Once, I had wanted to be on handbills all over Shanghai with this man. Once, I had yearned for a love that could release me from my weaknesses.

But someone had put a curse in our drinks. We were broken, and we needed surgeons to fix us.

R

Saining went out to the suburbs of Beijing with a pair of scissors and cut a large quantity of marijuana and brought it back here. We sat around every day with our milk shakes while he used a big wicker sieve to pick out the seeds. I'd sit beside him rolling. I would work awhile, smoke a joint, and drink some milk shake. And then I'd work a little more and smoke another joint, and after that, we'd sleep some more. There isn't any nice scenery in this city, but we have music.

Today, Saining made some kind of soup with all kinds of Chinese medicinal herbs in it. After we'd finished our soup, I said, Saining, let's play dueling DJs, OK? I'll put something on upstairs, and you can put something on downstairs. First you play something, and then I'll go, and we can just take it from there. How 'bout it?

And we started to play records. We played records for five hours straight, not stopping for even one minute.

Afterward I went and took a bath. After my bath, I saw that Saining was chatting with someone on the Internet. Can I join you? I asked. Saining introduced me to the other person, and then he said he was going to go take a bath. I waited until he'd come out of the bathroom to say, I don't feel like playing anymore. Saining said, Why? Didn't we agree that we'd talk together? I said, I don't want to play this game. I want to watch a DVD.

Saining came downstairs at once and sat down beside me. I knew from his expression that he was angry, so I turned off the computer and looked at him.

He said, Why do you think this is a game? Don't you realize there's another human being on the other end?

I said, Don't be so serious. I don't think it's a game, either. I was just saying that. I don't want to play this way, because I'm not used to not being able to hear or see the person I'm interacting with.

Saining said, So why do you still use the word *play?*

I said, It was just something I said. I didn't mean anything by it.

Saining said, I don't believe for a second that you just say things, and that's all there is to it.

I said, I apologize. I am truly sorry.

Saining said, I don't need your apology, but I do think that you need to think carefully about what you say.

Saining used to be a beautiful young man — even his anger used to be beautiful in the old days. But nowadays, for some reason, when he got angry I found it hard to take, and it made me sick at heart.

He stayed angry at me for the rest of the evening, and at bedtime I said, Saining, don't be angry. Haven't you always said that I brought you to life in my stories? I'm promising you right now that I'm going to write a book for you. I already know that writing it is going to make me cry, and this isn't something that I just decided to do today. I decided to do this a while ago, and if it doesn't make me cry, I won't publish it, OK? Is that all right with you?

Saining said, Is it about me?

It's about how all the good children will have candy to eat.

Just promise me you won't try to make any money from it.

What do you mean by that?

What I mean is, don't use me to puff yourself up.

Is that all you get out of my writing? Then I've failed.

You *are* a failure. Because you don't tell the truth.

Writing fiction isn't about telling the truth.

Then you're not a writer.

Don't be cruel, Saining. I have to have been wounded before I can commit something to paper. I'm just trying to express myself, and the truth is that nobody is obligated to read the product of other people's self-expression. Writing is simply the thing that gives me the strength to keep on living. It's an exercise that's full of feeling, it's a kind of love, and it's one of the easiest things in the world — and easy things can be liberating. We all live such meager lives, and we may still love people who don't deserve our love. Writing is just something a person might do. There is no absolute truth or falseness, and writing can't guarantee my safety. It's like music is for you, and I can't prove my honesty by going back and inserting some. The difference between you and me is that I've published my books, while you haven't published your music. That's the only difference between us.

That's only the biggest difference. I don't have any ambitions for my music. I'm not looking for an audience, and I don't expect to get anything back. My music is simply the shape of my spirit. That's all I want. There's nothing else I could want, because that other stuff isn't me.

Fine! As far as I'm concerned, you're the only person who has the right to talk to me this way, because I understand you. But you're the only one. I do want an audience, because I'm more passionate than you are, and I like people more than you do. But I don't expect to get anything back either, and I don't think there's anything wrong with that.

Let's have a baby! Maybe it could teach us what love is.

Don't even suggest it! Why would I want to have a child with you?

We're both the products of totally stupid ideas, but our child could be a revolution.

You're dreaming. Have a child with you? You're making me nervous. How long has it been since we last saw each other? Are you even fit to be a father? Our child could easily find itself without a roof over its head or clothes on its back.

You can always go down to Huating Road and buy some cheap counterfeit duds for it.

Very funny. You don't know anything about love. Nothing ever seems to touch you, you're so cold. You've never even given me an orgasm. It took someone else to do that.

Is that so?

I don't like having to tell you this, but it's true, I swear.

Who is "someone else"?

That's not important. The point is that it definitely wasn't you.

Why are you treating me this way?

Because you're an idiot. You've got a beautiful cock, but you're a piece of shit who doesn't know the first thing about love. You're still a sexy, crazy, poetic, selfish musician, but the girl who lost her head over that guy doesn't exist anymore. My world and my body always belonged to Saining. I'm such a stupid girl! Out of all the years, and all the nights we spent together, why was it that we couldn't manage to give me just one orgasm on just one of those nights? Why didn't you care? You were so full of yourself that you didn't even think of me as a human being. Had you talked yourself into believing that you could make me come if you'd wanted to? Or were you so stupid that you thought I always came? Or was it just that I played with myself too much when I was a kid and wrecked my body, and now God's getting back at me? I still love you, but it's only because the two of us are equally stupid. The problem is that even though we were together all those years, we never really dealt with this problem. Is that your fault? Or was it my own stupidity? Why am I so stupid? I wonder how many people are as dumb as I am. I'm ashamed of it, and sometimes it just makes me want to die.

How was I supposed to know that you didn't know what an orgasm was? I thought everybody knew.

When I was with you, I definitely didn't know, and nobody told me either, not even my male friends. Frankly I really don't care whether or not I come. If I have an orgasm, fine; if I don't, fine. Fuck me from the front, fuck me from behind — it's all the same to me. Only the useless are tough, only the feeble can have sexual climaxes, and only a dumb fuck would watch a big-screen television. I figured it all out a long time ago. The problem is that whenever I think of the past, I feel sad. You make me feel so pathetic. You don't understand love, and you don't understand my body. Neither of us does.

I think I understand love. When I've loved, I've never asked for anything in return. I think my love is pure, and it's simple. I think that means my love is real love. But you're not like that. You use love to explain everything, and you have many kinds of love. Your love is complicated, and you're much too physical, so I don't understand your love. You say you want to die. You'll never die. Paranoid people like you never die. Apple died, but you, who have tried to kill yourself more times than I can count, you won't die. I bet you could drink rubbing alcohol and you still wouldn't die. I bet if you bought a shotgun and tried to do yourself in, the bullets would get jammed. No matter what you tried, you wouldn't die. You'll never be satisfied. You use everyone, you're cruel, and you want everything. You're a broken-down slut; you've slept with enough men to fill an orchestra. You've searched for my face at countless concerts. You even took a brainless heavy-metal rocker home with you just because he looked like me. Ten years! And you tell me you've never had an orgasm with me. You're a phony. That's why you can't die.

Do you want me to die?

I've lost count of how many times I've wished for your death and imagined how you would look in death. I loved fantasizing about that.

But if I died, where would that leave you? Aside from me, everybody else thinks you're a piece of shit, a fool who goes through life with his eyes shut tight. Someday you're going to have spent all the money your mother left you. Someday you're going to die of cold and hunger. I'm your only friend. Doesn't it strike you as just a little bit odd? That after all these years you still have only one friend — me? You don't think of Sanmao as a friend anymore; you say he's gotten fat and ugly. You have no feelings. You don't like anyone; you don't love people.

If you die, I'll love you forever.

What are you crying about? Our Romeo cried. If you die I'll always love you, so you'd better hurry up and die, and soon! But we're alive. And the only reason we're alive is that we still want to live.

That night, Saining never seemed to stop crying.

He said, I love you, but I'm telling you I can't love you anymore. You're a phony. I can't love you anymore. You're a con artist.

He said, You're a first-rate actress. You like anything that's fake.

He said, I'll never be able to love you again. You're pathetic. You've always been so enigmatic and such an expert at deception.

He also said, I'm sorry.

I felt remorseful and afraid. Perhaps all we have is our innocence and confusion, and to lose these would be to lose everything. What the hell had we been up to all those years? That night, I obliterated all of the good that we had shared in the past. I destroyed it all.

Stars were twinkling brightly overhead, and maybe the clouds were white. We were losing ourselves because the moon had been extinguished. And another substance was bringing light to humanity, red clouds in the east.

I was crying too.

Saining said, I'm so sad. And I said, I feel sad too.

Saining went out.

I watched the early-morning light as it filtered through the curtains and scattered. In the past this was the hour when we made love, and at this moment it was as if I could see his face, like that of an angel, flashing in and out of view among the ordinary people down in the street. This was the loneliest time of day for him, and the most anxious. It was the time I felt the most moved by him. At night, when we got totally fucked up, our greatest fear was of being jostled around among those calm and virtuous morning faces. Honestly, he just liked to have a good time. He was completely clueless about everything, but at the same time, he understood everything. He was a child, but a child with a world of his own. Saining said that idiots were actually his favorite kind of people. He didn't find them pathetic at all. On the contrary, he thought that they were free, because they would take anything of value and smash it to bits. And they didn't care.

One morning several days later, Saining went out into the courtyard to play violin. As I listened to him playing the violin and watched him from behind, it suddenly struck me that this man had truly loved me and that he truly didn't love me now. I thought about the first

time we'd met. Outside, it was pouring rain, and I've long since forgotten what music was playing. Nor do I remember what made me
look at the overgrown boy who was swaying there, swaying from
side to side, and smiling at nothing in particular. An oversize white
short-sleeved T-shirt and multicolored pants made of corduroy.
The pants were really baggy, like a skirt, but they were obviously
pants. He was by himself at the bar, rocking from side to side, a glass
of whiskey in his left hand, while his right hand swung back and
forth. And as I watched his legs, his footsteps moved him toward
where I was sitting. He was wearing a pair of light blue sneakers.
The soles were very thin, and these shoes made him seem to stumble
as he walked. His hair was long and glossy and perfectly straight —
the tips brushed his shoulder blades. His face was very pale, and
although I couldn't see his features clearly, I was certain that he was
smiling. Still, I didn't know whether or not he was looking at me. I
kept eating my ice cream. A little while later, I noticed a man's hand,
with a whiskey glass in it, just to my right. It was a large hand with
sturdy fingertips, and I knew at a glance that he bit his nails. I bit my
nails too. His hair tumbled down right in front of me. I smelled its
fragrance, and I looked up and saw him. I swore it was the face of an
angel! He had on a strange smile, and the naked innocence in his
eyes threw me off balance. And ever since that night, I've never
been able to take my gaze away from the face I saw in that moment.
Perhaps that's why I'm still alive today, because I believe in that
face. I trust it.

Out of the blue, Saining announced that he was going back south
to get our dog.

I said, It's only a dog. It's a child that will never grow up. It's like an idiot — do you understand the meaning of the word *idiot?*

Saining was drinking cough syrup as I spoke. He said, The way this medicine feels as it rolls down my throat is just like saying good-bye.

S

You're gonna say that love is Romeo and Juliet
But you're talking about a book
You're gonna say that love is the angels in the Sistine Chapel
But you're talking about a painting
You're gonna say that love is what your neighbor feels for Maria
But you're talking about a story

'Cause I want to know
If you ever felt it
The tornado inside
The earthquake inside
But you can't tie down all the dishes in your cupboards
There's a seaquake inside
But you can't find a thousand life vests to save you from drowning

'Cause I know
Love is drowning
It's pain and light, thunder and magic, it's a joke!
Has it ever happened to you?

'Cause you're gonna write a story where you'll be Juliet
'Cause you're gonna paint a thousand blue angels playing harp
'Cause you're gonna jump into that river of yours
And get soaked to the skin

Get to drown together
Get to cry together
Get to hold hands together
Get to get lost in her arms

And I'll be there
In the audience
Learning an Eastern patience, and the patience of the fisherman
Until my turn comes

I am a ditch where water has collected after the rain, my name is Mian Mian, and this story is not the story of my life. My life story will have to wait until I can write nakedly. That's my dream.

Right now my writing just falls apart.

Right now the real story has everything to do with my writing, and nothing to do with my readers.

My CD player is always spinning around, like inexhaustible hope. My ears bring me this perfect world. Perfection has always been in the present. This remembered world is mine, I possess it, and it is everything to me.

Right now it's early in the morning, on April 21, 1999, and the only thing that's clear in this shattered piece of candy is the poem I received last night, in a note left for me. It has a sweet name, "I'll Talk to You Tomorrow."

This time, he didn't go away. It's as if he really likes Shanghai. Maybe our eyes will witness the last dawn of this century together.

But we don't know for certain where we are. He's a person, and I'm a person. That proves that we aren't really so far apart.

Altered, my life plays at several speeds. The mortal guitar goes on weakly, trying to express everything with some sort of tonality, trying to use one thing to stand for all things.

No matter how hard I try, there's no way I can become that plaintive guitar. No matter how hard I try to make up for my mistakes, the sky will not give me back the voice that I once offered it. I've been defeated, so writing is all I have.

Sometimes we have to believe in miracles. The voice in my writing is like the reverberations of a bottle breaking at midnight. Listening over and over to the Radiohead CD I stole from a friend, on this uniquely pure and stainless morning, at the age of twenty-nine, here at S. I come to the end of this piece of candy.

SHANGHAI, 1995–99

ACKNOWLEDGMENTS

First, I must give heartfelt thanks to my father and mother. My father is my hero. What's more, he never stopped saying: "She's a good kid — she just loses her way every now and then." My mother has this to say: "I am grateful to God for giving me this child. What she writes is so beautiful."

I also wish to thank my agent William Clark for helping me bring this book into print. I haven't been to America, but he has made me long to see it. My editors at Little, Brown, Judy Clain and Claire Smith, have been enthusiastic about publishing this book from the start, and I am deeply grateful to them.

Thanks to all my friends, as well. Thank you, Caspar, Tina Liu, Coco Zhao. All of you have given me the strength to love this world and have taught me that darkness always ends in light.

Thanks also to Jim Morrison, Radiohead, and PJ Harvey. Their music has brought its deeply loving caresses into my life.

And last but not least, I wish to thank "my poor George." He is the King, and my best friend. I can never be hurt again by any kind of love.

TRANSLATOR'S ACKNOWLEDGMENTS

A big thank-you to William Clark, who called me out of the blue one day and brought me into this wonderful project. From start to finish, he was always there when I needed him. Thank you to our wonderful and indefatigable editors at Little, Brown, Judy Clain and Claire Smith.

Thanks to Josh Salesin for the list of effects, and to all of the friends and friends of friends who gave me pointers on everything from raves in China to medical info. Thanks to my readers, Davi Grossman and Chris Sanford. Your comments on the early drafts of this translation were invaluable.

I wish to express my gratitude to the late Jeri Wadhams, who gave me my first opportunity to read Chinese literature and pointed me down the path I have taken. And I will always be grateful for the generosity and dedication of Mrs. Ping Hu, who taught me the Chinese language, and Dr. William Tay, who inspired me to explore the complexity of modern China.

Lastly, I give my undying love and gratitude to my family — to my husband, David, whose patience and gentle nature sustain me even in stressful times, and my children, Oona, Isaiah, and Eleni, who fill my life with their sweetness, their love, and their brimming imaginations.

ABOUT THE AUTHOR

Mian Mian lives in Shanghai and works as a writer and nightlife promoter. She is the author of two books, the story collection *La La La* and the novel *Candy*. She has become a cultural icon to a generation of Chinese youth who value her authenticity and honesty in portraying the new face of contemporary China.

ABOUT THE TRANSLATOR

Andrea Lingenfelter has translated such novels as *Farewell My Concubine* and *The Last Princess of Manchuria* as well as film subtitles and poetry. She lives in Seattle.

CANDY

A NOVEL

MIAN MIAN

A READING GROUP GUIDE

"So many young people are getting lost," Mian Mian says. "I want to show them how freedom is exciting but also dangerous."

Mian Mian, thirty, is perhaps China's most promising young writer. Her stories deal with issues — sexuality, drug abuse, China opening to the world — that touch the core of her generation's experience. Too young to remember Mao's collectivist dystopia, they know only today's disillusioned consumerism and see self-definition, rather than nation building, as the focus of their lives.

Last year the Chinese government gave her its ultimate award: It banned her books, along with those of her nemesis, fellow Shanghai chronicler Wei Hui. Willy Wo-lap Lam, a former columnist for the *South China Morning Post* who is called China's Walter Winchell, says an enraged President Jiang Zemin personally recited to the Politburo one passage, a description of casual sex with a young Westerner.

But with "banned in Beijing," an irresistible sales pitch, for all the wrong reasons, translations are finally hitting the bookshelves: *Tang* (or *Candy*) appears next month in France, from Les Bonbons Chinois, Editions de l'Olivier, and in 2003 in the United States, from Little, Brown.

Mian Mian's stories tend to circle around the years she spent in Shenzhen in the early to mid-1990s, the most lawless and chaotic time in that notorious border town's short history. Running away from her native Shanghai at age seventeen, she drifted into the city's nightlife scene, falling in love with a series of feckless musicians and acquiring a serious heroin habit along the way. With the help of her parents, she returned to Shanghai in 1995, went into rehab, and started to write. "There are no old people in that city," Mian Mian says of Shenzhen. "Everyone was so young."

Her imagined Shenzhen is an extravagant intensification of reality, much like the Shanghai of earlier Chinese popular authors like Eileen Chang, a threepenny opera of gangsters, prostitutes, and beautiful doomed musicians — women with a past, as the saying goes, and men with no future.

"A lot of lost people came to Shenzhen from elsewhere," Mian Mian says. "They all dreamed of using money to save their life." That kind of existential void, in a place with no history and consequentially no family or community ties, resulted in a cannibalistic society. "It is such a cruel city," she says. "It has no heart. There is no such thing as friendship there. No one is your friend."

Shenzhen's tabula rasa is also present in her prose — she's more likely to quote Jim Morrison than the Tang poets, something rare in a culture burdened by thousands of years of literary allusions. It is this, as much as her content, which has made her the poster child of "spiritual pollution."

Nowadays Mian Mian enjoys a domesticity remote from the milieu of her fiction, commuting between Shanghai and the English countryside with her British husband and their one-year-old daughter. Born Shen Wang, Mian Mian attended Shanghai's elite Yanji school at the behest of her father, a famous engineer. Teenage growing pains hit hard; when, at sixteen, a classmate had to be institutionalized, she felt saddened but almost relieved: "Until then, I thought I was uniquely weird."

Those years, the mid-1980s, witnessed a *wenhua re* or "culture fever" as the Communist Party leader Hu Yaobang's relatively liberal rule electrified a society traumatized by Mao's social experiments. Rock music and other products of Western pop culture became available after a thirty-year absence, and "modernist" writers like Xu Xing reintroduced irony, sarcasm, and black humor into fiction. "Xu Xing's work opened my eyes," she says. "He wrote about his real feelings. It was very black and very funny but also very sensitive. Until then, I didn't know what writing could be."

This, along with a Madonna video and her own classroom experiences, led to "Like a Prayer," which was chosen for publication by *Shanghai Wenxue,* a prestigious literary magazine of the time. But this wasn't to be. Deng Xiaoping fired Hu in 1987 and an "anti-rightist" campaign ensued. Teenage suicide was too controversial in this new environment, and the story was dropped. Devastated, she ran away from home. "I thought I had no chance in this world," she says. "I had no education, no degree. The only thing in my life was writing, and I had failed at that. There was only one thing left. I could make money. So I went to Shenzhen."

She arrived in a city carved out of rice paddies and banana plantations just a few years earlier. Its sweatshops were moving farther into the Pearl River Delta, and Shenzhen boomed as it morphed from a factory town into a service hub part Las Vegas, part Panama City. Such quasi-capitalism had yet to hit Shanghai or other cities, so for a while Shenzhen attracted the ambitious and the desperate from all over China, creating a flamboyant demimonde. Mian Mian thrived in this world until a broken love affair drove her to heroin. "I didn't know what danger is," she says. "And I didn't know what freedom is. I just did whatever I wanted."

For three years she lived as a recluse, watching television shows from the black-and-white era every night until dawn. Finally her parents brought her back to Shanghai and checked her into a hospital. Rehab in China employs crude but effective forms of therapy: They put her in a ward for the criminally insane. "It was such a horrible memory," she says. "I never took drugs again."

She started to write again, in 1997 publishing *La La La* in Hong Kong, from where it seeped into the Mainland. A series of four interlocking stories, it spoke (not surprisingly) of love, music, drugs, and despair in

Shenzhen. In 1999 *Candy,* her first full-length novel, appeared on the Mainland. "My books are not for intellectuals," she says. "My readers are in the streets, in a disco, listening to cool music." This differs markedly from the role Chinese intellectuals usually arrogate to themselves. "I don't want to teach anybody," she insists. "My only message is: This world is cruel. But you can survive."

Jonathan Napack's article on Mian Mian, headlined "Banned in Beijing: A Rebel Writer's Message," first appeared in the International Herald Tribune *on Thursday, February 8, 2001. Reprinted with permission.*

READING GROUP QUESTIONS AND TOPICS FOR DISCUSSION

1. The novel's narrator, Hong, idolizes figures like Jim Morrison and Kurt Cobain. Do you think Saining shares any of their characteristics? Does this help illuminate Hong's relationship with him or only further obscure it?

2. What is the biggest difference between Hong's and Saining's personalities? What are the largest sources of conflict between them?

3. Do you think that Hong would have gotten involved with heroin if she had not been in love with Saining or someone like him? Do you think that Hong will stay clean? What about Saining?

4. Do you think that Hong and Saining will stay together? Do you think Hong's happiness is dependent on Saining?

5. How does Hong's relationship with her own sexuality change over the course of the book? Do you think that sex plays a larger role in Hong's life than it does in most people's lives? Or is this novel just more open and honest about it?

6. What does the book's title, *Candy,* mean to you? How do you interpret the final sentence of the book?

7. What aspect of Bug's AIDS scare was the most surprising to you?

8. The Communist Party is still firmly in control of China's government. Judging from what you read in *Candy,* to what extent do politics affect daily life in China today? How?

9. Were you shocked by this story? Were your reactions in any way determined by the novel's setting? How might your response to the book

have been different if *Candy* had taken place in New York or Los Angeles, for example?

10. Do you think Hong's life would have been different had she not moved to "the South"? To what extent do you think the relatively new freedoms found there influenced the course of her life?

11. Toward the end of the book Hong describes writing as a "prescription." Do you believe in the redemptive power of art and expression?

BROWNSVILLE
Stories by Oscar Casares

"A fine debut. . . . Probing underneath the surface of Tex-Mex culture, Casares's stories, with their wisecracking, temperamental, obsessive middle-aged men and their dramas straight from neighborhood gossip, are in the direct line of descent from Mark Twain and Ring Lardner."
— *Publishers Weekly*

"Oscar Casares does for Brownsville, Texas, what Eudora Welty did for Jackson, Mississippi." — TIM GAUTREAUX, author of *Welding with Children*

SUPER FLAT TIMES
Stories by Matthew Derby

"Imagine *The Matrix*, but funny, or a neurotic *Metropolis*, and you might get some sense of what this weird, beautifully written book, made by someone who has watched far too much television, does to your brain."
— NEAL POLLACK, author of *The Neal Pollack Anthology of American Literature*

"A vital and astonishing writer. . . . Matthew Derby stages a brilliant wagon circle around everything dull and earthbound in American fiction."
— BEN MARCUS, author of *Notable American Women*

Available wherever books are sold

HOUSE OF WOMEN
A novel by Lynn Freed

Irresistible. . . . An unusual and unusually satisfying novel."
— KATHRYN HARRISON, *New York Times Book Review*

House of Women is surprising and inevitable, often in the same sentence.
t illuminates and, at the same time, deepens the human mystery. I don't
sk for more from a book."
— MICHAEL CUNNINGHAM, author of *The Hours*

THE DRINK AND DREAM TEAHOUSE
A novel by Justin Hill

Justin Hill knows China inside out. Every sentence is filled with knowl-
dge, affection, and a poignant sense of loss."
— CAROLYN SEE, *Washington Post*

Hill understands, like Tolstoy, that human nature cannot change along
ith the times. . . . This is a book of exoticisms, intoxicated by the
uman landscape of the Far East, a place of firecrackers and lotus
ots. . . . A first novel filled with sensual delight."
— EDWARD STERN, *Independent on Sunday*

Available wherever books are sold

THE BLACK VEIL
A memoir by Rick Moody

"Compulsively readable. . . . A profound meditation on madness, shame, and history. . . . One of the finest memoirs in recent years."
— JEFFERY SMITH, *Washington Post Book World*

"Ferociously intelligent, emotionally unsparing. . . . Verbal invention capers and sparkles on every page."
— DAVID KIPEN, *San Francisco Chronicle*

SIMPLE RECIPES
Stories by Madeleine Thien

"*Simple Recipes* introduces a writer of precocious poise. . . . The austere grace and polished assurance of Thien's prose are remarkable. . . . The trajectories of Thien's stories are unpredictable; though her characters dream of following simple recipes, they are themselves undeniably original creations."
— JANICE P. NIMURA, *New York Times Book Review*

"This is surely the debut of a splendid writer. I am astonished by the clarity and ease of the writing, and a kind of emotional purity."
— ALICE MUNRO

Available wherever books are sold